IDENTITY

BY SHAWNA SEED

CONTENTS

PART ONE

Sharlah

ONE

NAÏVE.

When the cop first said it, Sharlah wasn't sure what he meant. It was one of those words she'd read but never actually heard anyone say. In her head, she always rhymed it with "cave."

"Sweetheart, if you believe that, you are some kind of naïve," he said. "Wise up."

Sharlah leaned toward the wire mesh that separated her from the officer in the front of the parked cruiser. "I'm telling you, this is a mistake. Brian's working at a construction site in Houston today."

Construction accident—that had been her first thought when she rounded the corner on her way home from work and saw all the cars in front of the house. She thought the police were there to tell her something terrible had happened to Brian.

One minute she was driving along, half-listening to the news—something about President Reagan and El Salvador—and trying to decide whether the clutch in her Colt felt mushier than it had that morning. The next minute, she was met at the curb by a cop who ushered her into the back of his car.

He said Brian was being charged with drug trafficking, whatever that meant, and they were searching the house. He showed her the warrant, but he wouldn't tell her anything.

Sharlah shifted uncomfortably in the back seat and tried, discreetly, to pull her skirt away where it was sticking to the backs of her thighs. It was 3:30, getting on toward the hottest part of the day, and her waitress uniform was 100 percent polyester. That was great for repelling bacon grease and ketchup stains, but not so comfortable on an August afternoon. She was glad she'd at least peeled off her pantyhose in the car and changed into her flip-flops before she drove home from work.

She'd been sitting in the back of the stifling cruiser for 10 minutes, silently fuming after answering an initial barrage of questions.

Sharlah Marie Webb. Yeah, Sharlah with an h on the end. Nineteen. Yeah, she lived here. No, she never saw any drugs. No, she never saw Brian with lots of cash—she wished! Guns? No. Not even to hunt? He kept his deer rifle at his folks' house, she said, not bothering to add that Brian liked fishing better than hunting.

Tired of waiting, she aimed a question of her own at the back of the cop's neck. "How long do I have to sit out here?"

"Go on up if you want," he said without turning around. "Nobody said you couldn't."

That made Sharlah mad, because if anybody had told her she could go on in, she sure as hell wouldn't have been sitting outside all this time. She didn't say anything, but she made sure to slam the car door extra-hard when she got out.

A dark-haired cop with an impressive mustache and mirrored sunglasses was on her front step. He gave her the once-over, lingering on her chest, then smirked at her like he'd gotten away with something. Sharlah, who'd needed a bra since fifth grade and had dealt with worse, glared at him and pushed through the front door.

She stepped inside the house and gasped. Every piece of furniture in the living room had been turned upside-down. The lining of the couch had been slashed and pulled back. Albums spilled across the floor. The back of the TV had been removed, exposing the wiring.

It was a shotgun house, and all the doors were open, so Sharlah could see straight through the bedroom and into the kitchen at the back of the house. The cops had tossed every room.

Two of them stood in her living room going over some papers. One was older, with gray hair and a soft, jiggly gut that slopped over his belt. Sharlah recognized the younger one, who came to the restaurant sometimes. Never wanted a coffee refill, 15 percent tip to the penny, didn't stare openly at her boobs—pretty much an ideal customer in her book.

Another cop stood in the doorway to the bedroom with a pair of her panties in his hand.

"Hey!" Sharlah's foot hit the squeaky floorboard in the living room, and all three cops looked up. "Goddammit! Put those down!"

The expression on the older cop's face soured. He said something to the one in the bedroom, who put the panties down, then sidled past Sharlah and out the door.

"Pervert," she said under her breath as he walked by.

Sharlah turned to the older cop. "Are you in charge? Where's Brian?"

He took a few steps toward her. "So you're the suspect's girlfriend? I'm going out to the car to finish the paperwork. You'll need to sign."

The suspect's girlfriend. Sharlah didn't like the sound of that. She called after the retreating cop. "Are you done? Can I start picking up?"

"You can pick up," the younger cop said, the same way he said, "Eggs over easy, bacon, wheat toast, coffee." Flat. No expression.

Sharlah knelt and gathered albums into a neat stack, unconsciously alphabetizing as she went. She slotted Def Leppard after The Clash, Joan Jett between Joe Jackson and Billy Joel, all three of them before Journey.

"Did you guys really have to make such a goddamned mess?"

Loverboy, Men At Work, Metallica…

The Men At Work album belonged to her friend Missy and needed to be returned. Sharlah set it to one side.

The cop was looking out the front door, pointedly ignoring her. He was tall and wiry, with strawberry blond hair, cut short. His neck was sunburned.

Redneck jerk, Sharlah thought. He'd always seemed nice when he came to the diner, but now she regretted the effort she'd put into getting his orders right.

The dark-haired cop with the mustache called through the screen door. "Clearing out. See you later."

The red-haired cop bobbed his head once. "Later, Moreno."

Sharlah couldn't believe the way the cops went about their business like it was no big deal to make a mess of someone's house. She spotted a library book—*Mistral's Daughter*—sprawled under the coffee table, her bookmark a foot away. "You lost my place in my book," she snapped at the redhead. "Thanks a lot."

"What's the red stain on your steps?"

"Grenadine," she said, which was basically the truth. "It's hard to get out."

"It smells bad. You should try bleach." The cop turned around and studied her for a minute. Then he walked toward the couch. "Take the other end," he said.

Working together, they righted it. He glanced toward the front door.

"Morgan's coming back. Don't cuss in front of him. He's born-again. It'll just make things worse."

"Worse than this?" Sharlah said, sweeping her hand around the room. "Must be nice to be a cop and get to bust shit up whenever..."

"Your boyfriend's in the county jail."

Sharlah had been working up a head of steam, but she stopped. "Can I go get him now? Or will they keep him overnight?"

The cop shook his head. "He's looking at felony charges. If he can't afford a lawyer, they'll give him a public defender in time for his arraignment. That's when they'll set bail, but it won't happen until Monday."

Sharlah's shoulders slumped. "Not until Monday?"

6

She didn't know how much a lawyer cost, but she suspected the $65 she had in savings wasn't enough. She didn't even know where to start. Pick one out of the phone book?

She hated to admit it, but she was going to need help, and that boiled down to two choices. She could call Brian's older brother, Kevin, or she could call his friend Cliff.

One advantage to calling Cliff was that he lived in town, and Kevin was an hour away in Houston. Cliff was pretty much an honorary brother, anyway. He grew up on the same street and was right between the two Lowry boys in age. The way Brian told it, after divorce tore through their neighborhood in the early '70s like one of those plagues in *The Ten Commandments*, Cliff practically lived at their house.

The disadvantage to calling Cliff was that he didn't have a regular job, which made him hard to track down.

Kevin, on the other hand, would be easy to find. He'd be at his desk at the family business, where he was his dad's right-hand man. And that was the problem with calling Kevin—he would probably tell their parents.

Brian had a rule about not asking his folks for help, because he figured if he didn't take anything from them, they couldn't boss him around.

Sharlah walked through the bedroom, willing herself to ignore the mess the cops had made, and into the kitchen. It was a disaster, too, but she couldn't focus on that yet. She headed straight to the phone mounted on the wall next to the back door.

Deciding that Cliff was the better bet, she called the condo he shared with his girlfriend, Missy, but the phone just rang and rang. Then she called the restaurant where Missy worked, to see if she knew how to get Cliff, but the bartender said Missy wasn't due in until 5.

The clock on the stove said 4:35. It was Friday afternoon, and it seemed to Sharlah that if she didn't do something soon, it would be too late to do anything before Monday.

She ran her finger down the list of numbers taped next to the phone. Brian was terrible at numbers, could never keep them straight.

The last two entries were for his parents' house and the family business. Sharlah had added them, though she really shouldn't have bothered. One visit to the Lowrys' house in Houston had made it obvious they wanted nothing to do with her.

Sharlah took a deep breath and dialed.

"Lowry Marine," a woman's voice answered.

"Hi, I need to speak to Kevin Lowry, please."

"Who shall I say is calling?"

"My name's Sharlah Webb," Sharlah said, hoping the woman wasn't going to wave down Brian's dad as soon as she heard the name.

The woman paused, just for a beat, then said, "I'll connect you."

In the stories Brian told about growing up, he and his brother were always getting into mischief together, and Kevin specialized in finessing things with their folks afterward. He could talk his way out of trouble when the boys got caught wrapping the neighbor's house in TP or breaking a window playing ball in the street.

Now that they were grown, Kevin was still the one who knew how to please. He graduated with a business degree and married his college sweetheart. He and his wife, Lynn, had bought a house near his parents and were about to produce the first Lowry grandchild.

The hold music stopped abruptly. "Sharlah?"

"Hi, Kevin. I hate to call like this, but Brian…"

"Is in jail. Yeah, I know. He used his one phone call on Dad."

Until Kevin said that, Sharlah had been holding onto the idea that maybe Brian wasn't in too much trouble. She thought it might be like the time a friend got hauled in for drunk and disorderly. He was out the next day, fined $100.

If Brian called his dad, though, it had to be bad. Really, really bad.

"Sharlah, was that all you wanted to tell me? Things are crazy here, and I need to get going." Kevin's voice began to fade, and Sharlah pictured the phone receiver on its descent to the cradle on his desk.

"Is Brian OK? The police who searched the house wouldn't tell me anything."

Kevin snapped to attention. "They searched the *house*? Did they find anything?"

"They didn't take anything that I saw," Sharlah said. "They said something about drugs? What's going on?"

"Brian got pulled over this morning, and like a moron he let them search the truck," Kevin said.

Sharlah bristled at "moron" but let it go. "Did they find a joint in the ash tray or something?"

"It's worse than that," Kevin said. "Look, Dad's down there trying to straighten this out. Mom's losing her mind, and I promised to get over to the house. I'll get Dad to call you, OK? I don't really know anything else. I have to go now."

With that, he hung up.

Not knowing what else to do, Sharlah started cleaning up the mess the cops had made of her kitchen. She put the lid back on the Folgers can and swept the spilled coffee into the trash. She did the same with the flour and sugar. She shut all the drawers and cupboards that had been left standing open.

Sharlah picked up a bottle of tequila from the counter and eyed the golden liquid left at the bottom. Uncapping the bottle, she tipped it back and drained it.

Eyes watering, she tossed the empty bottle in the trash.

Nothing anyone said squared with the Brian she knew. She'd known bad guys, and Brian wasn't like that.

That had been one of the things that drew her to him when they met, right after she'd moved to town. She'd come because a girl from her hometown talked up how great it was. It was only after Sharlah arrived that she realized the girl was just talking big. She didn't want Sharlah to room with her—in fact, she didn't even want to be her friend.

Sharlah found a job waiting tables at a beach joint where Brian hung out. She liked his blue eyes, his easy smile and the way his Levis hung on his hips. But mostly she noticed that he was a good guy, always getting keys away from people who shouldn't drive, heading off fights, steering drunk girls away from guys who were trouble.

Brian wasn't perfect, but he wasn't trouble.

She moved to the bedroom, where all of their clothes had been tossed from the dresser to the floor. The sheets were pulled off, and the mattress was askew. Brian's guitar was dumped on the bed; the case was sitting open on the floor. The cops had slit the lining.

"OK, that just pisses me off," Sharlah said out loud in the empty room.

There weren't any drugs in the house, she was sure of that. She did all the cleaning—Brian was basically a slob—and she'd never seen so much as a joint. She sure as hell hadn't seen any big stacks of cash.

It had to be some kind of mistake.

Didn't it?

Sharlah sat down on the bed with an armful of clothes.

Brian *had* been different lately. He was tired and grumpy, and he never wanted to go out or see their friends. Cliff and Missy had been over the weekend before, but that was the first time they'd all hung out since summer started, even though Cliff was Brian's best friend. And Brian had hardly seen Kevin at all since Lynn got pregnant.

Sharlah had noticed the drifting, but she didn't know what to make of it. When they were growing up, the boys were so close that people called Cliff and Brian and Kevin the Three Musketeers. In high school, they had matching T-shirts made with a picture of the candy bar, kind of an inside joke.

Cliff had been wearing his Three Musketeers shirt the week before, when he and Missy showed up with a pizza and the new Men At Work album. They also brought beer for the guys and all the ingredients for Tequila Sunrises for the girls. Brian, who never got mad about anything, seemed annoyed at Cliff over the shirt.

It should have been the kind of night the four of them had shared hundreds of times: listening to records, drinking, laughing, just hanging out.

But something was not right that night, and it wasn't just Brian's mood. Missy drank way too much and started needling Cliff. When they were leaving, she threw up all over the front steps and Cliff's shirt.

Brian carried Missy to the car while Sharlah cleaned Cliff off with the hose. He didn't even try to save his shirt. He just stuffed it in the trash can at the curb.

By the time Sharlah had cleaned the worst of the mess off the steps, Brian was asleep.

She should have known right then that something was very wrong, because when had Brian ever just gone to sleep on a Friday night without wanting to make love?

TWO

BRIAN'S PARENTS WERE COMING to town to meet with his lawyer, and Brian's dad said they needed Sharlah to be there. *Needed*, he'd said. Not *wanted*. Sharlah wasn't sure which was better.

Of course her manager was being a pain in the butt about letting her out of work early, because Saturday was such a busy day.

Sharlah had been worried about explaining the situation to her boss, and she even considered making up some kind of cover story. But everyone at work seemed to have heard about Brian's arrest.

The diner's worst gossip pumped her for information to round out what she'd already heard: Brian had a million dollars' worth of pot in his truck, more arrests were coming, supposedly some cops were in on the whole thing.

Everybody acted surprised she hadn't called in sick, an idea that hadn't even occurred to Sharlah. She didn't really feel like being at work, sure, but she couldn't afford to skip. She needed the money.

Usually Sharlah didn't mind her job. Oh, sometimes the customers stiffed her on tips, and sometimes the cooks yelled if they couldn't read orders. But mostly it was just the same thing day after day—running around like crazy during the breakfast and lunch rush, then refilling ketchup bottles and rolling napkins until it was time to clock out.

She'd been at the diner almost two years, ever since she left the beach place where she'd met Brian. That job hadn't really worked out. She was 17 when she started—not old enough to serve alcohol, which was where the big tips were. The assistant manager had said he could let her work the bar when the manager wasn't around, but from the way he made the offer, Sharlah could tell he'd want something in return.

So she quit and went to work at the diner. Starting at 5 a.m. wasn't fun, but it put her on the same schedule as Brian, and Sharlah usually liked the job OK.

She didn't like it this morning, though. Everything annoyed her—requests for refills, for strawberry jelly instead of grape, for more time to study the menu. It was good the cop who'd searched the house hadn't come in. Sharlah would have enjoyed burning his toast.

By 2, the lunch crowd was thinning out, and Sharlah made another run at her manager. Joan lectured Sharlah about how she couldn't expect special privileges just because her boyfriend was in jail, but then she gave in with a sigh and said Sharlah could clock out.

There was no time to run home and change. She was going to have to meet the Lowrys and Brian's lawyer in her stupid orange waitress uniform.

Sharlah hustled out to her car and maneuvered in carefully, trying not to touch anything metal. Usually she'd open the door and wait a minute to let the heat escape, but today she didn't have time.

Even though the humidity made her feel like she was breathing through a wet washcloth, Sharlah didn't bother with the air-conditioner. The lawyer's office was 10 minutes away, and the Colt's creaky AC needed longer than that to get going.

The office was on the top floor of a two-story building a few blocks from the courthouse. Sharlah took the stairs two at a time; she arrived sweating and out of breath. If she hadn't been late already, she would have found a bathroom and freshened up. She wondered which Brian's mom would think was worse: being late or being sweaty.

The door was unlocked, but there wasn't a secretary up front or anything. Brian's dad said they'd made "special arrangements" to meet with the lawyer right away, which Sharlah supposed involved money. She'd never been in a lawyer's office before, and she wasn't sure what to do. She waited a couple seconds and then called out, "Hello?"

A man poked his head out of a doorway down the hall. He had long brown hair and was wearing a white shirt, a tie and blue jeans. He looked to Sharlah like a hippie who'd cleaned up his act. "Miss Webb? Come on back to the conference room."

Brian's family was sitting on one side of a big table. His mom, Renee, was in the middle, flanked by his dad and brother, Mitch and Kevin.

The guy with the tie held out a chair for her. "I'm George Ingersoll, Brian's attorney."

"Hi. Sorry I'm late," Sharlah said. "I was working."

Renee said something under her breath that Sharlah couldn't make out.

Mitch put his hand on his wife's arm. Kevin stared at the table like he hadn't heard anything.

Sharlah sat and dropped her purse on the table. It made more noise than she expected in the quiet room, and she immediately felt like she'd done something rude. "Sorry," she muttered. She moved her purse to the floor beneath her chair.

Ingersoll smiled at her, which made Sharlah feel better. "As I was just telling the Lowrys," he began, "I had my first meeting with Brian this morning."

"How is he?" Sharlah blurted out.

"He's holding up," the lawyer said. "I was just explaining what I call the rules of the road. You're all here because Brian has asked me to speak with you. That's my role here, to act in Brian's interest."

Renee shot Mitch a dirty look, and Sharlah wondered what that was about.

"When Brian's released on bail, there will be aspects of his case he can't discuss with you. You all need to understand that," Ingersoll continued. He looked around the table at each of them.

Kevin didn't look up. Renee just glared, her arms folded over her chest. Only Mitch acknowledged Ingersoll, nodding once in agreement.

"Sure," Sharlah said when his eyes fell on her.

"So, what happens now is that there will be an arraignment Monday morning," Ingersoll said. "The judge will set the bail, and then we'll arrange bond and get Brian released."

He paused for a moment. "Everybody with me so far?"

Sharlah thought it was strange that Brian's parents weren't saying anything. Did they already know all the details? Was she the only one in the dark?

She turned to the lawyer. "Is it OK to ask you about his case? A girl at work said Brian had a million dollars worth of pot in his truck. Is that true? She said other people are getting arrested, and some cops are in on it."

Renee Lowry exhaled in one long, hostile puff and looked at her husband. "Do we really have to sit here and listen to every rumor the truck-stop waitresses are spreading?"

Just like that, Sharlah wished she hadn't asked. It was always this way with Brian's family. It took about 10 seconds for her to feel stupid and know she didn't belong.

All she had to do was look at them. Even though it was a Saturday, Mitch and Kevin were dressed up in khakis and long-sleeved button-down shirts, white for Mitch and dark blue for Kevin. Despite the heat, Kevin had a T-shirt on underneath—Sharlah could see the white band of it beneath his open collar. Renee was wearing a crisp yellow blouse and white slacks. Her hair was styled just so, nothing out of place.

And here Sharlah was, in her polyester waitress uniform that smelled like sweat and bacon grease, her hair scraped into a ponytail. She'd let Missy talk her into a feathered haircut, which looked like hell unless she spent 20 minutes on it with a curling iron, and who had that kind of time at 4:30 in the morning? The shorter parts wouldn't stay out of her face at work, and she had to bobby-pin them back.

Ingersoll held up a palm. "It's fine, Mrs. Lowry."

He turned his chair toward Sharlah. "The police say they found about 130 pounds of marijuana in Brian's truck, concealed under a load of lumber," Ingersoll said. "We can assume they are looking to arrest other people involved."

"Are they sure Brian knew it was there? Because that doesn't seem like Brian at all. It's not like him to do something so..." Sharlah paused, searching for the right word.

"Stupid," Renee Lowry supplied. "And it is *exactly* like Brian to do something stupid."

Mitch opened his mouth to say something, then thought better of it.

Sharlah glanced at Kevin, hoping he'd defend his brother, but he just stared at the table.

The lawyer acted like Renee hadn't said anything at all.

"Now, the one arrow we have in our quiver is that Brian wisely declined to answer questions when they arrested him," Ingersoll said. "The police will be looking for help making cases against other people involved, so we've got something to bargain with."

Sharlah liked him for sticking the word "wisely" in there. She hoped Renee noticed.

Kevin spoke for the first time. "Brian's going to rat people out?"

"That's an unfortunate way to put it," Ingersoll said. "When I talked to Brian, he was not open to the idea of cooperating. But that attitude usually changes once the gravity of the situation sinks in. He'll have to do what's best for him."

Sharlah glared at the Lowrys assembled across the table. *Stupid? Rat?* What was wrong with them? Didn't they care about Brian? His mom, OK, that was to be expected. But Kevin? Brian would be crushed if he knew what Kevin said.

His family might not stick up for him, but Sharlah would. "Is there anything we can do for him right now? Is there anything he needs from home?"

"He can have a Bible, but that's about it," Ingersoll said.

"He wouldn't really have any use for that," Sharlah said.

Renee's eyes blazed. "Are you saying my son's not a Christian anymore?"

"That's not what I meant," Sharlah said, trying to keep her voice even. "He just wouldn't have any... I mean, what's he going to do with it? It's not like he can read it."

"I have no idea what you're talking about," Renee said, sitting up straighter.

"Yes, you do," Sharlah said, a little surprised that she was talking back to Renee. "Brian can hardly read—don't pretend you don't know."

"That's not true!" Renee spit out.

"It *is* true," Sharlah said, "and you know it. You all know it." She glanced around the table. "Kevin?"

Kevin said nothing, which Sharlah couldn't believe. He was always the one who smoothed over things between Brian and his parents, and now he acted afraid to say anything at all.

She turned back to the lawyer. "He only got through high school because teachers passed him so he could play baseball and his friends helped him with homework."

That, finally, prompted Kevin to look at her, a flicker of recognition in his eyes.

It was Kevin, of course, who had done the most to help Brian, starting in elementary school. Brian was always in trouble over his grades, and Kevin basically did his homework for him. Brian told Sharlah once that Kevin's help was the only thing that kept him from getting spanked every single night.

Ingersoll took a pen from behind his ear and made a note on a yellow pad. "That's good to know," he said. "If Brian's functionally illiterate, that could help us."

"My son is *not* illiterate!" Renee rounded on her husband. "Mitchell! Say something!"

"The man's just thinking out loud, Renee, trying to do his job," Mitch said.

"Brian's not dumb," Sharlah said. "He just can't read much. That's why he messed up at college, because he couldn't keep up."

Renee stared hard at Sharlah. "Brian failed at college because he's lazy and undisciplined and always has been," she said.

"Right, he's not as good as Kevin," Sharlah said, returning Renee's glare. "I'm pretty sure he got the message. You've only been telling him that his whole life."

Kevin slid lower in his seat, like he was embarrassed, and Sharlah thought he should be. She couldn't believe Kevin wasn't sticking up for his brother, even a little bit. She knew he thought their folks were hard-asses, too. She'd heard him say so to Brian.

"I won't apologize for wanting Brian to set his standards higher," Renee said. "His behavior might be acceptable in your world, but in our family..."

Sharlah was about to ask exactly what she meant by that, but the lawyer interrupted.

"I think we're getting off track here," Ingersoll said. "Now, about Brian's bond..."

Mitch Lowry perked up. "How much do you think we're looking at?"

"I can help," Sharlah said. "I have $65 in savings."

Renee rolled her eyes. "I'm not having this conversation with her in the room."

Mitch put his hand on her arm. "Renee," he said. He gave Sharlah an apologetic look.

"Our financial situation is private, Mitchell, and I will not discuss it with her here."

Sharlah waited, not sure what to do. She glanced over at the lawyer.

"We can get into that in a few minutes," Ingersoll said. "Arraignment is at 11 Monday morning at the county courthouse. Let's meet in the second-floor hallway about 10:50. The hearing will take 10 or 15 minutes. Miss Webb, did you have other questions?"

Realizing she was being shown the door, Sharlah reached for her purse and pushed her chair back from the table. "I'll have to see about getting off work."

Ingersoll stood and opened the door for her.

Sharlah waited in the doorway for some kind of goodbye from Brian's family, but none came. "OK. I guess I'll see you guys on Monday if I can make it."

Only Mitch met her eyes.

Sharlah paused in the reception area to take a deep breath. Seeing Brian's parents even under normal circumstances freaked her out, and these were not normal circumstances.

She heard footsteps in the hall and turned to see Kevin heading toward her.

"I was hoping to catch you," he said.

Sharlah crossed her arms over her chest. "Why?"

"I'll walk you out," he said, keeping his voice low.

Sharlah pointed toward the door. "I can find my own way, thanks."

"Don't be that way," Kevin said.

Brian said sometimes she was too quick to take offense, and Sharlah knew he was right. But at that moment, no one could talk her out of being mad at the Lowrys.

"Be what way? Pissed off?"

"Come on, Sharlah." Kevin glanced over his shoulder, like he was afraid Renee was right there, listening. He pushed past her and opened the door to the stairs.

Sharlah reluctantly followed him down to the street.

Kevin stopped on the sidewalk outside the office. "Look, I'm sorry. I know Mom was kind of hard on you back there, but..."

"Never mind what she said about me," Sharlah said. "She said terrible things about Brian, and you just sat there! You know he's not lazy! You know why he had so much trouble at school. But you didn't say anything!"

Kevin held up both palms, warding her off. "You have to understand, she and Dad hardly slept last night…"

"You think I did? Anyway, it's not like she needs a reason to pick on Brian—she does it all the time. You're supposed to stick up for him, and you didn't do anything! You know how much Brian looks up to you and how he counts on you!"

Kevin's face crumpled, and Sharlah realized—with a little zing of satisfaction—that she'd wounded him.

"What do you expect me to do, Sharlah?"

"You have to help him!"

Kevin braced one palm against the building and stared down the street, considering Sharlah's words.

"And how do you expect me to help him, exactly?"

"I don't know!" Sharlah said, exasperated. "Talk to your folks. Make them understand Brian's side. Get them to ease up."

"I don't know Brian's side," Kevin said. "Do you?"

He had her there. Sharlah's anger drained away.

"No," she said. "It doesn't make any sense to me at all."

"Look, you know I'll do anything to help Brian," Kevin said. "But this isn't like breaking a lamp wrestling in the living room, you know? It's not even like dropping out of college. I can't talk his way out of this for him. This is… The thing is, I don't know if this can be fixed."

*

Back home after the meeting, Sharlah turned on the AC, stripped out of her uniform and took a long shower. For the first time since Brian's arrest, she allowed herself to cry.

Normally, she thought crying was a waste of time. It never changed anything, and it gave her a headache.

But she hadn't realized how hard it would be to face Brian's folks without him. Sharlah wasn't surprised Renee was mean, because she was always mean. But when Brian was around, he'd sneak her sympathetic looks or make a point of putting his arm around her. Without him, Renee Lowry was pretty hard to take.

After she cried, Sharlah reminded herself that a pity party was useless. She couldn't just sit around and moan.

Saturday was laundry day, so she gathered up the dirty clothes and a stack of quarters. Brian would come home to clean clothes, at least.

Sharlah took along a book to help pass the time. It was the kind of novel she usually liked, with lots of romance and exotic places like France and New York, but she found herself just turning the pages until she got to the end, not really enjoying it.

She wished she'd brought her other book, the one the librarian had pushed her to try. But she'd left it at home and had nothing to keep her occupied but her thoughts.

Brian usually came to the Laundromat with her. Sometimes he brought his guitar and played while she read. Other times, they'd just talk.

He liked to tease her that their first date was at the Laundromat, although that wasn't really true. They never actually had an official first date.

She'd been in town a few months that first night she ran into Brian doing his laundry. They'd been friends awhile, chatting at her work or running into each other at parties. Once, at a cookout, they talked for three hours. Sharlah thought for sure he was going to ask her out, but then he didn't. She thought Brian was cute, but she'd also heard that he had a girlfriend in school up at San Marcos.

Sharlah was feeling pretty down that night. She'd thought leaving her hometown would change her luck and make her life better, but it wasn't really turning out that way. Her job was bad, and her living situation was worse.

She was still crashing with the girl from back home, and the roommate's boyfriend was turning into a big problem. He was hanging around the apartment more, coming by when his girlfriend was at work and pretending like he thought she'd be there. He always managed to brush up against Sharlah when he squeezed by her in the hallway.

Sharlah had heard him try the door while she was in the shower. She knew the lock wasn't much good, and if he caught her alone in the bathroom, she didn't stand a chance.

Talking to her roommate went nowhere, which didn't surprise Sharlah. She knew how these things went. The girl always got the blame.

Sharlah was trying to save up first month's rent and a deposit for her own place, but she was a long way from having enough money. She'd already bought a pocketknife at the Army-Navy store and kept it with her all the time, even when she slept. She wasn't sure what else to do.

Brian had brought his guitar to the Laundromat that night, and he was goofing around, taking requests. Sharlah asked for something by Jimmy Buffett, thinking he'd play "Margaritaville," the one song that every guy at the beach with a guitar seemed to know. But he'd surprised her by playing an older ballad, "Come Monday."

The lyrics—full of longing for someone—made Sharlah sad. Her whole life, she'd been leaving people behind or had been left behind herself, and no one had ever missed her like that.

Later, when the Laundromat was mostly empty and they were folding their clothes, Brian asked her what was wrong, and she told him the whole story about the roommate's boyfriend.

Brian hadn't interrupted her or acted like it was her fault. When she was done, he'd told her she could sleep on his couch for as long as she wanted. He said he wouldn't try to bust in on her in the shower. He held up his hand and said, "I swear on a stack of Bibles," which made her laugh.

She never went back to her friend's place.

Brian lived in a drab concrete-block fourplex then, an apartment so small the bedroom barely had room for a twin bed. It was messy, and the bathroom was downright gross. But he was true to his word—he didn't even try to hug her.

She worked nights then and Brian worked days, so they didn't see each other much. One morning, though, he got up at 4 because he had a long drive to his job site. Sharlah was still awake, reading a book, unwinding from her shift.

She talked to him while he packed his lunch: two sandwiches, a banana, a bag of chips and a two-pack of Hostess Cupcakes. They joked about how the cupcakes were the perfect food to stockpile in case the Russians started a nuclear war.

Brian stopped on his way out of the kitchen, and for a minute Sharlah thought he was going to kiss her. But he'd just squeezed her arm and told her to go to sleep.

When she got home from work that night, she discovered that Brian had saved her one of the cupcakes. It was perched on the kitchen counter, the plastic wrap tucked under it.

She ate the cupcake standing up, then took a shower to wash away the smell of cigarettes and fried fish.

After her shower, she went to the fridge and got out a beer. She stood in the kitchen for a long time, the unopened beer in her hand.

Finally, she put the beer back and tiptoed down the hall to Brian's room.

She stood by the bed awhile without saying anything. Brian was sleeping with one arm thrown back, and to Sharlah he looked like a little boy. Sweet. Defenseless.

Brian stirred and opened his eyes.

"Sharlah?" He stretched and yawned. "What's up?"

"I wanted to tell you thanks for the cupcake."

"You're welcome." He smiled then, a lazy grin that started with his eyes and slowly took over his face. "Is that it?"

"It's cold on the couch."

Brian threw back the covers and scooted over to make room for her.

She found that she could talk to Brian about anything, because he never judged her. After a few weeks, curled up together in the dark one night, she told him everything— about her folks, her brother in prison, all the ugly things in her life.

Because she was the one to tell Brian about them, she got to decide, for once, what those things said about who she was.

She was 17, and for the first time she could remember, Sharlah was happy.

THREE

SHARLAH WAS UP EARLY Sunday morning, even though she had the day off.

She'd had a hard time sleeping, turning everything over and over in her head. No matter how she looked at it, though, Brian and 130 pounds of pot just didn't make any sense.

She'd never seen Brian get high. He always said it made him stupid and he was stupid enough already. And he knew how she felt about breaking the law.

Everybody made it sound like there was a lot of money involved. But if Brian had extra money and spent it, she didn't know where.

His truck was five years old and paid off. His parents gave it to him when he turned 16 and then made Brian take over the payments when he quit college.

The house she and Brian rented was the nicest place Sharlah had ever lived, but that wasn't saying much. It was basically a wooden shack—one bedroom, one bathroom, nothing special—set on a narrow, weedy lot in a so-so part of town.

Their furniture was second-hand. The most expensive thing in the house was the stereo, Brian's high school graduation present.

The truth was, Brian wasn't into making money and buying stuff. He wasn't envious of other people's new cars. He didn't care that they couldn't afford cable and didn't get MTV like all of their friends. The thing he worked hardest at was learning to play "Jack and Diane" on his guitar.

Sharlah always teased him that his favorite things were drinking beer, playing guitar and making love, "not necessarily in that order." Brian would smile at her and say, "Definitely not in that order."

Brian had no ambition, that's what his folks said, like that was the worst possible thing. Brian told her that's what his college girlfriend had said, too, when she dumped him—that he wasn't trying to "do anything" with his life.

It didn't help that he was constantly compared to Kevin, one of those super-confident people who always seemed to come out a winner. It was easy for Kevin to please his parents, because the stuff they wanted came naturally to him.

Brian wasn't good at the things his parents thought were important, and the things he was good at, well, Mitch and Renee thought those things didn't matter. He could never make them happy.

Sometimes when Brian was down, he said he felt like all his friends were leaving him behind—Kevin was settled down, and Cliff had quit his construction job and was trying to put together a deal to open a bar.

Sharlah told Brian that everybody did things on a different schedule and he shouldn't worry. But she also noticed that Kevin and Cliff didn't seem to call much anymore.

In fact, Sharlah hadn't heard from Cliff and Missy since Brian's arrest, which annoyed her. People at Sharlah's work had known about it, and she imagined it was all over the bar where Missy worked, too. If something bad had happened to Missy or Cliff, Brian would have been checking in to see whether he could help. He was loyal like that.

Instead, it looked like it was up to Sharlah to get in touch with them.

Sharlah took her cereal bowl to the sink and washed it. She'd been looking forward all week to her one day off with Brian, and now she was at loose ends. It was too early to call Missy; she never got up before noon.

The bathroom needed cleaning, but that wouldn't take more than 20 minutes. She also needed to go by the diner and let her boss know about Brian's hearing. She wanted to get some new books at the library—she was hoping *Cinnamon Skin* was back on the shelf, finally—but the library didn't open until noon on Sundays.

Brian laughed at the way she had the library schedule memorized, but she always told him it was his fault, because getting a library card had been his idea in the first place.

He'd seen the way Sharlah pored over the used paperbacks at the thrift store and was disappointed when she couldn't find something good. Now she went to the library at least once a week and always came home with an armful of books.

At first, she'd stuck to authors she already knew—Sidney Sheldon, Jackie Collins, Judith Krantz. Eventually, though, she got to know one of the girls who worked at the library, and Jeanie started making suggestions.

Now Sharlah read all kinds of books, although mysteries were her favorite. Lately she'd been reading John le Carré, because Jeanie recommended him. The only problem was that he used a lot of words she didn't know, and she had to keep a list and look them up in the library's big dictionary. She'd been a little embarrassed about the list at first, worried that Brian would make fun of it, but he never did.

After Sharlah cleaned the bathroom, she decided that she might as well do the kitchen floor, since she had the mop out already. Everything else in her life might be falling apart, but at least the house could be clean.

Then she took a pail of watered-down bleach out to the front porch and spent an hour on the patch of red Missy left when she threw up an evening's worth of Tequila Sunrises.

As she scrubbed, she worked up a head of steam about Missy. It was just like her to leave a big mess at somebody else's house and not even think about who would clean it up. Sharlah decided that she wasn't going to worry too much about what time Missy would wake up. She'd head over there to return Missy's album when she felt like it, and if Missy was asleep, well, she'd just have to get up.

⌁

Missy and Cliff had just moved to one of the new condo developments down on Seawall Boulevard, a sparkling white stucco complex with two pools and Gulf views. Missy said they got a deal on the rent because Cliff's stepdad knew one of the developers.

Every time she pulled into their parking lot, Sharlah had to tamp down her jealousy. Missy always tried to pretend the place wasn't that great, complaining that the closets were too small for all her clothes and that the long entry hall wasted space.

Sharlah walked past Missy's yellow Datsun parked crookedly in its assigned space—and part of the adjacent space—and climbed the stairs to the second floor, shaking her head. It was just like Missy to take two spaces.

From the walkway, the development was a solid white wall with a series of identical blue doors. At No. 217, Sharlah stopped and raised her fist to knock.

She noticed that the door was open about an inch; Missy was up early. Sharlah was a little disappointed. She'd been looking forward, in a mean way, to waking Missy up.

She knocked once and pushed the door in another inch or two. "Missy?"

Sharlah heard voices inside, and for a minute she thought Missy might be on the phone. But then she heard a laugh track and realized it was the TV.

"Missy? Hey, it's Sharlah."

For no reason that she could explain, Sharlah's heart began to pound. She was tempted to put Missy's album down inside the door and take off. Instead, she forced herself to push the door all the way open, into the long entry hallway.

The condo looked like her house after the police had searched it, only Missy—being Missy—hadn't bothered to clean up. The door off the hall to the bedroom was open, and Sharlah glanced in. The sheets were half pulled off, and the bedspread pooled onto the floor. Pieces of a broken lamp littered the carpet.

"Missy?"

The name stuck in Sharlah's throat. She swallowed hard and tried again. "Missy?"

Then she saw a bare foot with hot pink toenail polish jutting into the hallway from the kitchen.

Sharlah crept forward and reached out, her hand shaking, to touch the sole.

It was cold.

Sharlah snatched her hand back.

When she was 13, Sharlah cleaned house every other week for Mrs. Whiting, a neighbor lady. One Saturday, Mrs. Whiting hadn't answered the door, and when Sharlah let herself in, she found the old woman in her recliner. She looked asleep, but when Sharlah touched her arm to wake her, it was cold, just like Missy's foot was cold.

Sharlah reached out again. She had to be sure. She closed her hand around Missy's ankle and waited, hoping to feel a pulse, some sign of warmth or life.

There was nothing.

*

Sharlah had to knock on six doors before she found somebody home. The man in No. 229 said she could come in to wait, but she didn't.

The police found her outside on the concrete walkway, her back against the metal railing, knees pulled up. She faced the door of No. 217, the Men at Work album clutched to her chest.

The officers walked into Missy's apartment to see for themselves. After a couple seconds, they walked out. One stationed himself in the doorway and unclipped his radio.

Sharlah caught a few of the words: White. Female. Deceased.

The other cop took Sharlah's arm and helped her up, which surprised her, because she had no memory of sitting down. He guided her down the stairs to a police car.

"We're going to wait here," he said, opening the passenger door of the cruiser.

For the second time in three days, Sharlah was sitting in a police car, spelling out her name, where she lived, how old she was. This cop, at least, was being nice and turned on the AC.

He scribbled down everything she said. "I know this is upsetting," he said. "The girl upstairs, who is that?"

"Missy Burke," Sharlah said. "That's my friend Missy."

"You got a good look at her, then?" he said. "You're sure?"

"I didn't see all of her," Sharlah said. "I only saw her foot. I went to the edge of the hall and felt it, and it was cold. I assumed it was her. Is it somebody else?"

Hope flickered briefly in her chest, but one look at the cop's face extinguished it.

A van marked CORONER pulled into the parking lot.

Sharlah answered a few more questions—why she'd come by Missy's place, when she'd last seen her, where Missy worked.

Another car pulled up, this one unmarked, and the cop told her the detectives had arrived. He said she should wait in the car, and he got out to talk to them.

More police were showing up by the minute—in uniform, not in uniform. People started wandering out of their condos and over from the pool to check out the commotion.

Suddenly, Sharlah felt exhausted and shaky.

Brian was going to take this really hard. He and Missy had been friends forever.

A cop tapped on the passenger window and then opened the door.

"The detectives want to speak with you."

Sharlah got out of the car, nearly dropping the Men at Work album. She'd forgotten she was still holding it. The cop gently took it away.

He walked Sharlah to the foot of the stairs and introduced her to another cop. He wore baggy brown dress pants, a white short-sleeved shirt and an ugly green tie. He was old, with broken veins in his nose and cheeks. Sharlah didn't catch his name.

He asked a few of the questions she'd already answered— what time she'd arrived, why she'd come, what she'd seen. He didn't write anything down, just watched her as she repeated everything she'd said earlier.

"And you only saw the foot, correct? You never looked around the corner and saw the rest of the body?"

"Her foot was cold," Sharlah said, "so I went for help." She'd thought that was the right thing to do, but now the cops had asked her about it twice, which made her wonder if she'd messed up somehow.

The detective watched her for a moment. He seemed to be weighing something.

"The victim suffered what we call blunt force trauma. Most of the damage is to the back of the head." He put one hand behind his head, near his neck, demonstrating. "Would you be willing to look at her face and make the positive identification for us? We haven't tracked down her folks yet, and we'd like to get this done."

Sharlah's instant reaction was no, she didn't want to look at Missy's dead body. But then she thought again. "If I do it, then her mom or dad won't have to, right?"

"That's right," the detective said.

Sharlah took a deep breath. "OK."

Missy's body came out of the condo on a wheeled stretcher, zipped up in a black plastic bag. The detective led Sharlah over to the stretcher.

"Ready?"

Sharlah nodded.

One of the attendants unzipped the bag a little, just enough to show Missy's face and neck, down to the edge of her white T-shirt.

She had a purple mark above her right eye and another on her cheek. Her hair on one side was matted with blood, turning it from blonde to rust. The strangest thing, Sharlah thought, was how her lips seemed to have no color at all.

"That's her," Sharlah said. "That's Missy."

The attendant zipped the bag. The detective told her that an officer would drive her downtown to the police station to answer more questions.

The ride went by in a blur. At the station, the officer showed Sharlah to a small room with two chairs and a table and left her there.

The AC was turned up high, and Sharlah was dressed for running errands on a hot, humid day in a car with a weak air conditioner. It didn't take long for goose bumps to rise on her bare legs and arms.

She hugged herself for warmth. She didn't have her watch, and the room didn't have a clock, but everything seemed to be taking a long time.

She guessed that someone had to tell Missy's mom. What a horrible job that would be.

Sharlah had met Missy's mom once. She seemed young and cool, more like an older sister than a mom. She and Missy shared clothes and fought like sisters, too. Sharlah had witnessed some of their screaming matches over the phone.

Missy had terrible temper tantrums. She was like a little kid that way, but she could also be really sweet. It was hard to believe anyone would kill her.

When Missy was in a good mood, nobody was more fun. Mostly, Missy just needed to be the center of attention. Brian said it was because she hardly saw her dad after the divorce and her mom was running around dating instead of spending time at home.

Sharlah hoped Missy's mom had the money for a big funeral with lots of flowers. Missy would definitely want that.

About the time Sharlah was thinking she should go find somebody, in case they'd forgotten she was there, the detective she'd met earlier came into the room.

First, he asked Sharlah a bunch of questions that she swore she'd answered twice already. Then he asked how long she'd known Missy and how they'd met.

Sharlah did her best to explain it, how Missy and Brian and Cliff had all known each other since grade school. Cliff moved to town first, to work for a friend of his stepdad's. Brian moved down to room with Cliff after he left school. Then Missy came and Brian had to move out, which was why Brian lived by himself when Sharlah met him. She probably went into more detail than the cop wanted, because she'd always felt like Cliff and Missy screwed Brian over on the roommate thing.

How did Cliff and Missy get along, the detective wanted to know.

"They've been together since high school," Sharlah said. "They get along fine."

"You sound like you're not so sure about that."

"Why are you asking me this?"

The detective put down his pen. "Who do you think might have done this to Missy?"

Sharlah realized where the questions were going, and she was shocked. "You think Cliff did this?" She shook her head. "No way."

"I'm just exploring possibilities," the detective said. "Did you ever witness any physical fights between them? Did Missy ever confide in you about anything like that?"

"Cliff would never hit her," Sharlah said. "If anything, it was the other way around."

"Tell me about that," the detective said, raising an eyebrow. "Missy was violent?"

"No! Missy was just…" Sharlah trailed off, trying to think how to explain.

It seemed unfair to paint Missy in an unflattering light when she was dead.

"She was insecure. If she didn't think Cliff was paying enough attention to her, she'd find something to have a hissy fit about. Mostly she just said mean things, but sometimes she'd throw stuff or try to kick him."

"And how did Cliff respond to that?"

"Cliff's a big guy, so it's not like she ever really hurt him," Sharlah said. "He'd just catch her wrist and tell her to calm down. He was good with her."

"So you never saw him respond with violence?"

"Never. Brian wouldn't have been friends with him if anything like that had gone on. He doesn't believe in hitting women."

The detective turned a page. "So, if you don't think Cliff could have done this, any thoughts on who might have? Anyone she had trouble with?"

"I don't know," Sharlah said. "I mean, it's not like she hung around a rough crowd or anything."

"What about this drug situation your boyfriend's involved in?"

Sharlah's temper flared. "Are you saying Brian had something to do with this? That's bullshit! Brian wouldn't hurt anybody! Anyway, you've had him locked up since Friday."

"I'm asking whether you think the two things could be related, that's all."

"I'm not convinced Brian had anything to do with drugs," Sharlah said, her voice rising. "I don't have to believe it just because you all say so!"

It seemed as though the madder she got, the calmer the detective was. He eyed her steadily. "If you know something, you need to tell. We're talking about a murder now."

"I don't know anything!"

The detective waited and watched.

"Honest to God, I don't," Sharlah said. "I never heard anybody talk about drugs. I never saw any money. Brian and me, we're broke. Ask anybody. Ask our landlord how often we're short for the rent and pay a couple days late. Ask my boss how often I pick up extra shifts."

"OK," the detective said, holding up his palm to slow her down. "OK. Do you know where Cliff Knorr is? We've been trying to locate him since Friday."

"Since Friday? Why?"

Suddenly, everything became clear to Sharlah. Brian would never go out and do a drug deal on his own, but Cliff? He was trying to come up with money to open a bar.

Now she could see how it all might have happened: Cliff talked Brian into it, and Cliff probably had the money, and Cliff was the reason Brian wouldn't talk to the police.

The detective was watching her closely, but she wasn't going to let on that she'd figured anything out. She was determined not to make things worse for Brian.

"If Cliff's not at his mom's, or his dad's, then I don't know where he is," Sharlah said.

"Let's change gears," the detective said. "In your experience, how conscious of her personal safety was Missy? Was she careful? Did she always lock the door?"

"Oh, yeah, definitely," Sharlah said. "I used to work nights, and we talked about how you have to walk out with other people and have your keys already in your hand. She even talked about getting a gun, but I don't think she did."

"If I told you that she appeared to be dressed for bed, in a big T-shirt and her underpants, and that it didn't appear anyone broke in, what would you surmise?"

Sharlah looked at him blankly.

"Guess," he said, "what would you guess, based on those facts?"

Sharlah crossed her arms. "You're trying to get me to say it was Cliff."

"No," the detective said. "I'm just asking, what do you think that means?"

"That it was someone she thought she was safe with," Sharlah said quietly.

There was a tap at the door, and a man stuck his head into the room. "Notification's done. Patrol's got your witness. We're waiting for his lawyer."

"Cuff him in the waiting area," the detective said. "Have the patrolman come get her."

He slid a business card across the table to Sharlah. "I'm going to check out what you told me, and if I find out you're lying about anything, you're going to be right back down here, OK? If you think of anything else, you call the number on that card. We're getting a patrolman to drive you back to your car. Wait here."

He got up and followed the other man out of the room.

A minute or two later, the door opened again. Sharlah recognized the uniformed officer—he was the one who had helped her right her couch, the one who came to the diner.

"I'll take you back to your car," he said, all business, as usual.

"I know you," Sharlah said. "You were at my house the other day." She peered at his name tag. R. ZUK, it read. "How do you say your name?"

He looked down at the tag, as though he needed to read it. "Rhymes with book." He held the door open. "This way, please. Down the hallway and…"

Sharlah stepped out of the room and then, at the end of the hallway, she spotted Brian. He was sitting on a bench, staring at the floor.

"Brian!"

Without even thinking, she sprinted toward him.

Brian looked up when she called his name. He tried to stand, but his right wrist was handcuffed to a metal ring bolted into the wall.

"Miss Webb! Stop!" Zuk called after her.

Sharlah reached Brian and awkwardly threw her arms around his neck. Brian wrapped his free arm around her. "Hey, Shar," he murmured.

Zuk came hustling up behind, all the equipment on his belt rattling and squeaking. "Miss Webb," he said. "Step back, please."

Sharlah ignored him. Ever since she found Missy, she'd been trying to keep it together and do what the cops asked her to do, but she'd had enough.

Another cop came around the corner and stopped short. "What the hell is going on here? Break that up!"

Brian put his hand on her shoulder and gently pushed her away. "Shar, you have to do what they say."

Sharlah sank to her knees and began to cry, big heaving sobs. Embarrassed, she put her hands to her face.

"She's a friend of the dead girl," Zuk told the other cop. "She ID'd the body."

Brian leaned over, as close as he could get to Sharlah without touching her. His free hand twitched on his knee, inches from her head. "Shar, don't cry. Please don't cry."

That just made Sharlah cry harder. Then Brian's breath became uneven, like he was crying, too.

"Get her up," the second cop said. "Now."

Zuk squatted down and took Sharlah's elbow. "Miss Webb, you have to stand up."

Sharlah reluctantly allowed him to pull her to her feet. She looked up at Zuk, then the other cop, her eyes still brimming with tears. She didn't have a tissue; she dragged her hand across her face and wiped it on her T-shirt.

"Sorry," she said.

Zuk exchanged a look with the other cop.

"Oh, for God's sake," the second cop said, sighing. "OK."

Zuk fumbled on his belt for a key and unlocked Brian's handcuff. "You can have a minute," he said.

"One minute," the other cop said, holding up one finger. "That's it. And no talking!"

Freed from the cuff, Brian jumped up and wrapped his arms around Sharlah, pulling her in tight. She rested her head against his shoulder and buried her face in his neck.

The fabric of the jail shirt was rough against her cheek, and Brian smelled wrong—a harsh, chemical odor.

It didn't matter.

"OK, that's all," the second cop said.

"I'll see you tomorrow," Sharlah said into Brian's neck. "At court."

"I love you," Brian whispered. "Hang in there." Then he let her go and backed away.

6

When Officer Zuk dropped Sharlah at her car, he told her he was going to follow her home. She didn't think that was necessary and told him so, but he seemed determined.

At the house, he offered to come in and take a look around, which Sharlah thought was weird. She told Zuk thanks, but she was fine. She'd stayed in the house without Brian before—he was gone three days for his brother's wedding, and his mom always insisted he had to spend one night at home at the holidays. She wasn't worried.

Zuk told her to be sure to lock her doors, and then he left.

Sharlah did that right away, but she would have anyway. She didn't need reminding. How did the detective put it? Sharlah was very conscious of her personal safety.

After she'd locked up, she went to the kitchen and surveyed the contents of the refrigerator and cupboard, trying to come up with something for dinner. She hadn't eaten anything since a bowl of cereal at breakfast.

She didn't have much to choose from. Friday was supposed to be payday for Brian; they'd been counting on his check for grocery money.

There was a box of macaroni and cheese, but no margarine or milk. Sharlah knew from experience that substituting water for the milk produced a runny, inedible mess. There were four slices of bread, counting the heel, and a little bit of peanut butter. Looked like she'd be having PBJ again. She thought there might be an apple left in the crisper drawer, but then she remembered that she'd packed it in Brian's lunch Friday.

As soon as Brian made bail and came home, they were going to have to figure out what to do about money.

Sharlah fished an envelope and a pencil out of the junk drawer and did a little calculating while she ate her sandwich. She could pick up two or maybe three extra shifts a week, but it would be hard to get more than that unless somebody quit.

Assuming nothing else went wrong, they'd be OK for a couple weeks, especially since she had money in savings. If something went wrong—and Sharlah was pretty sure her clutch was just about shot—they'd be out of money a lot sooner.

She didn't know whether Brian could work when he was out on bail, but she could look for a second job. In the corner of the envelope, she jotted down other things they could do. The record store bought albums back. They could sell the TV. She scanned the living room, looking for anything else they could do without.

It was important to come up with a plan. If she didn't, Brian's parents would impose one, and it didn't take a genius to figure out what that would be. They'd want Brian to move home and work for his dad, like he had summers and Saturdays all through high school. They'd try their damnedest to make it impossible for him to see Sharlah.

Of course, they were paying the lawyer, so Brian's parents might do all of that anyway.

Sharlah found herself getting really mad at him for giving them the opening, but then she made herself stop and take a deep breath. She was trying hard not to be angry until she heard his side of things. For all she knew, Brian wasn't even aware of the pot under the lumber in his truck. It would be just like him to do somebody a favor and not ask questions.

The phone rang then, a welcome distraction from her calculations.

It was Kevin. He'd already heard about Missy; Sharlah was glad she didn't have to break the news. Like Brian, Kevin had known Missy a lot longer than Sharlah had.

He asked her what happened at the police station. She tried to keep it short, because she really didn't feel like rehashing all the details.

"So I guess it had to be Cliff," Kevin said when she was done.

"I don't believe that," Sharlah said. "I know they argued, but he loved Missy. I don't think it's fair to Cliff to say that."

"Hey, I'm just saying that's what the police think," Kevin said. "Anyway, that's not really why I called. I need to talk to you about Brian's court appearance tomorrow."

That was just like Kevin, cutting to the chase. That was the difference between him and Brian. Kevin was always focused.

"It's at 11, right? And we're supposed to meet the lawyer in the hallway at ten of?"

Kevin took a deep breath. "Here's the thing, Sharlah. Mom thinks it's really important to make a good impression on the judge. She wants him to see Brian's not just a drug dealer, he's..."

"Brian's not a drug dealer!"

"Well, the police say he is. Mom wants to show he's from a good family and..."

Sharlah should have known this was coming. She stamped her foot and fought the urge to cuss Kevin out.

"And she doesn't want me there."

"It's not that she doesn't want you there," Kevin said. "It's more like..."

"She never wants me around, Kevin. I'm not stupid."

"No one's saying you're stupid, Sharlah."

"So what *are* you saying?"

Kevin sighed. "Look, don't shoot the messenger here, OK? I talked to Dad, and what we were thinking was, if you could maybe not wear your work uniform and..."

"I can't skip work, Kevin. I need the money. I'm already leaving early."

"Nobody's asking you to skip work. But it would be great if you could change before you came to the courthouse."

Sharlah added up in her head how much money she'd lose taking an additional 15 minutes off her shift. "Fine. I can change first."

"Just make sure it's not shorts or jeans. It needs to be something nice, like a skirt, but not a short skirt. Nothing that would look..."

"Like I'm Brian's trailer-trash girlfriend?" That's what Renee called her: Brian's trailer-trash girlfriend. Sharlah knew this because Missy had told her.

"Sharlah, I'm trying to help you here."

"Thanks, Kevin. I appreciate the help. I'll see you tomorrow."

Sharlah slammed the receiver back in the cradle.

FOUR

SHARLAH SET HER ALARM a half-hour early so she'd have time to blow-dry and style her hair. Even as she carefully curled each section, watching herself in the mirror, she knew it was a waste of time. The first time she walked into the hot kitchen at the diner it would wilt. Anyway, Renee would probably give her the evil eye no matter how she looked.

Two sets of clothes were laid out on the bed: her uniform and her outfit for court.

She'd gone through her closet the night before and pulled out a plain blue cotton skirt that came to her knees and a yellow polo shirt. Missy had helped Sharlah shop for the clothes when she decided to try for an office job. The yellow was a terrible color on her, but the shirt had been marked down to $4, too cheap to pass up.

It was good she was getting another use out of the clothes, because she didn't get the job. The ad in the paper said it was just answering the phone and filing, no typing necessary, but when Sharlah filled out the application, the woman said they couldn't consider anyone without a high school diploma.

The only shoes Sharlah had that would work were a pair of Candies that hurt her feet, the ones Brian called her Barbie shoes. She'd borrowed a pair of blue espadrilles from Missy when she went to see about the job.

She'd dreamed the night before about shopping with Missy. Missy came out of the dressing room and said, "How do I look?" And when Sharlah looked, one side of her head was spurting blood.

"Ouch!" Sharlah yanked the hot curling iron away from her neck. She pushed her hair back and leaned up on her tiptoes to take a look in the mirror. Her neck was a little red, but it seemed like the burn mark would fade.

God only knew what Renee would say if she showed up with a red mark on her neck. She'd probably try to convince Brian some other guy put it there.

It was so stupid, the way Renee always got worked up over how Sharlah looked. It had been that way from the very beginning, since the first Thanksgiving Brian took her home. They'd only been together a few weeks, and she didn't know that Brian's mom expected everybody to dress up until she saw him putting on a sweater and khakis that morning.

Sharlah was in jeans and a sweatshirt. She didn't own anything nicer, and there was no place open to buy anything, not that she could afford to. Brian told her not to worry and even changed into jeans to make her feel better, but it didn't matter. His mom was pissed.

By their first Christmas, Sharlah had the job at the diner and volunteered to work. That's what they always did now for holidays. Sharlah worked, and Brian packed his nice clothes and went to Houston the night before, to keep his mom happy.

Sharlah stopped and made herself take a deep breath. Sometimes just thinking about Brian's mom made her so mad that her hands shook.

❡

Sharlah knew her manager, Joan, didn't like to think about anything too complicated until she'd had her first cup of coffee. Sharlah poured the cup herself and took it to Joan. She waited 10 more minutes before she went to explain about Brian's court date.

Joan heard her out, but Sharlah could tell from her expression that she wasn't happy.

"This is two times in three days you've asked me to let you go early, Sharlah, and both times with no warning."

"I know," Sharlah said, "and I'm sorry about that. But after today, Brian's out on bail, and then I'll have more notice before the next thing."

Joan had little glasses that she wore on a beaded chain, and she liked to stare at people over the top of them when she was displeased.

"When did you find out about this?"

"On Saturday."

"So why am I finding out today, which is Monday?"

"I was going to ask yesterday," Sharlah said. She looked around and dropped her voice. "But a friend died, and I had to talk to the police. I was at the station all afternoon."

Joan drew back in surprise. "That girl in the condo down on Seawall?"

Sharlah nodded.

"Let me look at the schedule. Get back to work now."

Fifteen minutes later, Joan found Sharlah setting out salt and pepper shakers. "Come talk to me in the office," she said.

Sharlah followed her down the hall, past the restrooms and the pay phone into a little cubbyhole next to the kitchen.

"Shut the door," Joan said.

Sharlah scooted up against the desk and closed the door.

Joan had the morning paper spread out before her on the desk.

"It says here the body was found by a friend." Joan looked up. "Was that you?"

"Yes."

"Oh, Sharlah." Joan settled her bulk back in her office chair. "It says that the police can't find her boyfriend, and then there's all this business about maybe her death is tied to a violent drug ring. Is that what Brian's mixed up in?"

"People are saying a lot of things about Brian," Sharlah said. "He's innocent until proven guilty."

Joan gave her a pitying look. "Sharlah, I like you. You're reliable, and you try to do right by this job. I just wish you'd try as hard to do right by Sharlah."

All she wanted was permission to leave work early, and now Sharlah was going to be stuck listening to one of Joan's lectures. She tried not to let her impatience show.

Joan took off her glasses and turned her head. She pointed to a star-shaped scar on her temple. "My ex-husband did that to me. Bashed me in the head with a glass ash tray."

Sharlah couldn't let that go. "Brian would never hit me! He's nicer to me than anybody's ever been. Don't judge him because of what's in the paper."

Joan sighed and put her glasses back on. "I know a thing or two about letting men drag you down, Sharlah, and I hate to see it happen to you. You've got so much potential."

"Brian's not dragging me down," Sharlah insisted. "He loves me."

She and Joan stared at each other across the small desk.

"Nobody wants unsolicited advice, Sharlah, but I'm going to give you some anyway. You need to ask yourself whether being with Brian is the best thing for you. I know you might think you're nothing without him, but you're wrong about that."

Sharlah started to get mad, but then she reined herself in. There was no point in arguing with Joan, especially not when she was trying to get a favor from her.

"I guess that's something to think about," Sharlah said, hoping to get Joan off her back. She waited for more advice, but Joan seemed to have run out of steam.

"Try to get your tables wrapped up by 10:30," Joan said, finally. "And the next time you need to leave early, you let me know ahead of time."

"I will," Sharlah said. "I promise. Thank you. I won't do this to you again."

Joan waved her hand in dismissal. "Get back to work."

Sharlah hesitated a moment.

"What?" Joan said.

"Can I have the paper?"

*

At 10:30, Sharlah was still waiting for her big table of the morning, eight older women, to quit lingering over their coffee and settle the bill. At 10:35, one of them flagged her and asked for a refill. Then everybody wanted a refill.

At 10:40, Joan told Sharlah to go, that Robin would wrap up the table. Sharlah hated to give up on such a big table, because she knew Robin would lie about how much they tipped and shortchange her. But she didn't have any choice.

She sprinted to her car and grabbed her clothes. Back inside, she locked herself in the biggest stall in the restroom and peeled off her uniform and pantyhose. She pulled the polo shirt over head, stepped into the skirt and jammed her feet into her sandals.

She stopped at the mirror to fluff up her hair and then dashed out to her car. It was 10:48, but she thought she'd probably still be OK on time.

And she would have been, if she'd found a parking place closer to the courthouse.

Instead, she pounded up the stairs and arrived in the hallway outside the courtroom at 11:12, seconds before Renee Lowry burst out of the courtroom, trailed by Mitch, Kevin and Brian's lawyer.

Sharlah rushed down the hall to catch up with them.

"Sorry I'm late. Is it over already?"

Renee glared at her. Mitch looked haggard. Kevin's expression was unreadable.

"Let's find a quiet spot down the hall where we can talk about this," Ingersoll said.

Sharlah looked back toward the courtroom, confused. "Where's Brian?"

Ingersoll looked at Mitch, then Renee. When they didn't speak up, he took a step toward Sharlah. "Brian was denied bail."

"What? Why?"

"It's a lot of things," Ingersoll said. "The seriousness of the charges, but mostly..."

"My brother *killed* a guy, and he got bail!"

Renee Lowry actually staggered. "Dear God," she whispered.

Belatedly, Sharlah realized that Brian had never told his parents about Wayne.

"Not here, Renee," Mitch said, taking her elbow. "Not here."

Ingersoll pointed toward an empty bench down the hall. "Let's have a seat down there and discuss this."

They all filed down the hall and sat on the bench. Sharlah picked the spot next to Kevin. That seemed to be the safest place to be.

Ingersoll squatted in front of them. "This is a temporary setback. We'll ask for a new hearing."

Sharlah had just begun to realize that Brian wasn't coming home. "But why won't they give him bail? I don't understand."

"The main thing is that the judge found Brian to be a flight risk," Ingersoll said.

"But Brian doesn't even like to fly!"

Renee snorted, and Sharlah swiveled from Renee to the lawyer, unsure what she had said wrong.

"It doesn't literally mean flying," Ingersoll said. "It means running away. They have evidence Brian was planning to leave the country. Something about Costa Rica."

"He talked to someone about that? He never told me," Sharlah said.

"Maybe his plans didn't include you," Renee said. Mitch reached for her hand, but Renee jerked it away.

Kevin started to say something and got as far as, "Mom…" before thinking better of it.

"No, I know he likes to talk about Costa Rica," Sharlah said, "but that wasn't for real! It was just something we imagined doing, like me wanting to go to New York City."

"This is crazy," Mitch said. "Brian's never even been out of the country."

Sharlah sneaked a glance at Kevin. That wasn't true, and he knew it. When Brian was 16, he'd tagged along with Cliff and Kevin to South Padre Island, and the three of them had gone over the border to Matamoros. The older boys tried to get Brian to go to a brothel, but he wouldn't do it.

Kevin didn't meet her eyes. He was studying the floor, as though some important message were spelled out in the tile. Sharlah had never seen Kevin so subdued.

"They're playing hardball, and for now the judge is going to let them," Ingersoll said. "They're trying to make a big case, and Brian's all they've got. They think sitting in jail will make him more cooperative."

Kevin abruptly checked his watch. "Dad, I have to go. Lynn's doctor's appointment is at 1:30. I promised her I'd make this one."

"That's all right son, you go on," Mitch said. "I'll call you later. Give Lynn our love."

Kevin strode down the hall and stabbed at the elevator button with his thumb. He waited for a second, then turned and started down the stairs.

With Kevin gone, Sharlah scooted down the bench a little closer to Brian's dad, but not too close. "Does it take a long time to get a new hearing?"

"Hard to say," Ingersoll said. "In the meantime, there's jail visitation on Mondays, Wednesdays and Saturdays. Brian's allowed two visits per week, and two people can visit at a time."

He opened his briefcase and pulled out a sheet of paper, which he handed to Mitch. "This covers the rules. Brian could use a visit. He needs support."

He closed up the briefcase. "I'm sorry we didn't get better news today, but this is just one battle. Don't get too discouraged."

He shook hands with Mitch, then nodded at Renee and Sharlah. "I'll be in touch."

He was barely down the hall when Renee hissed, "Mitchell, that man..."

"Not now, Renee."

Sharlah held out her hand for the visitation schedule. "Can I look at that?"

Mitch absentmindedly handed it to her.

"You saw Brian in court, right?" She leaned forward, trying to make eye contact with Mitch. "How did he seem?"

Renee answered before Mitch could say anything. "Oh, honestly, Sharlah, how do you expect he seemed? He's an inmate."

"Renee," Mitch said. He patted her knee. Renee crossed her arms and stared off into the distance.

"I'm so worried about him," Sharlah said. "I saw him for a minute at the police station yesterday, when they had us there about Missy. He didn't seem good."

Mitch looked her in the face for the first time. His eyes—the same blue as Brian's—were bloodshot, and he looked pale despite his tan. "Seems like we get a fresh piece of bad news every day," he said. "That just breaks my heart about Missy."

She always thought Brian's dad looked pretty good, for an old guy in his forties, but today he seemed like all the starch had gone out of him.

Sharlah wished she knew what to say. She never could figure out how to talk to Brian's parents.

She looked at the visitation schedule. "It says here that you can go Monday from 4 to 6 p.m.," she said. "Did you all want to go this afternoon, since you're already in town? I could go on Wednesday, but it's noon to 3, and I have to work. Saturday might be better for me, maybe with Kevin, if he wanted to go?"

She hoped the Lowrys would say that they had to get back to Houston, that she could see Brian by herself.

She didn't want to wait until Saturday to see him, but she also wanted the Lowrys to realize she was willing to work with them, for Brian's sake.

"Let me see that." Renee stretched her hand out across her husband, and Sharlah gave her the schedule.

Renee put it in her purse, which she snapped closed. The click echoed in the empty corridor.

"Are you going to go this afternoon, then? Or should..."

Renee cut Sharlah off. "Brian's schedule is not something we need to discuss with you."

Sharlah stuffed her hands under her thighs so that Renee wouldn't see them shake and steadied her voice. "I think Brian should get a say in this."

"Brian is in no position to dictate to us," Renee said, biting off the words. "And you certainly are not, not after getting him into this immoral lifestyle of yours. No one in our family had a minute's trouble with the law before you came along."

"Excuse me?" Sharlah sprang up from the bench. "You're saying this is my fault somehow, because of my brother? I was in sixth grade when that happened!"

Mitch stood and positioned himself between the two women. "Renee, honey, that's enough. Sharlah, this has been a tough time for everybody and we're all on edge. Go on home. We'll work this out, and we'll give you a call."

Sharlah didn't budge, and Mitch put his hand on her arm. "We'll work this out. You have my word on it. Go on home now."

❡

Back in her car, Sharlah leaned her head against the steering wheel and cried.

Then she got mad.

If she didn't hear from Brian's dad, she would call Kevin and enlist his help. She would call Brian's lawyer, too. He'd said his job was to represent Brian's interests. Brian wanted to see her, and his parents shouldn't be allowed to stand in the way. If she had to, she'd go to the jail during visiting hours and dare the Lowrys to throw her out.

Sharlah tried to start the car, but her hands were shaking, so she sat for another minute trying to calm down. Her head was pounding, probably because she cried but also because she hadn't eaten anything since her sandwich the night before.

She needed groceries. She didn't really want to go to the store in these stupid shoes that hurt her feet, but it was a waste of gas to go change first.

With a sigh, she opened her purse and counted her tips, mentally setting her budget.

Sharlah didn't think of herself as having a lot of talents, but she was good at keeping a running tally in her head at the store. Brian tried sneaking things into the cart to mess her up, but she always knew, within a quarter or so, how much the bill would be.

She pushed her cart quickly down the aisles, adding in her head as she went. Milk. Bread. Cereal. The ground beef, she decided, was too high. She rooted around in the case, hoping to find a package closer to expiration marked down, but no luck.

She started feeling better about the money situation as she shopped. Brian was the big eater in the house. She could get three meals, maybe four, out of one box of mac and cheese. She'd eat PBJ and cereal and apples. She didn't need meat.

Back home, Sharlah put away the groceries, made herself a sandwich and sat down on the couch to read the paper she'd bummed from Joan.

There wasn't a whole lot in it about Missy that she didn't already know. The story said her death might be linked to a ring that moved drugs up the I-45 corridor. The ring was tied, the paper said, to a violent gang suspected in several murders.

Sharlah read the story twice, trying to reconcile the facts there with her Brian.

Brian had never even yelled at her. He quit football after eighth grade because he didn't like hitting people. That took guts, too, because Kevin had been a star linebacker, and Brian was supposed to be just like him.

Brian was a big guy—6-2, close to 190 pounds—but he didn't *act* like a big guy. He never tried to intimidate anyone. Sharlah thought it was because Brian, tall and muscular as he was, had always been smaller than Kevin.

Sharlah leafed through the rest of the paper, but there wasn't anything interesting. President Reagan was visiting Mexico. A trough of low pressure had formed in the Gulf.

She had just flipped to the help-wanted ads when someone knocked on her door.

When she opened it, Mitch Lowry was standing on the walk with one foot on the bottom step of the porch. A brown Oldsmobile—Renee's car—idled at the curb. She was in the passenger seat, staring straight ahead.

"Hi, Mr. Lowry," Sharlah said. Even though in her head she always called them Mitch and Renee, Sharlah never addressed the Lowrys that way in person.

"I'm sorry to drop by without calling, Sharlah. Can I come in?"

Sharlah stood back to admit him. "Does Mrs. Lowry want to come in?"

"She'll wait in the car." Mitch took a step inside and looked at the coffee table. "I've interrupted your lunch."

"It's just PBJ," Sharlah said. "It's not going to get cold or anything."

Sharlah was a little unnerved to have Mitch Lowry in the house. Neither of Brian's parents had visited before, because they didn't approve of living together. Sharlah thought that was kind of a joke, considering anyone who could count knew Brian's mother was pregnant with Kevin when she got married.

But they disapproved, and so they hadn't come to the house.

Sharlah tried to remember what she'd seen people on TV do when they had company. "Do you want something to drink? Ice water is about all I've got."

"A glass of ice water would be nice," Mitch said.

Sharlah picked up her plate and went to the kitchen. She let the water from the tap run for a few seconds to get cold while she cracked the ice tray and put four cubes in a glass, checking to make sure it wasn't one of the ones with a chip. Brian liked a lot of ice in his drinks, and she figured his dad might be the same. The Lowrys had an icemaker; they never worried about running out.

She carried the glass back to the living room and stopped, dumbstruck.

Mitch Lowry was sitting on her battered plaid couch, his face buried in his hands, his shoulders heaving in silent sobs.

She took a tentative step toward him. "Mr. Lowry? Are you OK?"

He pulled a handkerchief from his pants pocket and mopped his face. "Sorry," he mumbled into the hankie. "Don't know what's gotten into me."

Sharlah put the water in front of him on the coffee table and retreated across the room to sit in the armchair. She pulled her bare feet up under her and waited.

Mitch took a long drink of water and caught his breath before he spoke.

"Sharlah, it's no secret that Brian's mother and I don't approve of this relationship. Even before this happened, we felt like he was wasting his potential. To be honest, we just don't think you're right for him. But I think you'll agree that we all have to work together here."

He fixed her with those eyes that reminded her so much of Brian. "Renee and I, well, we don't hold a lot of sway right now. Never have, I suppose."

"That's not true," Sharlah said. "Brian cares a lot what you think."

Mitch smiled weakly. "I wish that was true. The person with the most influence over Brian right now is you, whether we like that or not. We think it's best if you go see Brian this afternoon."

Under different circumstances, Sharlah would have been thrilled to have Brian's parents acknowledge her place in his life. Now, though, she felt a little awed by the responsibility.

"I'll make him see what he has to do," Sharlah said, expressing more confidence than she really felt. It would be hard to talk Brian out of covering for Cliff. He was loyal to a fault.

"I have no idea what he's thinking, telling his lawyer he won't play ball," Mitch said. "I have no idea what the hell he's thinking, period. What do you make of all of this?"

"I'm as surprised as you are, Mr. Lowry. I never saw any drugs." She waved her hand around the sparsely furnished living room. "I sure as hell didn't see any money."

"His mother thinks this is Brian's way of thumbing his nose at us."

Of course she does, Sharlah thought, because she assumes everything is about her.

"Brian's not spiteful like that," Sharlah said. "None of this makes sense. It says in the paper the drugs are tied to some violent gang. You *know* that's not Brian."

"I don't know what I know anymore," Mitch said. "I can't imagine why Brian would get mixed up in something like this, unless…"

Sharlah waited, halfway expecting a suggestion that the whole thing was her fault.

But the look Mitch Lowry gave her was more confused than accusative. "I wondered if Brian got into drugs himself, you know, and somebody made him do this because they had their hooks into him. One of our neighbors, her nephew up in Dallas got addicted to cocaine, and when he couldn't pay for it anymore, he stole from his own grandmother."

Mitch put his glass on the table. "Could it be something like that? Is Brian on drugs, and he needed money for them?"

"Brian's not on drugs. He couldn't have hidden that from me," Sharlah said, not quite believing she was having this conversation with Brian's father. "I see all his paychecks. I pay the bills and I know where all the money goes."

She didn't tell Mitch that she'd taken over their finances after the one big argument she and Brian ever had. She filled out Brian's deposit slips and balanced his checkbook, because he tended to get numbers turned around.

Mitch nodded slowly, looking relieved but also sad. "It's hard to realize you don't know your own son," he said.

Sharlah almost felt sorry for him, but she couldn't help thinking that if he didn't know Brian, Mitch Lowry had no one to blame but himself.

"Well, I've taken enough of your time," Mitch said. He started to rise, but then he sat back down.

"Sharlah, you've got to make Brian understand how serious this is. His lawyer told me that if he doesn't take a deal, he could go to prison."

Mitch's voice broke. "He's my baby, Sharlah, and I'll do anything to protect him. He's only 21 years old. He has his whole life ahead of him. We can't let that happen."

"It won't," Sharlah said. "I'll make him see, Mr. Lowry."

Mitch sat for another second, hands resting on his thighs, then he sighed and got up. "I guess I've kept Renee waiting long enough. I appreciate you hearing me out."

Sharlah walked him to the door. "Could you explain to Mrs. Lowry that I didn't know anything about this?"

Mitch opened the door and glanced outside. "Brian and his mother, they've always been oil and water. Renee loves him, don't get me wrong, but right now she's so angry that it just… she says things she doesn't mean. Don't take it to heart."

6

Brian looked smaller in jail.

That was the first thing Sharlah thought when he came shuffling through the door and sat down on the other side of the glass.

He picked up the phone receiver on his side of the glass, and Sharlah did the same.

"Hi, Brian."

"Hi. You need to know they tape all the calls here."

"I know, they gave me a whole list of rules to read while I waited." She mustered a smile for Brian. "Sorry I missed you at court. I was late getting away from work. I had a whole table of old biddies who kept wanting coffee refills."

"I'm just glad to see you."

The rules said they'd have only 20 minutes, so Sharlah decided she'd better get straight to the point.

"Brian, we need to talk about what you're going to do."

"I don't want to talk about that," Brian said, looking miserable. "I've been so worried about you. Are you OK? It scared me, the way you cried yesterday. You never cry."

That was just like Brian. Here he was, sitting in jail with no prospect of getting out soon, and he was worried about her.

"I was upset about Missy."

Brian's voice dropped to a whisper. "I'm sorry you had to see that. All that blood."

"I only saw her foot, and then I ran for help," Sharlah said. "Did they tell you it was really bad?"

"They showed me pictures."

"They showed you *pictures*?"

A guard walked into view and pointed at Sharlah, then held his finger to his lips.

Chastened, she lowered her voice. "Why?"

Brian stared at the table, and his voice was so soft Sharlah struggled to hear it. "They said it was my fault. My lawyer made them stop."

"Brian, that's not right," Sharlah said. "Look at me."

Brian slowly raised his head.

"I know you never would have let that happen. You were a good friend to her," Sharlah said.

Brian shrugged, like he wasn't convinced.

"You got out of bed to change her tire that one night. And what about that time she cut her foot at the beach and you piggy-backed her all the way to the car?"

"You were mad at me when I did that."

"I wasn't mad at you, I was mad at her for flirting and trying to make Cliff jealous."

Brian frowned at the mention of Cliff, and Sharlah thought her guess about Cliff's involvement was probably right.

Brian sighed. "This is such a mess, Shar."

"I know it looks that way right now, Brian. But we'll figure it out. We're a team—us and your lawyer. You need to listen to him."

"Are you OK for money? You should get Kevin to pick up my last check."

It was nice to know Brian was worried about her, but Sharlah was frustrated that he kept changing the subject.

"I'll call Kevin. And I have that money in the bank. I'll be fine." She wasn't sure that was true, but it was what Brian needed to hear.

"That's for you to take classes," Brian said. "I don't want you to spend that."

"I'll see about extra shifts. I can get a second job, at night after I get off at the diner."

Brian slumped in his chair. "I don't want you working in a bar, guys hassling you."

"I'll figure something out," Sharlah said. "We need to focus on getting you out."

"I don't want to talk about it."

"Brian..."

Brian slowly shook his head from side to side. "I really screwed up this time, Shar."

"It doesn't matter now," she said. "What's done is done. You need to listen to your lawyer and do what he says, Brian."

"You know the worst part? It's not my parents, because they expect me to screw up. It's..." Brian's voice cracked, and he swallowed hard. "I let you down. I told you I'd take care of you, and I let you down."

Sharlah didn't want to cry again in front of Brian and make him feel worse, so she tried hard to smile. "You know me. I'm tough. I'll be OK."

After a painful silence, Brian took a deep breath and composed himself. "I was going to replace your clutch over the weekend. How is it?"

"OK. Maybe a little mushy."

Brian grimaced. "Somebody should look at it. It's going to go out on you."

"You shouldn't be worried about stuff like that right now," Sharlah said. "You need to be looking out for yourself."

Brian went quiet. He seemed to be thinking about what to say.

"There's all this stuff I promised you. We were going on that trip to Austin. You weren't going to have to work nights ever again. I was going to help you go to school. I was supposed to fix your clutch and that squeaky board in the living room."

"Brian, it's OK. Really. None of that matters."

"It *does* matter," Brian said. "I wasn't just blowing smoke, Shar. I meant all that stuff—all of it. It's important." He leaned forward. "It's all really important."

A buzzer sounded, and Sharlah jumped in her chair.

"I think that means we have to wrap it up," Brian said. "I'll try to call you tomorrow. We get calls on Tuesdays and Thursdays."

Brian looked over his shoulder. The guard had opened the door to the hallway.

He managed a smile for Sharlah and mouthed one final message.

"I love you."

$

Sharlah stopped by the library on the way home. She still had the books she'd meant to return Sunday in her car, and *Mistral's Daughter* was going to be overdue soon.

She also needed something else to read. The only book she had left from her last batch was the one Jeanie at the library pushed her to try, and Sharlah didn't feel like tackling something big and complicated right now. She wanted something familiar and satisfying, the book equivalent of a hamburger.

Jeanie was helping another person check out. Sharlah put her books on the return pile and quickly walked away. She didn't know whether Jeanie had seen the story in the paper, or whether she'd make the connection that the Brian Lowry with a long list of charges after his name was Sharlah's Brian.

Jeanie spotted her and waved enthusiastically.

Sharlah pasted a smile on and headed back to the counter.

When she'd first met Jeanie, Sharlah thought she must be Assembly of God or some other strict religion, because she always dressed so plain and never wore makeup.

Today, she had on a white blouse with a little round collar, buttoned up all the way, and an old-fashioned slip underneath it. Her brown, shoulder-length hair was pushed back behind both ears. She could pass for 14, but Sharlah knew she had to be at least 22 or 23. She'd already been away to college and come back home.

If Jeanie was religious, she didn't let it affect what she read. She wasn't too keen on Sidney Sheldon or Judith Krantz or some of the other writers Sharlah liked, but plenty of the books she recommended had sex in them.

"Did you read it? Did you love it?" Jeanie asked as she sorted through the books Sharlah had stacked on the return desk.

"I haven't started it yet," Sharlah said.

Jeanie looked up from checking in books. "But you're going to read it, right? Sharlah, I promise you're going to love it. It's amazing!"

Sharlah scanned the spines on the desk. Technically, people weren't supposed to take books off the return pile, but Jeanie usually let her. "Is *Cinnamon Skin* back in yet?"

She had recently discovered the John D. MacDonald series featuring Travis McGee, and now that she was caught up and ready to read the latest book, it always seemed to be checked out.

"I've been keeping an eye out, but it's not back yet." Jeanie transferred an armload of books from the counter to a rolling cart. "Why don't you start on Styron, and when MacDonald comes in, I'll bury it on the bottom of a return cart for you?"

Sharlah grabbed a book off the counter and held it up. "Would I like him?"

Jeanie wrinkled her nose and shook her head. "Try the Styron."

"It looks so long," Sharlah said. "I'm not sure I'll even get it."

"It's worth it," Jeanie said. "And it's not over your head. Don't be silly. There's a lot of New York City—you'll like that. Really, just read 25 pages and see if you don't love it."

♪

Sharlah called Brian's folks when she got home, figuring they'd want to hear about the jail visit.

Renee answered and didn't even let Sharlah say four words before she cut her off.

"You have no right to call here," Renee said. "I can't stop Mitch from being played for a fool, but I won't be a party to it. You ruined Brian's life. Don't call my home again."

Then she hung up.

Hands shaking, Sharlah slammed the receiver down. "Bitch," she muttered.

Once her anger subsided, Sharlah realized nothing had really changed. She'd always known Renee hated her. It was good, in a way, to have the cards right there on the table.

She ran her finger down the phone list taped on the wall, found Kevin's home number and dialed.

Lynn answered, and she and Sharlah chatted for a few minutes while Kevin came to the phone.

Sharlah hadn't seen Lynn since May; she'd had a miserable pregnancy and mostly stayed home. Brian said Kevin complained about her, saying he had to get out of the house a lot because Lynn was crabby, but Sharlah had a hard time picturing that.

As far as Sharlah could tell, Lynn was nice to everybody. She invited Sharlah to the wedding—wrote her name on the envelope with Brian's and everything. Brian's mom said Sharlah couldn't come, because it wasn't "appropriate," but it meant a lot to Sharlah that Lynn had asked.

When Kevin came to the phone, Sharlah told him about her conversation with Brian and asked him to update his dad, because Renee said she couldn't call the house.

"Huh," Kevin said, but he didn't really sound surprised.

She also told him what Brian said about getting his last check from the contractor. Kevin said he'd look into it but he didn't know when he'd have time. He acted like it was a favor she was asking, rather than his brother, and that made Sharlah mad.

"Kevin, this isn't me asking," Sharlah said. "It's for Brian."

That seemed to get his attention. "Sorry—I'll see what I can do," he said. Then he said Lynn needed him and he had to go.

Sharlah was the first to admit that she wasn't an expert on how families were supposed to work. But she really didn't get the Lowrys sometimes. Maybe it was like Mitch said—the whole mess had everybody on edge.

After the phone call, she sat down on the couch and opened her book. Then she got back up without reading a word.

The house was too quiet without Brian around. "Too quiet," Sharlah said aloud, just to hear the words echo in the empty house.

People thought Brian wasn't a big talker. But he was good at helping her figure out how to get along with the girls at work, making her see the other person's side and realize when she took things the wrong way or was holding a grudge.

He had a way of teasing her out of a bad mood. The way he did it wasn't mean, and Sharlah never felt put down by it. It was more that he really knew her and could see the funny side of her faults.

Sharlah flipped through their albums, thinking music would make her feel a little less lonely. She finally settled on Journey and put the record on the turntable.

Brian always said Journey sucked; her taste in music was one of the things he made fun of. Sharlah didn't really care. She loved the song "Open Arms," because it reminded her of the way Brian accepted her and all the messed-up stuff in her life. She thought of it as their song, although she would never say that to Brian.

Tonight, though, it just made her sad. She turned the stereo off and went back to reading in silence.

After 90 pages of *Sophie's Choice*, Sharlah knew that Jeanie was right about the book. She'd managed, while she was reading, to put her worries about Brian aside. But she needed to go to bed. She had a bad habit of getting so into a book that she lost track of time, and then she'd be miserable when her alarm went off.

She washed her face and brushed her teeth, and her thoughts returned to Brian and what she could say to change his mind. Maybe she could make him see that cooperating was a way of keeping his promise to take care of her. The most important thing was fixing his situation, not her clutch or the living room floor. That might work.

She put on one of Brian's old T-shirts for bed. She checked the back door and turned off the lights in the kitchen.

She was replaying the whole jail conversation in her head as she checked the front door and crossed the living room to turn off the lamp.

Her foot hit the squeaky floorboard in the living room, and she stopped.

◊

The thing was, Brian had never promised to fix the squeaky floorboard.

When she'd asked him to do it, he'd told her it was too much work. It would take practically a whole Saturday, he said, and she should just avoid stepping on the board if it bugged her so much.

So why would Brian say he'd promised to do it?

Sharlah shook her head. She read too many mysteries. Brian was probably just feeling bad about blowing off something she'd asked him to do.

But then she remembered the way he'd leaned forward, insisting that all the things he'd promised were really important.

Sharlah double-checked that the curtains were closed tight, then she moved the coffee table. She rolled up the rag rug, a castoff from Kevin and Lynn.

She studied the squeaky floorboard for at least 10 minutes. After looking at it from every angle and seeing nothing amiss, she decided the whole idea was crazy.

Brian was going to have a good laugh about that when he got home.

Sharlah was rolling the rug back into place when she noticed a nick in the floorboard next to the squeaky one. She sat back, thinking about a Saturday when she'd come home from work and found Brian—who *never* cleaned—putting the broom and dustpan away. He told her he'd spilled potato chips.

She needed something to pry the board up. Brian's tools, unfortunately, were in his truck, which was in the police impound lot. She tried three different table knives from the kitchen, bending one nearly in half, before she decided that wasn't going to work. She needed something stronger.

Her pocketknife would do the trick. Sharlah got the knife and went to work on the board. It took a little effort, but she finally got the angle right, and one end popped up.

She tugged the floorboard loose and peered down, through a hole in the sub-floor, into the dark crawl space under the house.

Brian kept a flashlight in the kitchen junk drawer. Sharlah fetched it and aimed it into the hole.

Something was down there, something metal and square.

Sharlah rocked back on her heels. "Oh, Brian," she whispered. "What did you do?"

She shined the light into the hole again and tried to gauge the dimensions of whatever was down there. Another floorboard was going to have to come up.

She checked all the adjacent boards and found the one Brian had pulled up—it had a nick in one end, too. She pried it up and set it aside, then reached into the hole.

She couldn't quite reach. Brian, at 6-2, had much longer arms than she did at 5-3. Lying face down on the floor worked, though. She ran her hand over the cool metal until she brushed against what felt like a handle. She grasped it and hauled with all her might.

It was a metal briefcase, like something out of a James Bond movie. It was covered in cobwebs and a layer of grime.

A car door slammed on the street, and she startled. Sharlah got up and peeked out the curtains. The neighbor across the street was headed up his sidewalk with a six-pack of beer under his arm.

Spooked, she lugged the briefcase into the bathroom and locked the door.

Sharlah sat on the linoleum floor, took a deep breath, and popped the lid.

The cash was in twenties, each stack held together by a rubber band. She pulled out a stack and counted. It held 50 twenty-dollar bills—a thousand bucks. Sharlah had never seen a thousand dollars in her life, and here was a suitcase full of thousand-dollar stacks.

She pulled each stack out, adding as she went. She counted twenty stacks of $1,000 each. That made $20,000, stuck in a hole under the house.

There was a gun, too. She carefully put it to one side, puzzled. When Missy made noises about getting a handgun, Brian had talked her out of it.

Underneath the money was a plain manila envelope. The metal fastener was splayed to keep it closed. Sharlah pried it open with her thumbnail and dumped the contents into the emptied briefcase.

Her own face was staring up at her.

It was a Louisiana driver's license, bearing her picture and the name Elizabeth Louise Ellsworth. The birth date made Elizabeth, whoever she was, a few months younger than Sharlah. The other statistics were right—blonde hair, blue eyes, 5-3, 110 pounds.

Brian's picture was on a license for James Robert Coughlin. His address was in Slidell, and he was 22—a year older than Brian.

There were Social Security cards and birth certificates and passports.

The cops were right. Brian had been planning to run.

But his mother was wrong. He was going to take Sharlah with him.

Sharlah was leaning against the tub, trying to take it all in, when she heard a footstep crunch on the gravel driveway outside and froze.

She jumped up and shut off the bathroom light. Then she sat in the dark and waited.

One more footstep sounded, coming closer to the house. Then nothing. She held her breath and waited for what seemed like forever.

Finally, she heard footsteps again, retreating this time, followed by the soft click of a car door.

Sharlah tiptoed out to the living room. She pulled the curtains aside, just a little, and scanned the street.

Red taillights receded in the distance. The car stopped at the corner, then turned. As it passed under the streetlight, Sharlah saw the lights on top and the police department seal on the door.

FIVE

SHARLAH SAT UP most of the night, puzzling over the briefcase and its contents.

Brian must have wanted her to find it—why else would he mention the squeaky floorboard? But what did he expect her to do with it? Obviously she couldn't just tote $20,000 cash down to the bank and deposit it.

The photo for the driver's license and passport, she realized, had been taken on a trip to Houston earlier in the summer. They'd been driving around, joking about all the places in the world they'd see one day, and Brian spotted a place that took passport photos. When he'd dragged her in to get her picture taken, she'd thought it was just Brian being his sweet, goofy self.

Now she saw that he'd planned the whole thing—found the photo place ahead of time, figured out how he'd convince her to go in.

That meant Brian had been working on an escape plan since June, at least. At Kevin and Lynn's housewarming in May, he'd blown up at his mom over a cutting comment she made, which totally wasn't like him. Was he involved with drugs then? Had he been doing it the whole time Sharlah had known him?

Sitting on their couch staring at the briefcase, Sharlah reviewed her nearly two years with Brian, searching for other clues that he wasn't the person she thought he was, but nothing really clicked.

No answers came to her. Not sure what else to do, she put the money, gun and passports back in the briefcase and snapped it closed. Sharlah eased the briefcase back into its hiding place, replaced the boards, rolled out the rug and tried to catch a couple hours of sleep.

$$\mathit{6}$$

Her alarm clock rang way too soon, but Sharlah got up and went to work, yawning the whole way.

The diner was busy, and she was glad for the distraction and the tips.

She always liked the working guys who came in early—utility employees with their names sewn on their uniforms, delivery drivers with clipboards, construction workers with steel-toed boots. They left nice tips and never acted like they were better than anybody else.

The next wave was always office workers and retirees, people who didn't have to be anywhere until 9 if they had to be anywhere at all. After that would come the stragglers—usually tourists, a mix of families and college students.

Some of the girls liked waiting on the families with little kids, despite the slime trails of spilled milk and dribbled syrup. Sharlah was happy to trade those tables.

She didn't dislike kids, but she didn't go nuts over them the way some of the girls did. She and Brian had a little scare after they'd been together about a year, and the whole time she was waiting for her period, Sharlah watched the parents at the restaurant and tried—without success—to picture her and Brian in their shoes.

Brian was worried what his parents would say and what they'd do for money, but he wasn't as upset as she was. Sharlah couldn't imagine herself as somebody's mother. Brian, on the other hand, talked about how he was going tuck his kids in when he was a dad, not come home from work at 10 o'clock every night like his father had.

After the working guys plowed through their three-egg omelets and mountains of hash browns, things got slow. The waitresses all congregated by the kitchen to lean against the wall and gossip. They weren't allowed to sit, no matter how empty the diner was.

Sharlah grabbed the newspaper left by the guy who drove the Dr Pepper truck and stood off to one side, reading.

There wasn't anything new on Missy, except that police were awaiting the autopsy. The big news was that the trough of low pressure in the Gulf was now a tropical storm named Aileen. It had been the talk of the waitresses all morning.

Tami confidently predicted it would turn out to be nothing. "A bunch of people cleared out for Allen, when was that? Three years ago? Nothing happened. Big waste of time."

Donna called over, "Hey, Sharlah, what does the paper say about the storm?"

"You guys pretty much covered it," Sharlah said.

"Anything new in there on that girl that got killed?"

Sharlah shook her head. "No."

That was all the invitation Robin, the diner's main gossip, needed. "And there won't be anything new, either," she said. "The cops are covering everything up."

Tami laughed. "Why would the cops do that?" She was just as opinionated as Robin, which often led to arguments, especially when there weren't customers needing attention.

"The police are in on it," Robin said.

"I heard it was Mexicans," Donna put in. "I heard they tied her up and they cut her from…"

"She was hit in the head."

Three faces swiveled toward Sharlah.

"Missy was my friend," Sharlah said. She tossed the paper in the trash. "I'm going to make fresh coffee."

*

The lunch rush was just winding down around 1:30 when the cop, Zuk, came in.

He talked to Joan, and then they walked over to Sharlah at the drink station, where she was refilling Cokes for a table of teenagers. She'd been tracking him across the room, afraid that she knew exactly why he was there.

"Miss Webb?"

Sharlah slowly put a plastic glass of soda on her tray, concentrating very hard so that her hands wouldn't shake.

"We need you to come down to the station."

Sharlah cut her eyes toward Joan.

"It's OK, Sharlah," Joan said. "Go on. I won't dock you."

As she walked back to get her purse, Sharlah saw Robin sidle over, tea pitcher in one hand, to say something to Donna. The diner gossips had new material to work with.

Sharlah couldn't figure out how the cops knew she'd found the money. Obviously they'd been watching the house, but she didn't understand how they could have seen inside. All the curtains had been closed, and the only window in the bathroom was tiny and frosted.

They did listen to everything at the jail. Did Brian say too much when he talked about the squeaky floorboard? That seemed unlikely—even Sharlah didn't get the hint right away. If she hadn't stepped on the squeaky board, it wouldn't have occurred to her to investigate.

Then she remembered something she'd seen when they were searching the house. One of the officers had come around from the back, dusting himself off. Maybe he'd been in the crawl space and found the briefcase? Could the cops have left it to trap her?

Sharlah decided that if the police started asking about the money, she'd say she wanted a lawyer. She was pretty sure they had to give her one, even if she couldn't pay. She'd seen that on *Hill Street Blues*.

At the station, they put her back in the same room she'd been in on Sunday. The detective she'd talked to that day came in a few minutes later.

His short-sleeved shirt was blue this time, but otherwise he looked pretty much the same—messy, like an unmade bed. He introduced himself again, and this time Sharlah held onto the name: Detective Downs.

"I appreciate you coming in," he said, which Sharlah thought was weird. Did she really have a choice?

And that was it for the pleasantries. "I'm afraid I've got some bad news," he said. "A body was found late yesterday in a ditch up by League City. This morning, it was identified as Cliff Knorr."

Sharlah leaned forward in her chair, not wanting to believe what she'd just heard. "Cliff's *dead*?"

"He was shot in the head."

Sharlah wrapped her arms tight around her torso and, without meaning to, began to rock back and forth. "Oh, poor Cliff," she said. And poor Brian, she thought. He was going to take this really hard.

Downs pushed a box of tissues across the table toward her, but Sharlah had no tears.

"We believe he died Friday afternoon, Friday evening at the latest," Downs said. "Do you understand what that means?"

Sharlah stared at him, uncomprehending. Cliff was dead. What difference did it make if he died at 3 or 8 or midnight?

"Missy Burke was at work until 11 p.m. on Saturday, at which point she received a phone call at the bar and asked permission to leave early," Downs said.

"Cliff didn't kill her," Sharlah said, finally grasping the point. "He was already dead."

"That's right."

"Good," Sharlah said. "I didn't want to think that he did."

"We also got the results of her autopsy this morning," Downs said. "It appears that sexual intercourse took place shortly before her death."

Sharlah's stomach flip-flopped. "She was raped?"

"We believe it was consensual. The coroner found a contraceptive in place, one of those new things, a sponge."

"She told me she was going to switch to that," Sharlah said. "She read about it in *Cosmo*. She thought the Pill was making her gain weight."

Then she stared down at the table, embarrassed. Why on earth had she mentioned that?

"She confided in you about personal things, like her choice of birth control, then?" The detective's voice was neutral, professional. "Is it accurate to say she talked to you about her sex life?"

Profoundly uncomfortable, Sharlah said nothing.

Missy did talk about it, had almost from the time she and Sharlah met. At first, Sharlah was flattered. Missy's confessions made her feel like they were close, and Sharlah had never really had a friend like that.

At one point, Sharlah worked up the courage to ask Missy for advice. *Glamour* and *Cosmo* didn't cover everything, and Sharlah hoped Missy, who seemed more experienced, might help. Missy answered Sharlah's question, but she also joked about it later, in front of Brian and Cliff.

Sharlah was sick with embarrassment. Brian wasn't happy, but he was sweet about it. He said Sharlah shouldn't ever tell Missy something she didn't want repeated, because Missy couldn't keep a secret.

"Miss Webb?" Downs jolted Sharlah out of her memories. "Did your friend talk about things of that nature?"

"Sometimes," Sharlah said. "Why are you asking me this?"

"Do you have any idea who Miss Burke might have been involved with?"

"Someone other than Cliff? No."

"I'm not saying this person killed her," Downs said. "But he might have seen or heard something that was important, and we really need to talk to him."

Sharlah shook her head. "I can't believe Missy would cheat on Cliff."

"She never mentioned any problems?"

"Well..." Sharlah thought about the best way to phrase things. "Cliff had been spending a lot of time in Houston lately, and he would stay over at his dad's or mom's maybe a couple times a week. Missy would complain sometimes that he wasn't, um, paying enough attention to her."

Actually, what Missy had said was that she had a disease

called "Lackanookie," but there was no way Sharlah was going to tell the detective that.

"And she never talked about another man in a way that made you wonder? Maybe someone from work, or a friend that she mentioned a lot?"

"Not really," Sharlah said. "Missy had a lot of friends, and she could be a flirt, but I don't know anything about her having another boyfriend."

The detective flipped back a few pages in his notebook and scanned it. "One of her co-workers said she hinted about being involved in another relationship and he got the idea that something about it was secret or taboo. Does that mean anything to you?"

"Well, she would have kept it secret from Brian and me," Sharlah said. "Cliff is Brian's friend, and Brian would have been caught in the middle. Everybody knows he hates that."

"The person who heard this got the idea it might be a man of another race, for lack of a better word. Can you think of anyone that might be?"

Sharlah shook her head. "They're wrong."

"You seem really sure about that."

Sharlah tried to think how she could answer without making Missy look bad.

"Missy was really against that. I'm not saying I agree or anything, but she was... prejudiced, I guess. Brian says it's the way she was raised. You couldn't even talk to her about it. We tried."

"Can you think of anyone new who has been hanging around, maybe not around Missy necessarily, but a new friend for Cliff, or even Brian?"

It was pretty sneaky, Sharlah thought, the way he tried to slide a question about Brian in there, not that it mattered. "I don't know of anyone new around Cliff or Missy," Sharlah said. "We hadn't seen much of them lately. For sure Brian didn't have any new friends."

She didn't say so, but at the moment, it didn't seem that Brian had any friends at all.

♪

The same cop, Zuk, took Sharlah back to her car. She thought, since he was dropping her at the diner, he might mention the times she'd waited on him, but he didn't. Maybe he didn't remember. Maybe she'd been just an orange blur with a coffee pot to him, even though he'd been enough of a regular that she knew his order by heart.

To the cops, she knew, she was "the suspect's girlfriend" or "the dead girl's friend." It was just like her hometown, where she was known for things she couldn't control—"Arvin Webb's kid" or "the sister of the guy who killed Danny Ott."

The only identity she'd ever chosen for herself was the life she'd made with Brian, and now it felt like other people— maybe even Brian—were trying to change that, too.

She could accept that Brian had done something wrong and would be punished for it. But she felt like she was being punished, too, and that didn't seem fair.

Brian was the only person she could turn to—really, the only person she'd been able to count on in her life. And now she could see him only through glass, with someone listening in.

Tears stung her eyes. Sharlah hated to cry, and lately she seemed to be doing a lot of it.

She turned the radio on, hoping music would make her feel better, but every station was full of talk about Tropical Storm Aileen. She switched it off. She was so distracted that she was practically in her driveway before she noticed the Lowry

Marine truck parked in front of her house and the two men arguing beside it.

Kevin Lowry was trying to get in his truck. A neighbor was blocking Kevin's way, his arms crossed over his chest, his thick legs planted wide. Kevin had several inches and at least 50 pounds on him, but the neighbor wasn't giving ground.

She and Brian didn't really know the neighbor—he worked an evening shift at the post office and was hardly ever around. He was an older guy with long hair and a fondness for tie-dyed T-shirts, and, in cooler weather, a green Army jacket. Brian said he was one of those hippies who got stuck in the 1970s and never got out. Sharlah thought he was kind of creepy and didn't like the way he always seemed to watch her. She didn't even know his real name. Everybody just called him Well.

She got out of her car and walked up to the men. "Kevin? Well? What's going on?"

The tension immediately went out of Kevin's body. He turned to Sharlah and smiled. "Hey, Sharlah."

"You know this guy?" Well poked his finger at Kevin. "I saw him looking in your windows."

"He's Brian's brother." Sharlah turned to Kevin. "What are you doing here?"

"Looked to me like he was trying to break into your house," Well said.

"You didn't answer when I knocked, but I thought I heard music, so I was looking to see if you were home," Kevin said, addressing Sharlah and ignoring the neighbor. "Must have been coming from next door."

Well still seemed to be spoiling for an argument. "Her car wasn't here."

"You're right," Kevin said. "I should have noticed that." He shook his head. "Sorry to alarm you. I wasn't thinking.

"We've got a lot on our minds, don't we, Sharlah?" Kevin smiled at her then, a tired, sad smile that reminded her of Brian.

"We're OK here," she told Well. "Thanks for keeping an eye out."

"No sweat," Well said. He took a couple tentative steps toward his house. "I saw the cops crawling all over here and I read about Brian in the paper. Real sorry about that."

Other than the girls at work, nobody had tried to talk to Sharlah about Brian, and it wasn't a conversation she really wanted to have with a neighbor she barely knew.

"Thanks," Sharlah said, hoping that would be the end of it.

"Seems like a lot of hassle over some weed," Well said. "Nancy Reagan and all this 'Just Say No' crap has gone too far, you know?"

Kevin caught Sharlah's glance and raised an eyebrow.

"It's just a diversion," Well said, and it seemed like he was just getting warmed up. "So we don't notice what's going down in Central America, you know?"

Kevin put his hand on Sharlah's elbow and started toward the house. "Sharlah and I need to talk, so you'll have to excuse us now. Sorry about the misunderstanding."

"Like, in El Salvador, we're..." Well caught on, finally, that Kevin and Sharlah intended to walk away. "Right," he said. "Enough about Bonzo."

He retreated across the street and up the rickety steps to his porch, where he sat down in a battered director's chair.

"What a weirdo," Kevin said under his breath as he and Sharlah walked away.

Sharlah unlocked the front door and gave it a hard shove. The wood always swelled in the summer, making the door stick.

"I don't know why you guys live in such a shitty neighborhood," Kevin said. He took a step inside the house and stopped. "Jesus. Don't you have AC?"

"We turn it off when we're not home," Sharlah said. "It keeps the light bill down."

"Well, turn it on. It's a fucking sauna in here."

"I'll just be a minute," Sharlah said. "It won't take long to cool down."

"Mind if I get a drink?"

One of the things Sharlah hated about their house was the way the rooms were laid out one after another. People had to walk through the bedroom to get to the kitchen or the bathroom, which opened off the bedroom. She hadn't minded so much when it was friends like Cliff and Missy, but it felt strange to have Kevin walk through her bedroom.

"It's this way," she told Kevin, leading him through the bedroom doorway. She stopped to turn on the window AC unit, waving him on to the kitchen. "Help yourself. I'm just going to duck into the bathroom."

Sharlah was dying to get out of her work clothes, but she settled for wriggling out of her pantyhose. Usually she took them off in her car in the parking lot at work, but Zuk had been sitting there in his cruiser, watching her. There really was nothing worse than pantyhose on a hot day. Joan's insistence that all the girls wear them was the one thing Sharlah could say she definitely hated about her job.

When she came out of the bathroom, Kevin was standing with his head in her refrigerator. "Don't you have any beer?"

"We're out." She pulled a glass down from the cupboard. "Do you want ice water?"

"That's OK," Kevin said. He slammed the refrigerator shut and leaned against it, looking straight at Sharlah in a way that made her nervous.

Sharlah never knew quite how to take Kevin. He looked so much like Brian, but he was so unlike him in other ways. She liked his take-charge attitude in getting rid of Well, and sometimes, honestly, she wished Brian had a little more of that. Brian would do anything to avoid confrontation. But the way Kevin banged around cussing and criticizing their neighborhood and griping about the AC put her off.

He and Brian were really close, which Sharlah thought was great. She barely knew either of her brothers. But sometimes she felt like it was a one-way street, that Brian paid more attention to what Kevin thought than Kevin did to what Brian thought. Lately, she'd thought that Brian was catching on to that, too, and he didn't seem to have such a bad case of hero worship when it came to Kevin.

Sharlah ran some cold water from the tap into her glass and drank it down. "We should sit in the living room," she said. "The kitchen is the last place to cool off."

Kevin followed her to the living room and sat on the couch. "I thought you'd be home from work earlier."

"I was at the police station again," Sharlah said, taking the chair. She'd started to say more, but then she realized that Kevin might not have heard about Cliff.

"Was it about Missy this time, or Cliff?"

Relieved again that she didn't have to break bad news, Sharlah said, "Kevin, I'm so sorry. I know you and Cliff were friends since you were little."

Sharlah noticed for the first time how rough Kevin looked. His color was off, he had dark circles under his eyes, and he'd hacked his neck shaving.

"It's hard to believe this is all happening," Kevin said. "What did the police want? You don't know anything about what happened to Cliff."

"It was more about Missy," Sharlah said. "I'm so worried about how Brian's going to take the news about Cliff."

Kevin leaned forward, balancing his elbows on his knees and clasping his hands together. "What a God-awful mess Brian's gotten himself into," he said.

She supposed Kevin was trying to be sympathetic, but it just made Sharlah mad, the way he seemed to blame Brian for everything.

"The police tried to make him feel like Missy was his fault. They'll probably do the same about Cliff," she said, hoping Kevin would take her point. "He's so sad, Kevin. I hope you can buck him up when you see him. Maybe we could go Saturday, unless your folks want to go?"

"Saturday's no good," Kevin said. "I have to work. Dad docs, too. We're going to have to sell a lot of boats to pay that lawyer. And no way is Mom going to see him in there. You should just plan to do the visiting for now."

Sharlah's first reaction—she couldn't help it—was happiness. She wanted Brian all to herself. But she knew that was selfish. It was important to do what was best for Brian.

"It would mean a lot to him if you would come," Sharlah said. "You guys are so close, and he listens to you. You know what the lawyer said—we all have to encourage Brian to cooperate with the police."

Kevin shook his head. "He's not going to listen to me, Sharlah."

"What makes you say that?"

"I think it would just make him feel worse if I saw him in there. It's always been hard for Brian, the difference between us," Kevin said. "Now, especially, you know. I have a wife and a house and a baby on the way... I think his resentment would get in the way of hearing anything I had to say."

Just like that, Sharlah was angry again. How could Brian's family understand so little about him?

"Brian doesn't resent you! He's happy for you! He's really excited about being an uncle," Sharlah said. "The only thing he resents is people wanting him to be some carbon copy of you instead of himself."

Kevin held his palms up. "I'm not trying to make you mad, Sharlah. Look, I know you love Brian, but you don't know everything about him. I'm just telling you the truth here."

"It's *not* the truth! You guys don't understand him at all! It's like your mom saying Brian got into trouble just to stick it to her. That's not why he did it."

Kevin cocked his head to one side and narrowed his eyes. "So why did he do it?"

"I don't *know* why he did it, Kevin. We can't exactly talk about it. He's in jail, remember?"

"What about before he was in jail? It's kind of hard to believe this was going on and you didn't notice anything."

Sharlah sprang to her feet. "You know what, Kevin? You can just get out." She marched across the living room and tugged the front door open. "Seriously. Just get out. I'm tired of your family acting like this is my fault."

Kevin slowly rose from the couch, like it took a big effort. "Sharlah, nobody is saying this is your fault."

"You mom said exactly that. She said I got Brian into an immoral lifestyle."

"Mom says a lot of things." He gestured toward the door. "You're letting the cold air out."

"How come you didn't say anything at the lawyer's office?"

"There's a way to deal with Mom," Kevin said, "and arguing with her or airing family business in public isn't it. I've told Brian that a million times." He smiled at her. "Shut the door, Sharlah. We're all on the same side here. We all want to help Brian."

Sharlah reluctantly shut the door, but she wasn't placated.

"Why are you here, Kevin? You could have told me over the phone that you don't care about seeing Brian."

That last part, Sharlah realized, might be a little unfair, but she wasn't in a mood to take it back.

Kevin let it go. "I wanted to see how you were getting along," he said. "I didn't get a chance to talk to you after court, and I was beat when you called the other night."

He sat back down on the couch. "So how *are* you doing, Sharlah?"

Sharlah held her spot by the door. "I'm OK."

Kevin chuckled. "Brian always says you're a tough cookie. He wasn't kidding. Don't be mad at me. I'm not the enemy."

He settled back against the couch cushions like he was planning to stay awhile. "I didn't have a chance to call yet about Brian's check. Are you OK for money? Things are a little tight right now for Lynn and me, but I could talk to Mom and Dad…"

"Your mother wouldn't give me a nickel, and I wouldn't give her the satisfaction of turning me down," Sharlah said. "I'll be fine."

"You sure? Your refrigerator seemed pretty empty."

"I haven't had a chance to go to the store," Sharlah lied.

Kevin slapped his hands against the cushions. "OK, look, there's another reason I drove down here. Mom thinks that at Brian's next hearing…"

"Brian has a new hearing? Nobody told me that! When is it?"

"No, he doesn't have it yet," Kevin said. "Mom asked me to come get some of his nice clothes so she can make sure they're clean and pressed when he finally does get it."

"She thinks I can't even get Brian's clothes ready? I've been doing his laundry for two years, but all of a sudden I can't do it right?"

"Jesus, Sharlah, everything Mom does is not meant as a put-down of you," Kevin said. "She needs to *do* something, and this is the only thing she can think of."

"She could try being nicer to him," Sharlah said. "That's something she could do."

Kevin's expression soured. "She's not going to turn into a different person overnight just because Brian got arrested, Sharlah."

The phone rang in the kitchen, and Sharlah jumped up, no longer interested in arguing with Kevin.

"That might be Brian," she said. "He said he'd call today."

"Better answer it, then," Kevin said. "I can grab his clothes while you're on the phone."

"Brian's stuff is in the top two drawers," Sharlah said, already halfway to the kitchen. "If it's Brian, do you want to say hi? I'm not sure how long he gets on the phone, but I know he'd love to talk to you."

The phone trilled again, and Kevin shooed her toward the kitchen

Sharlah picked up the receiver and then waited as an operator gave her instructions before Brian finally came on the line.

"Shar? Are you there?"

"Hey, Brian," Sharlah said. She stretched the phone cord as far as it would go, across the kitchen. "Kevin's here. He wants to say hi."

Clutching the receiver to her chest, she called to Kevin. "It's Brian. Come say hi."

Kevin poked his head around the doorway from the bedroom. "He only has 15 minutes," Sharlah said. She held the receiver out to him. "Please?" she whispered.

Kevin clearly wasn't happy, but he took the phone.

"Hey, Baby Bro," he bellowed, and Sharlah winced. This was Kevin the backslapping businessman, not Kevin the loyal brother.

"I just came down here to check on Sharlah, and she's doing great. You don't need to worry about anything there. Dad's got the lawyer working on a new hearing, so until then you just need to sit tight, OK? Everything out here is totally under control. Hope the chow in there is OK! Here's Sharlah again."

Kevin handed Sharlah the phone back and retreated to the bedroom. Sharlah didn't think he'd let Brian get in a single word.

She scooted back across the kitchen and sat on the floor with her back against the outside door. "Brian, are you there?"

"Yeah," Brian said quietly.

They talked about Cliff a little, but Brian's breath got ragged, like he might cry, so Sharlah let him change the subject. He asked about her clutch and her day at work. He wanted to know what was going on in her world, as if her life had room for anything but his problems at the moment.

Brian seemed so sad that she didn't have the heart to press him about cooperating with the police. Cliff was dead; maybe Brian would come around on his own without her nagging.

All too soon, they got a warning message letting them know they had one minute left.

"Come see me tomorrow?" Brian asked.

"If I do that, you'll have to wait until Monday for another visit," Sharlah said. "And I'll get there kind of late, too, because of work."

"I need to see you," Brian said. "Come tomorrow."

As she hung up the phone, Sharlah realized that her hands were shaking. She wanted to scream or cry, maybe even break something.

It was impossible to have a real conversation with Brian knowing someone could be listening in. She couldn't ask any of the really important questions.

Why did you do it?

What am I supposed to do with the money?

Brian simply had to get bail. Then they could talk—really talk—and figure things out. Until then, there was almost nothing she could do to help him.

She started to see Kevin's point about his mom, how it was important to feel like she was doing something.

Sharlah went to the bedroom and paused in the doorway, stunned.

"What are you doing?"

Kevin was pawing through one of the dresser drawers, spilling a waterfall of colorful T-shirts to the floor in his haste. Another drawer had been dumped out on the bed.

Kevin jumped at the sound of her voice. "Are you off the phone already? I'm looking for a T-shirt."

"The plain white ones are on top, with his socks and underwear." Sharlah opened the top drawer to reveal a neat stack of white tees.

"Don't know how I missed that," Kevin said, backing up and shaking his head. "Guess I got frustrated and made a mess. Sorry."

Sharlah handed him a white T-shirt from the stack. Then she began refolding and straightening everything he'd disturbed in the second drawer. "Did you find his button-down shirt and nice pants? Those are in the closet."

"Right," Kevin said. He opened the closet and began pulling out the clothes Brian almost never wore: khakis, white button-down shirt, blue blazer.

Sharlah finished straightening the second drawer and moved to the pile on the bed, thinking that Kevin must be a worse slob to live with than Brian. Poor Lynn.

"Where are his ties?"

"Look on the peg at the back of the closet," Sharlah said. She folded Brian's jeans and replaced them in the drawer. "I think there's only one."

"Found it." Kevin looped the tie over the neck of the hanger that held the shirt, then hung the jacket on top of that. "That should do it."

Sharlah handed him a pair of dark socks and pointed to Brian's dress shoes. "No, *that* should do it."

Kevin exhaled long and hard, like someone who had just climbed a flight of stairs. He had put on weight lately; Brian joked about his brother getting a belly just like his wife.

"You do a good job keeping up with laundry. It's really gone to hell at our house lately. I'm out of clean everything, seems like. I've had to dig deep." Kevin mopped his forearm across his brow. "Hey, can I buy you dinner?"

Sharlah looked at him skeptically. "Don't you need to get on home to Lynn?"

"She's got girlfriends over tonight," Kevin said. "They're addressing birth announcements or thank-you notes or something." He smiled at Sharlah. "Tell you what. I'll call her while you get changed, and then we'll go get something to eat."

Sharlah hesitated. "I have to get up early."

"You haven't gone to the store. There's nothing here to eat," Kevin said. He edged by her and out of the room. "Go on. Get changed."

Sharlah didn't want to admit it, but a meal on someone else's dime was appealing. She'd had to shorten her shift twice and was running far behind her back-of-the-envelope estimations. Dinner with Kevin would give her one extra day of groceries, and that was an offer she couldn't afford to pass up.

$$\varsigma$$

Kevin wanted to eat at one of the restaurants down by the seawall that catered to tourists, a place Sharlah and Brian avoided because it was too expensive. He tried to talk her out of it, but Sharlah insisted on driving her own car so Kevin could head straight home after dinner.

The place was busy. Their waitress already had at least four tables, including an eight-top, and when she came by to get their drink orders, she was friendly but frazzled.

Sharlah thought about a beer but decided to stick to water. Kevin ordered a Long Island Iced Tea. "You sure you don't want a drink? I'm buying," he said.

Sharlah shook her head. "I have to get up early."

Suddenly, a loud voice boomed across the restaurant.

"Aileen was upgraded today from a tropical storm, and a hurricane watch has been posted from Corpus Christi to Grand Isle, Louisiana."

The bartender had turned up the TV over the bar, and everyone in the restaurant paused for a moment to watch the weatherman from one of the Houston stations.

"...Category One hurricane, with sustained winds between 74 and 95 miles per hour. Residents are urged to take precautions..."

The bartender turned the sound back down when the report was over, and the chatter resumed in the restaurant.

"How was your call with Brian?" Kevin asked. "What did he have to say about talking to the police?"

"Whenever I bring it up, he says he doesn't want to talk about it," Sharlah said. "But I think he'll come around eventually. He just needs time."

By the time the waitress finally came to take their orders, Kevin had downed half of his drink. Sharlah got fried shrimp. Kevin ordered a combo plate, but with a bunch of substitutions. Sharlah felt sorry for the waitress, who kept crossing things out on her order pad.

Kevin was in a talkative mood. He gave her a long explanation about the difference between bail and bond and how the system worked.

"Mom and Dad are arguing a lot over the lawyer," Kevin said. "Mom thinks we need to get a big shot from Houston. She thinks Ingersoll is too casual. But Dad did his homework, and Ingersoll's supposed to be the best on drug cases."

Kevin took a big swig of his drink, and Sharlah thought about suggesting he should slow down. Instead, she changed the subject.

"How is Lynn? She sounded good when I talked to her the other night."

"Big as a house," Kevin said. "Cranky, weepy. But it'll all be OK once the baby's here. We can't wait to see him!"

Sharlah was glad to see Kevin excited about the baby. Brian had told her that Kevin freaked out when Lynn got pregnant because he'd wanted to wait a few years and save more money before they started a family.

Their food arrived, and Kevin asked the waitress for another Long Island Iced Tea. They chatted about the baby while they ate. Kevin had wanted the nursery blue, because he was sure the baby was a boy. Lynn wanted yellow.

"We ended up with green," Kevin said, laughing. "I think it looks gross, like a hospital room, but Lynn likes it, and that's all that matters."

Sharlah laughed, too. Then she caught sight of a cop at the hostess stand, picking up takeout food. It was Zuk. He saw her and tipped his hat. She nodded.

Kevin turned around. "Who's that?"

"His name is Zuk," Sharlah said, taking care to pronounce it right. "He was one of the cops who searched the house, and he's driven me home from the station a couple times."

To Sharlah's surprise, Zuk strode over to the table.

"Miss Webb," he said.

"Hi," Sharlah said. "This is Brian's brother, Kevin Lowry."

"Russ Zuk," the cop said, offering his hand. The men shook.

"You all set with your hurricane preparations?" Zuk looked down at Sharlah. "You should have your car gassed up, in case there's an evacuation order."

"Is it really supposed to hit us? The girls at work say these things always fizzle out," Sharlah said. "They say that if you leave, you'll just sit on the causeway forever and your house will get looted while you're gone."

"Evacuation orders are issued for a reason," Zuk said. "You should go to the gas station tonight. The lines are already long, and tomorrow's just going to be worse."

Kevin caught Sharlah's glance and rolled his eyes.

"That's good to know," Sharlah said. "Thanks."

"Yeah, thanks for the helpful advice, officer," Kevin said.

Zuk ignored Kevin's sarcasm. "I'll let you finish your dinner," he said. "Take care."

As soon as Zuk was out of earshot, Kevin said, "Does he think he's your dad?"

"He's been nice to me," Sharlah said, shrugging. "Weird to run into him here."

"You know the cops aren't your friends, right? They're trying to screw Brian over," Kevin said.

Even though she'd been careful not to say anything that would hurt Brian, Sharlah felt guilty and defensive. "I wouldn't do anything to hurt Brian," she said. "But I found Missy, remember? That makes me a witness. If I can help them find out who did that to her, I'm going to."

Kevin spotted the waitress and rattled the ice in his empty glass at her. "I'm just saying, you need to be careful with them," he said. "I know you want the best for Brian."

Then he smiled at Sharlah. "The Astros are playing Cincinnati. Want to hang out at the bar and watch a few innings? Lynn's girlfriends will be there awhile. Might be good to relax, take your mind off things."

"I'd better not," Sharlah said.

Even if she didn't have to get up early, she would have said no. Sitting at the bar with a married guy, even if he was Brian's brother, didn't seem right. Anyway, she'd been around Kevin when one of his teams was losing, and it wasn't pretty. She'd seen him throw a beer bottle when a last-minute field goal sailed wide right.

She wondered, too, whether three Long Island Iced Teas were a bad idea when Kevin still had to drive 45 minutes home.

She thought about saying something, but Brian could always handle more drinks than she could, and Kevin was even bigger than Brian.

She thanked Kevin for dinner and said goodnight. As she left the restaurant, he was headed to the bar with a drink in his hand.

6

Driving home, Sharlah wondered whether she should have told Kevin about the money, and she wished, for the millionth time, that she could just ask Brian what to do.

She turned on the radio and listened as the announcer ran through hurricane preparation tips. She decided that maybe she needed to get serious about the storm.

She made a mental list of things to do, starting with putting the TV back together so she could watch the news. According to the radio, she'd need to fill containers with drinking water and run the bathtub full so she'd have water to flush.

Even if they called for an evacuation, she would stay put. Where would she go? And she didn't want to worry about looters, not with $20,000 hidden in the house. Mostly, though, she didn't want to be stranded, unable to get back to Brian.

Fixing the TV the police had taken apart turned out to be a harder project than she expected. Two wires had been pulled loose, and Sharlah had to guess which wire went where. She got it wrong the first time, and, even worse, screwed the back of the TV into place before she checked.

She did get it right, eventually, and just in time to catch the news.

The broadcast had all kinds of graphics about the hurricane, but they didn't really help Sharlah—color-coded maps don't translate on a black-and-white TV.

The anchors went on and on about how serious the situation was. Except for the sports guy, who seemed mad that his report got cut short, everybody seemed amped up, like kids about to get ice cream. It made Sharlah wonder how seriously to take the whole thing. How bad could it be, if they were so obviously looking forward to it?

After the news, Sharlah went to the kitchen to find things to store water in. She pulled out every glass, pitcher and pan. Some of them didn't get much use and weren't clean. She filled the sink with hot water and dish soap.

Sharlah turned on the radio for company, the Top 40 station that Brian hated, and sang along with "Stray Cat Strut."

Out of the corner of her eye, she saw the trees moving in the back yard. It looked like the wind was starting to pick up.

When she heard the opening bars of "Every Breath You Take," she leaned toward the radio to turn it up.

Just as she reached for the radio, the window exploded.

$\mathbf{\mathcal{S}}$

Sharlah's first thought was that the hurricane had hit early, and how could the TV people get it so wrong?

Her second thought was to wonder how she ended up sitting on the floor.

Her third thought was that her arm hurt, like she'd burned it.

That was when she noticed the blood—lots of it.

She mopped at the blood with a dishtowel until she could figure out the source. On her upper arm was a spot where the flesh had been gouged away, leaving a divot.

What the hell? That was her fourth thought.

Sharlah was sitting on the floor, watching blood soak the dishtowel, when she heard banging on the front door. It could have been two minutes later, or it could have been 20—she couldn't say.

A man called out: "Police officers!"

He pronounced it "PO-leece," which for some reason struck Sharlah as funny.

She followed the squawk and chatter of a police radio as footsteps sounded along the side of the house. Then a familiar face appeared at her shattered kitchen window.

"Miss Webb? It's Officer Zuk. Are you injured? Can you get up?"

Sharlah tried to answer, but the words refused to come.

"I'm coming in," Zuk said. He used his flashlight to break a pane in the door, then reached in and flipped the deadbolt. His boots crunched on the glass that littered the floor.

Sharlah found her voice. "My arm hurts."

He knelt next to her. "Let's take a look." He peeled away the dishtowel, then pulled a microphone off his shoulder and called for an ambulance. Sharlah thought she heard him say something about a shooting.

"Who got shot?"

"Is there anyone else in the house, Miss Webb?"

"No," she said. "Who got shot? Wait... did I get shot? Someone shot me?"

Zuk got up. "Ambulance is on the way. Please stay where you are."

It hadn't occurred to Sharlah to get up.

Zuk was back moments later with another cop. He seemed familiar to Sharlah, a handsome guy with dark eyes and a mustache, but she couldn't place him.

Sharlah peered up at Zuk. "You're always around when something bad happens."

"We got an anonymous 911 call reporting a gunshot." Zuk pulled a notebook from his shirt pocket. "Can you tell us what happened?"

"I don't know," Sharlah said. "I didn't even know I was shot."

"I'm going to check the alley," the other officer said.

Zuk knelt next to Sharlah again. "You're in shock, Miss Webb, but it would really help us if you could tell us what happened. Walk me through it."

Sharlah closed her eyes and tried to concentrate. "I was washing dishes, to have stuff to put water in, for the hurricane. And then the window broke."

A siren wailed in the distance.

"Did you see or hear anything beforehand?"

"I didn't hear anything. I was listening to the radio. I was just leaning over to turn it up, because 'Every Breath You Take' was on, and that's when it happened."

The siren grew louder and then stopped. Sharlah heard doors slam.

"And you didn't see anything?"

"Just the trees moving in the back yard. I thought it was the wind," Sharlah said. "Can I ask you something?"

Zuk stopped writing and looked at her. "What?"

"How much does the ambulance cost?"

𝓼

The doctor in the ER was a woman, which threw Sharlah for a loop. She'd never seen a woman doctor before.

The doctor said the bullet "grazed" her, like it was no big deal. She cleaned and bandaged the arm. She gave Sharlah antibiotics and Tylenol 3 and told her she could go as soon as they finished her paperwork. A gunshot always involved a lot of paperwork, she said.

Sharlah lay back on the bed and tried not to think about how much blood there would have been if she'd been something more serious than "grazed."

There was a knock at the door, and then it opened.

Sharlah was expecting a doctor or nurse, but it was the detective, Downs, trailed by Zuk.

"Hello," Downs said. "Are you up to answering a few more questions?"

"Sure." Sharlah sat up, even though it made her woozy.

Downs went through a bunch of questions she'd already answered: what she'd been doing beforehand, what she'd seen, what she'd heard.

After 10 minutes or so, he asked Zuk to go find him a cup of coffee.

"I just want to make sure I've got the timeline right," Downs said, pulling up a chair to the edge of the bed. "Did you turn the TV off right after the news?"

"Yes," Sharlah said. "I went to the kitchen and got things out of the cupboard."

"How long did that take?"

"I don't know. Less than five minutes?"

"And then you started washing dishes? How long were you washing the dishes before the shot was fired?"

"Not very long," Sharlah said. "I think I only heard one song on the radio."

"And after the window shattered, then what happened?"

Sharlah was starting to feel a little fuzzy, but she tried hard to focus. "I guess I fell down or sat down on the kitchen floor. Then you guys were knocking on my door."

"Right. OK. I've got it all now." Downs put away his notebook.

"Was someone trying to kill me?"

"That's a good question," Downs said. "Do *you* think someone was trying to kill you?"

"I don't know why anyone would want to," Sharlah said.

"No?" Downs raised an eyebrow. "Well, moving to turn up the radio may have saved your life."

Downs yawned elaborately. "I wonder where Zuk is? He's usually quicker than this. Was he first on the scene tonight? Or was that Moreno?"

"Zuk," Sharlah said. Then she reconsidered. "Actually, I don't know. I didn't answer the door, and then Zuk came around back. Is somebody in trouble for not getting there faster?"

Downs laughed. "No, nobody's in trouble." He glanced up at the little window in the door. "Here's Zuk with my coffee. We'll have him drive you wherever you want to go."

⚡

By the time Sharlah walked through the muggy night and got into the police car, she was feeling light-headed.

"Uh-oh," she said. "I think I'm kind of f…" Sharlah caught herself. Was this the cop she wasn't supposed to swear in front of? She couldn't remember.

Zuk turned to her. "Where am I taking you? Have you called your folks?"

"You wouldn't ask that if you knew my folks."

"Brothers? Sisters?"

"Rod joined the Navy. Wayne's in Huntsville. He took a bat to a guy in a fight and killed him." She glanced over to see Zuk's reaction, but he didn't seem fazed at all.

"What about Brian Lowry's family?"

"They hate me," Sharlah said. "Well, his mom does. And she calls the shots."

"There's got to be someone," Zuk said. "A friend? Someone you work with?"

Sharlah thought, briefly, about calling Joan. But then she remembered Joan's lecture about not letting Brian ruin her life, and she shelved the idea.

"I'll be fine. Just take me home," Sharlah said.

Zuk didn't seem happy, but he didn't argue.

"I used to wait on you at the diner. Did you know that?" They rolled by the bank, and Sharlah did a double take at the sign. "Is it really 2:30?"

"Yes," Zuk said. Sharlah wasn't sure which question he was answering

"I can't believe I have to get up in two hours," Sharlah said. She leaned back against the seat and watched as the car slid past the darkened downtown.

She didn't remember closing her eyes. But then the car stopped moving, and she opened her eyes, and they were in front of her house.

Zuk shut off the engine. "I'll just walk you in and take a look around."

Sharlah had trouble operating the door handle; Zuk had to open it for her.

The house was a mess, like a lot of people had been in and out. The rug was crooked, and Sharlah bent to straighten it but thought better of it when she nearly lost her balance.

Zuk caught her elbow. "Why don't you have a seat while I take a walk around?"

Sharlah shook him off. "I have stuff to do," she said, trailing Zuk into the kitchen.

The broken glass from the window had been swept up, and plywood was nailed over it and the broken pane in the door.

She could see blood on the linoleum, though. She was going to have to get out the mop and clean that up.

"Thanks for fixing the window," Sharlah said.

"That wasn't us."

The sink was still full of water. Sharlah plunged her hand in and pulled the plug. She needed to wash all the dishes, she knew that, though she couldn't remember why.

"Miss Webb." Zuk said her name quietly, then louder. "Miss Webb, if I could…"

Suddenly the answer came to Sharlah. "There's supposed to be a hurricane."

"Miss Webb, they gave you a narcotic painkiller at the hospital. You need to sleep."

Sharlah realized that she still had the drain plug in her hand and felt a little bit stupid. "I guess maybe you're right," she said.

"Are you sure I can't take you somewhere else to stay?"

Sharlah shook her head.

"Walk to the front door with me," Zuk said.

She followed him to the door, noticing again that the rug was askew. Sharlah knew this was bad, but the reason eluded her.

Zuk opened the door. "You need to lock this after me. I'm going to stand on the porch until I hear the lock. Do you understand?"

"Duh," Sharlah said. "I'm not stupid." But even as she spoke, she realized she was slurring.

He stepped outside and closed the door. Sharlah locked the doorknob and turned the deadbolt. Then she leaned her forehead against the door and listened as his footsteps echoed away from the house.

SIX

THE PHONE WOKE Sharlah up.

It took awhile for her to realize what it was, and even longer for her to crawl out of bed and stumble to the kitchen to answer it.

"Hello?"

"Sharlah? It's Joan. Where are you?"

This struck Sharlah as a stupid question. She was home, wasn't she, if she was answering her phone? And why was Joan calling her in the middle of the night?

"Sharlah? Hello? It's 5:20. You're late. You're never late. What's going on?"

Sharlah glanced at the clock. Joan was right. It was 5:20.

Why was she so thirsty? Sharlah turned on the kitchen faucet, caught some water in her hand and drank it. Her arm hurt like hell.

"I'm sorry, Joan," Sharlah mumbled. "I don't think I can come in today."

"You what?"

"I can't come in today." Sharlah knew she needed to say more. She should explain about the trip to the hospital, the

Tylenol 3—especially about the Tylenol 3. But she couldn't seem to form the words.

"Sharlah, we are open 365 days a year. Our customers count on us. And I count on you." Sharlah vaguely recalled hearing Joan give this speech before, to someone else. "You are scheduled to work, and I need you to be here. Are you going to be here?"

"I don't think so."

Joan let out a long, exasperated sigh. "Sharlah, if you don't get here in the next 30 minutes, I'm going to have to let you go. Do you understand?"

"OK," Sharlah said, and hung up.

When Sharlah woke up the second time, on the couch, her arm still hurt like fire. She was still thirsty. But her mind was clearer—clear enough to wonder why she was asleep on the couch and to realize the light in the living room was wrong.

Only when she walked into the kitchen for water and saw that the clock read 10:30 did she remember the conversation with Joan.

She reached hurriedly for the phone and then moaned as pain shot through her arm. She'd have to remember to use her right arm as little as possible.

The phone in Joan's office rang 12 times, and when someone finally answered, it was one of the other waitresses, not Joan.

"Donna, it's Sharlah. I need to talk to Joan."

"You're dead meat." Donna relayed this news a bit cheerfully, Sharlah thought. "You know how she is about no-shows."

"I can explain," Sharlah said. "Would you please just get her?"

While she waited, Sharlah surveyed kitchen. She was going to have to call the landlord about the back door and window, and he was going to be mad. Sharlah didn't think it was her fault that someone shot her, but he probably wasn't going to see it that way.

Just thinking about saying those words aloud to Joan—I'm not at work because *someone shot me*—had a sobering effect on Sharlah.

"Sharlah, you still there?" It was Donna again.

"Yeah."

"Joan says you have to come explain in person. She'll be here until 3."

Sharlah thanked Donna and hung up. It was less than what she'd hoped for, but at least Joan was willing to hear her out.

It scared Sharlah to think what would happen if Joan didn't relent. No job, no Brian—she wouldn't be able to pay the September rent. She'd be out on the street with nowhere to go and no one to help her.

She'd get cleaned up and dressed and show Joan her hospital paperwork. Joan was basically a nice person. She would give her the job back.

They'd told Sharlah at the hospital that she could shower but should try to keep her wound dry. That was easier said than done, especially when she washed her hair. Water mixed with shampoo got under the bandage, and it stung so much it made her gasp.

If Brian were home, he would have washed her hair for her. He did that sometimes, and Sharlah thought that was one of the best feelings in the world. Brian thought it was sexy, and that had led to more than one good-natured argument in their shower, which Sharlah thought was too cramped for what Brian had in mind.

Sometimes she gave in, and Brian would tease her later about her reluctance. "See, you didn't fall and break your neck," he'd say. "I wouldn't let anything happen to you."

Ever since Brian's arrest, thinking this way had left Sharlah overwhelmed with longing for him. The feeling that overwhelmed her this time, though, was anger—a big, raging thing directed not at the police or Brian's family, but at Brian himself.

It was Brian who got her into this mess, who sat on the other side of the glass and stared sadly and refused to help himself or give Sharlah anything to hang onto at all.

The hell with this, Sharlah thought. Brian had asked her to come see him, and she would. But this time she was going to get some answers.

Sharlah finished rinsing her hair, turned off the water and yanked the shower curtain back so hard that it almost came off the rod.

She didn't bother with the hairdryer. The way the rain was pounding on the roof, she could tell there wasn't any point. She slid into her jeans and pulled a pink T-shirt over her head, the first one her hand had landed on when she opened the drawer.

Her hospital paperwork was sitting on the dresser along with the prescriptions they'd given her. She crumpled the one for Tylenol 3 and tossed it. No way she was taking that again. The other was for an antibiotic, and she put that one in her purse. She'd stop at the pharmacy to get it filled. God only knew how much it would cost.

She grabbed her car keys and stomped out to the living room.

She stopped when she saw the rug.

Vaguely, she remembered that something had nagged at her the night before, and now she knew what it was.

The armchair was moved about a foot from its usual spot, and the rug was off-kilter.

The money, Sharlah thought. What if somebody found the money?

She went to get her pocketknife.

Then she stopped. "This is crazy," she said aloud. If the police had found the money, they would have questioned her about it. In fact, they'd probably *still* be questioning her about it. She took a couple steps toward the front door.

But now the idea was in her head, and she couldn't quite shake it.

Pulling up the floorboard a second time was both easier and harder—easier, because Sharlah knew just where to apply the pressure, and harder, because her arm hurt with the slightest exertion.

She breathed a sigh of relief when she spotted the briefcase in the crawl space.

Sharlah started to put the floorboard back, but then she paused. Maybe it made sense to move the money to a spot where she could check on it quickly.

Or maybe she should leave it exactly where it was. The police hadn't found it the first time, which meant the crawl space was a good hiding place.

But they'd already searched the house once, and what were the chances they'd do it again? If she moved it, she wouldn't have to pry the floor up every time she got paranoid.

Even as she argued both sides in her head, Sharlah knew her desire to move the money had nothing to do with the cops' chances of finding it or not finding it.

She wanted to move the money so she could get to it more easily in case she wanted to use it. It really was that simple. She needed a new clutch; now she had doctor bills; the rent was due in two weeks.

Brian could turn to his parents if things got bad. They might impose conditions, but they would never let him go without food or end up on the street. Sharlah, on the other hand, didn't have anyone, nobody but Brian, and right now he wasn't helping her any.

Sharlah liked to think of herself as an honest person. She'd never stolen anything in her life, not even when she was really desperate. If anybody had asked her to deal drugs, she would have said no, no matter how much money they offered her.

But this wasn't stealing. The money was Brian's. The drugs had already been dealt.

Sharlah unfolded her pocketknife and pried up the second floorboard.

$$\text{\textbf{\textit{6}}}$$

Figuring out a new hiding place for the money wasn't easy. Sharlah thought about wrapping it in aluminum foil and putting it in the freezer. But the freezer held nothing but ice trays, and big square packages would stick out.

The broom closet was her next idea. But there really wasn't any way to conceal the metal briefcase there, so that idea was out.

She moved to the bathroom, and that's when she had an idea that struck her as brilliant.

In the cabinet under the bathroom sink, Sharlah kept several unopened boxes of tampons—she'd found a great sale earlier in the summer. Brian had been with her at the store, and he was horrified when she put all those boxes in their cart. He wouldn't even wait in the checkout line with her—he just handed her his wallet and went over to leaf through a car magazine until she was done.

Sharlah was pretty sure there was no way a cop would rifle through a tampon box, not when guys were so squeamish about that stuff.

She got a plastic bag from the kitchen and dumped all the tampons into it. Then she transferred the money from the briefcase to the tampon boxes, folded the tops closed and put them back under the cabinet, next to the plastic bag.

That left the envelope with the passports, and the gun.

Sharlah carried the briefcase to the bedroom and put it on the bed, thinking.

She knew she could tuck something flat up under the bottom of the dresser, because she'd found a *Playboy* there once when she moved the furniture to sweep.

Sharlah stared at the gun for a long time. She wished she could just get rid of it, but she had no idea how to do that.

Nothing came to her, and the morning was ticking away— visitation at the jail started in 20 minutes. She finally wrapped the gun in one of Brian's old T-shirts and stuffed it in her underwear drawer.

She took the briefcase to the alley and buried it under a big bag of trash in the next-door neighbor's bin.

9

The rain picked up as Sharlah drove from the house to the jail. Her clutch felt mushier than it had the day before, and she wondered if the weather could be making it worse. Maybe she'd ask Brian. Maybe that was a question he'd actually answer.

Sharlah wanted to be fair to Brian. She wanted to hear his side of things. But it was getting harder and harder for her to push away her doubts.

She'd thought they had a plan. She would get her GED, then take a typing course. She'd get an office job that paid better than waiting tables. She knew Brian was on board with that—he'd even told her she was smart enough for college.

The second part of the plan, in her mind, was finding a better job for Brian. He'd always shut her down when she'd tried to talk about it, but Sharlah thought that was just because flunking out of college had hurt his confidence. She assumed he needed more time before he was ready to challenge himself again.

The thing that bothered Sharlah most about being poor was the feeling that she didn't have control over things. That was her goal—more control. She didn't care about having more stuff, and she'd always thought Brian felt the same way.

Stacks of money hidden under the house, though, made her wonder whether she'd been wrong. Mitch Lowry liked to talk about how he'd built his business up from nothing, but Brian didn't remember any of that. For most of his life, they'd had a pool in the back yard and new cars and nice vacations.

Kevin and Lynn had honeymooned in Hawaii, and Brian and Sharlah couldn't even scrape together the money for a weekend in Austin. Had that started to grate? Had Brian come up with his own plan for his future?

Sharlah tried to shake off those thoughts and concentrate on her driving, because the weather was getting worse by the minute.

At one intersection, she plowed through water a foot deep, which spooked her a little. She knew it could just be a plugged storm drain, but the specter of a hurricane was starting to scare her.

The waiting area at the jail was deserted. Apparently the weather was keeping visitors away. Sharlah sat in a plastic chair, took her book out of her purse and tried to concentrate on *Sophie's Choice* while they processed her and fetched Brian.

After 20 minutes or so, they let her into the visiting room.

Brian smiled when he came through the door, but it didn't melt her heart. Not this time.

"I wasn't expecting you so early," he said when he picked up the phone. "I thought you had to work this morning."

"I didn't go in," Sharlah said.

Brian could tell something was wrong. "Is everything OK? You never skip work."

"I never got shot before."

"What?" Brian sat up straighter and leaned toward the glass divider.

"Why would someone shoot me, Brian?"

"Seriously? Are you OK? What happened?"

"I was standing in the kitchen and someone shot me through the window." Sharlah pulled up the sleeve of her T-shirt to show him the bandage. "Why would someone shoot me, Brian?"

Brian stared at her arm. "Is it bad? Did you call the police?"

"It grazed me," Sharlah said. "The hospital cleaned it up, gave me antibiotics and sent me home. You haven't answered me. Why would someone shoot me, Brian?"

"I don't know," he said softly. "God, Shar, you must have been so scared."

"Does somebody think I know something?"

Brian glanced toward the reminder on the wall that all visits would be taped.

"I don't care if they're taping us," Sharlah pointed to her arm. "Why did this happen?"

Brian was quiet for a moment. When he spoke, he was clearly choosing his words carefully. "I don't know. I just don't know."

"Could someone think I have something of theirs?"

Brian's eyes widened in alarm. "No," he said. "There's nothing like that." He glanced again at the warning sign on the wall.

Furious, Sharlah sank back in her chair. "I don't know why I'm even wasting time asking you, because you 'don't want to talk about it,'" she said, making air quotes.

She stared hard at Brian through the glass. He wouldn't look her in the eye.

"Maybe you should ask about how work's going, or my clutch, or the squeaky board in the living room, since those are the only things you ever want to talk about."

Brian's head dropped to his chest. "I'm sorry, Shar," he said. "I don't blame you for being mad. If you walked out right now and never came back, I wouldn't blame you."

Sharlah didn't answer. The clock on the wall ticked away their precious visiting time. She'd never felt so far away from Brian.

After a minute had gone by in silence, Brian put the phone receiver on his shoulder. He bowed his head and put one hand over his eyes. His shoulders began to shake, and Sharlah watched, chastened, as tears dripped off his chin and wet the front of his shirt.

Sharlah tapped on the glass that separated them. Brian wiped away the tears with the back of his hand and put the receiver back to his ear.

"I'm sorry I got mad. It's OK, Brian. It's going to be OK."

She wasn't sure she believed that, but it seemed important to say it.

"I'm helpless in here, Shar. I can't protect you." Brian gulped hard for air. "I'm useless. I know it."

"Brian, stop. You're not useless."

She'd come in angry, but now Sharlah was desperate to lift Brian's spirits. It tore at her heart when Brian got down on himself, and she'd do anything to make him feel better. He'd messed up, but he was a good person. She knew that.

Suddenly, an idea came to her, a way to help them both. "You don't have to fix everything for me. Like my clutch, I just have to go to a mechanic. And you were totally right about the squeaky floorboard."

Brian eyed her warily. "Yeah?"

"Yeah. I checked it out. It would be a lot of trouble to fix."

Brian nodded once. "When I get out on bail, I'll deal with it."

Did that mean he'd understood? Sharlah hoped so.

"So I guess in the meantime, I can just leave it be," she said.

Their eyes met, and then Brian's glance slid down to her arm.

"Are you sure you're OK? Does it hurt? What did the cops say?"

She shrugged. "They seem clueless, like they expect *me* to tell *them* who did it. They told me to call 911 if I see anything suspicious, although I think they're watching me or watching the house. I keep running into this one cop, and..."

The look of panic on Brian's face made Sharlah's heart lurch.

She glanced left, then right. No guards were visible. She mouthed a question to Brian. "Is that bad?"

Brian nodded.

She mouthed another question. "Can I trust them?"

Then, aloud: "Have you ever been in a hurricane?"

"No," Brian said.

A guard strode into view, and Sharlah wanted to stamp her foot in frustration. She'd thought it was crazy when Robin at the diner said the police were in on everything—the drugs, Missy's death. Robin thought *everything* was a conspiracy. But now it seemed that Brian was telling her she should be afraid of the police.

With the guard watching, Sharlah had to keep up the pretense of talking about Hurricane Aileen. "Everybody at the diner has been talking about whether it's better to leave or stick it out."

"I think it's a good idea to leave," Brian said, carefully enunciating every word.

Was he talking about the hurricane for real now? Sharlah couldn't tell. "Really? People say if it does hit, and you're not home, your house will get looted."

"You can take the stuff that's valuable, put it in the car and go," Brian said.

"But people say you won't be able to get back for days, and then I won't be able to see you. I don't even know where I'd go."

The buzzer sounded, indicating one minute left of visiting time. "I don't want to get stuck somewhere and not be able to see you, Brian. I don't *want* to go."

Brian put his palm against the glass dividing them. Sharlah did the same and tried to persuade herself she could feel the heat of Brian's hand through the glass.

"Don't worry about me," Brian said. "Keep yourself safe until this blows over. I'll see you when I see you."

The phone went dead, and Brian mouthed one final message to Sharlah.

"I love you. Go."

The door opened behind him, and Sharlah watched as the jail swallowed him up.

𖦹

The rain had intensified while she was inside, and water stood four inches deep in the parking lot. Sharlah paused under the building's overhang to roll up her jeans and then splashed to her car.

She switched on the radio and drove toward the diner to see Joan, her wipers on high.

Her anger at Brian seemed a faraway thing now. He'd helped her as much as he could, she could see that. The rest would be up to her.

The mayor was on the radio talking about the hurricane, and she turned it up. He sounded reassuring and not worried at all.

Then a guy from the weather service came on and seemed exactly the opposite, talking about flooding and storm surges. Ominously, he said the water in the bay had to rise only a few more feet and then the causeway would be underwater, cutting the island off.

Up ahead, she could see a steady stream of cars turning left to avoid a flooded intersection. If she wanted to get to the diner, she was either going to have to plow through the water or go the long way around.

Sharlah put on her turn signal and made a right, headed toward her house. She felt bad about blowing off Joan, because she'd always been fair. But Brian's instructions had been clear. The weather was getting worse, and explaining herself to Joan was a luxury Sharlah couldn't afford. When it was safe to come back, she'd go square things at the diner.

When Sharlah pulled up to her house, the street was deserted except for her neighbor Well, who was nailing plywood over his windows.

Inside, Sharlah went to the kitchen, planning to make a sandwich to eat while she packed.

First, though, she had to do something about the rain that was seeping in around the plywood covering the broken window and puddling on the floor.

As she sopped up the water with a dishtowel, Sharlah thought about the way Zuk showed up right after the shooting. He'd just happened to be at the same restaurant, and he'd insisted on following her home from the diner earlier in the week.

It was warm in the house, but Sharlah shivered.

She remembered, too, that Downs had sent Zuk out of the room at the hospital and then asked her which cop showed up first.

She'd liked Zuk from the start, because she knew him from the diner and because he helped her with the couch. But maybe he was *trying* to make her like him.

She wished she had someone to advise her, someone she could trust. She knew that most 19-year-olds would have called their parents already. But she hadn't talked to her dad in two years, and he wouldn't be any help anyway.

Would Brian's dad help her? Hadn't he come to see her here at the house and cried in front of her and begged her to use her influence with Brian?

Sharlah grabbed the phone and dialed Lowry Marine.

The phone rang for a long time before someone answered.

"Hello," she began. "I'm trying to reach Mitch Lowry. My name is Sharlah Webb."

"Sharlah? It's Kevin."

His voice sounded higher than usual, and rushed. "Oh, hi, Kevin. Is your dad there?"

"He's out on the lot," Kevin said. "It sounds like this storm's going to be rough. What did you need?"

"Yeah, it's getting bad here. I'm packing up to leave," Sharlah said. "And I'm worried, because last night someone shot at me and..."

"Someone *what*?"

"I got shot in the arm," Sharlah said.

"My God. Did you call the police? Did anyone see anything?"

"The police didn't tell me anything," Sharlah said. "I don't think they have a clue."

"But you're OK? You weren't badly hurt?"

For the second time in two days, Sharlah was pleased by Kevin's concern. "They let me out of the ER after a couple hours. But I'm worried about the storm. Brian said..."

"Come ride it out with us here in Houston," Kevin said, decisive.

This was what Sharlah had been hoping for—someone who would take charge, someone she could trust.

"Could I? I'm kind of afraid to be alone."

"How soon do you think you'll leave? You should get going before it gets worse."

"I can be on the road in 30 minutes. I don't know how traffic is going to be, though," Sharlah said. "And I don't remember how to get to your place. Brian always drove."

"Find a pay phone and call when you get to Houston," Kevin said.

"Maybe when I'm there... maybe we could talk about what's going on with Brian," Sharlah said. "There's some stuff I'm really worried about, and I don't know what to do."

She heard Kevin inhale sharply. "OK, Sharlah. Be careful."

𝓼

In the bedroom, Sharlah pulled her suitcase out of the closet and opened it on the bed. It was an ancient thing, a bright turquoise Samsonite that she bought at a yard sale for the trip she and Brian had planned to Austin.

She had no idea how long she'd be gone, but she figured she should pack clothes for three or four days, just in case.

In the bathroom, she swept up her toiletries and her makeup. After some hesitation, she pulled the boxes of money from under the bathroom sink. It didn't seem safe to leave the money in the house, and she might need to show it to Kevin.

The last thing she packed was the gun, still wrapped in Brian's old T-shirt. She put it in the corner of the suitcase, wedged between her socks.

The suitcase was hard to shut—one of the locks was dented and kept popping open. Finally, Sharlah put the suitcase on the floor, sat on it, and reached between her knees to close it. That did the trick.

She grabbed her raincoat and her purse and car keys and was halfway out the door when she remembered the envelope with the fake IDs. She dashed back to the bedroom to retrieve the envelope, not wanting to leave anything incriminating in the house.

When she stepped out onto the porch with her suitcase, Well was still out boarding up his windows. He spotted her and came trotting across the street, his hammer in his hand, catching up with her in the driveway.

"Hey, looks like we might really get hit, huh?" Well peered at her from under the hood of his slicker. "You taking off?"

"Yeah," Sharlah said. She shifted the suitcase so she could unlock the trunk.

"Let me help you with that," Well said, reaching for the suitcase.

"Thanks, I've got it," Sharlah said.

Well grabbed the handle. "Let me. You've got your hands full."

"I've *got* it," Sharlah said. She opened the trunk and tugged the suitcase away. The locks popped, and her clothes began to spill out. Sharlah wrapped both arms around the suitcase and heaved it into the trunk, hoping to keep her things off the wet ground.

"Whoa, sorry about that," Well said. He picked up a stray sock and put it in the trunk. "Can I help you there?"

Sharlah crammed things in her suitcase as quickly as she could. "I said I've got it."

"I was just trying to help you," Well said. "Don't get so uptight."

Sharlah leaned on the suitcase and managed to close it. She shut the trunk.

"Hey, like I said, I'm sorry," Well said. "Where you headed?"

"Out of here," Sharlah said. She opened the car door and got in.

"Stay safe," Well said, but she'd already slammed the door and started the car.

🌀

Traffic on the main road to the causeway was crawling. Everyone seemed to be grabbing the last chance to leave ahead of the hurricane.

Her windshield wipers could barely keep up with the rain, and the palm trees were beginning to bend in the wind. It was going to be a long, slow drive to Houston.

She came to a complete standstill a couple miles from the causeway, and Sharlah sat, fuming, for five minutes. Finally, things started moving again, and she stepped on the clutch. It went all the way to the floor with no resistance.

Sharlah let out a wail of frustration. The driver behind her honked.

She pumped the clutch a couple times, but nothing happened.

The road angled downhill, so Sharlah hit the flashers, put the car in neutral and coasted until she came to the entry to an office park. She rolled into the deserted parking lot.

Sharlah sat for a few minutes, trying to decide what to do.

She knew there was a convenience store with a pay phone in the next block. She could call the diner. Maybe someone would still be there. Robin owed her a favor—Sharlah had given her rides when her car broke down.

Of course, that would mean going back to the house and riding out the storm after Brian had told her to leave.

Maybe she should call Lowry Marine and explain the whole story—about finding the money, about the police, about Brian telling her to leave. If they knew the spot she was in, maybe Kevin or Mitch would come get her.

A big gust of wind swept through the parking lot, shaking the car and galvanizing Sharlah to action.

She rolled up her jeans and fastened her slicker all the way up the front. She put the hood up and stepped out into the storm.

$$\pmb{\varsigma}$$

The convenience store was jammed. Cars were 15 deep at the gas pumps, and the checkout line inside snaked through the aisles.

A girl wearing an Iowa Hawkeyes T-shirt and cutoffs had the one pay phone tied up. Sharlah put down her suitcase and tucked under the building's awning to wait.

"We're just getting gas," the girl said into the phone. "We're going to get as far north as we can tonight and find a motel room."

The girl paused to listen and kicked one foot impatiently against the wall of the store. "I don't know, Mom. Oklahoma is, like, really far. Maybe Dallas?"

She was wearing rubber flip-flops, the kind Missy always wore, and a wave of sadness rolled over Sharlah. Everything had been so crazy that she could almost forget sometimes that Missy was dead.

The Iowa girl went on arguing with her mother about why she hadn't called on Tuesday and why she hadn't headed inland sooner. "We were too watching the news, Mom!"

A cop car crept through the parking lot. Sharlah turned her back, hoping whoever was in the car wouldn't recognize her with her hood pulled up.

There was a newspaper rack behind her, and she made a show of studying the front page. The big story was about the storm, but a headline below it caught her eye.

Police Actions In Drug Case Questioned

Sharlah dug change out of her purse and bought a paper. She had just started to read the story when the Iowa girl hung up.

"All yours," she said.

PART TWO

Brian

SEVEN

BRIAN TAPPED TENTATIVELY on the office door and waited.

His father's secretary was deep in conversation with another woman, their heads bent over a set of photos. Both looked up at his knock.

"Sorry," Brian said. "Darcy, does he have a minute?"

The second woman hastily gathered up the photos. Brian would have greeted her, but he couldn't remember her name. He aimed a smile at her, but she didn't smile back.

"I'll show you the rest later," the woman told Darcy.

Brian stepped back, giving her plenty of space to leave the office. She walked quickly past him, her head down.

"He's on a call," Darcy said, glancing at the phone on her desk. "Shouldn't be long."

Brian hovered in the doorway.

"Come on in," Darcy said. "Have a seat."

Brian took a couple steps into the office and gestured toward his dirty work pants. "Better not." He edged up against the wall so people in the hall wouldn't see him.

It was the last business day before Christmas, and the mood of most Lowry Marine employees was festive.

Darcy smiled at him. "Do you have your Christmas shopping finished?"

Brian had hoped she would go back to her work and ignore him. He shrugged and stared at the carpet. "Pretty much."

He realized right away that his answer was rude and regretted it. Darcy had been his father's secretary as long as he could remember, and Brian had always liked her.

"I got my niece a Tonka truck," he volunteered, briefly looking up.

"Ashley," he added, then immediately felt like an idiot. Darcy knew who Ashley was—Kevin's office was right down the hall.

Darcy's eyes widened. "Oh, how cute! Four is such a fun age."

"I know it sounds weird for a girl, but she said she wanted one," Brian said.

Darcy glanced down at the phone. "Your dad's off the line." She cocked her head toward the inner office door. "Go on back."

"Thanks," Brian said. "Have a good Christmas."

Mitch Lowry was sitting at his desk sorting white envelopes.

"Hey there, son," he said, looking at Brian over his reading glasses. "Everything OK?"

Brian shut the door and held his spot a good five feet from the desk. "The parole office called. They need a drug test today."

"Today? Did they say why?"

"They said it's random," Brian said. "Is it OK if I go now?"

Mitch set aside the stack of envelopes and stared up at his son, frowning. "Right now? Don't you want to stay for the lunch?"

Every year, Mitch closed the office early for Christmas and treated his employees to a catered lunch where he handed out bonuses.

"There might be a wait," Brian said. "The sooner I go, the sooner I'm out. It gets dark so early now, and I still don't feel good driving at night."

"I wish you didn't have to miss the lunch."

"I'm sorry."

"Aw, don't be sorry," Mitch said, waving his hand. "I just hate the way the parole office says 'jump' and you have to say 'how high?' That's not your fault."

His father was wrong, though Brian wouldn't say that. Of course it was his fault that he had to go to the parole office. All of it was his fault.

"So I can take the truck and you'll catch a ride with Kevin?"

"More likely I'll be driving *him* home," Mitch said.

The Lowry Marine Christmas party was officially dry, but some of the guys had a long tradition of ignoring the rule, and Mitch had a long tradition of ignoring their drinking as long as nobody got out of hand.

Until the parole office called, Brian had been planning to keep an eye on Kevin so his dad could relax and enjoy the party.

"OK," Brian said, turning to leave the office. "Sorry."

"Hold up, son," Mitch said. He rifled through the envelopes and pulled one out. He walked around his desk and held the envelope out to Brian.

"This one's for you."

"I can't take that, Dad," Brian said.

"Everybody gets a bonus. It's not special treatment. Yours was calculated same way everybody else's was," Mitch said. "Well, in your case, I counted total time of service, before and since... since you came back."

"I still owe you for..."

Mitch put the envelope in Brian's shirt pocket and patted him once on the chest. "Thanks for all your hard work, son. I appreciate it."

Brian could tell he wasn't going to win. He'd have to deal with this later.

"Go by the break room and see if the caterers can fix you a plate to go," Mitch said, returning to his chair.

"OK." Brian put his hand on the doorknob, ready to leave.

"This thing today is just random, huh? Nothing to worry about?"

"It's fine," Brian said. "Don't worry."

$$\boldsymbol{\mathcal{S}}$$

Brian always felt conspicuous at work, even back in the shop, but he felt doubly so in the halls up front where the salesmen and secretaries and accounting clerks worked.

He hurried past his brother's office. Kevin wasn't in when Brian came by the first time—late again—but now his voice drifted out into the hall.

"So this thing's got a million pieces, and I told Lynn, we're just going to have to give it to her in the box, because there's no way I'm getting that put together after..."

A voice—not Kevin's—called out. "Brian? Hey, Brian!"

Brian froze. He exhaled and backed up a step.

Ray, one of the salesmen, was perched on the edge of Kevin's desk, a coffee cup in one meaty hand. He waved the other at Brian. "Come on in here!"

Brian cut his eyes to Kevin, who put down his own coffee cup and smiled. "Hey, Baby Bro. What brings you up from the shop?"

"I had to see Dad," Brian said.

"Come help us settle an argument," Ray said.

Ray tipped his cup toward him—it held a couple inches of clear, amber liquid—and produced a flask from his pants pocket. He waggled his eyebrows at Brian. "Care for..."

Kevin cut in. "Ray, he can't."

Ray quickly shoved the flask back in his pocket. "Sorry. I didn't know it was against your, um, rules."

"It's because of my concussion," Brian said. "That's all."

Recovering his composure, Ray picked up a large manila envelope from Kevin's desk and handed it to Brian.

"What's this?"

"Open it and flip to March," Ray said, winking at Kevin.

Brian looked to Kevin for guidance, but he just shrugged. Brian opened the envelope and took out a calendar, a freebie sent by a supplier.

Calendars like this one, which featured models in bikinis draped over boats, arrived every December at Lowry Marine. In junior high, Brian and Kevin had schemed to get their hands on them.

"March," Ray said, prodding.

Brian dutifully turned to March, which was graced by a blonde in an orange bikini with her elbows resting on a boat, her rump thrust out. She was staring back over her shoulder at the camera, and Brian thought her eyes looked dead.

Ray punched him on the arm. "She's something, huh? Who does she look like?"

Brian glanced at Kevin, looking for a hint.

Kevin silently shook his head at Ray and took a swig from his coffee cup.

"Heather what's-her-name," Ray said, stabbing a fat finger at the model's head. "From *T.J. Hooker*?"

Brian stared at him blankly.

"It's a TV show," Kevin supplied. "Nothing to do with actual hookers."

"I haven't seen it," Brian said. He offered the calendar back. "Sorry."

"Tell you what, why don't you keep that calendar," Ray said. "Your daddy won't let us hang 'em around the office because the secretaries bitched about it, and sure as shit the warden's not going to let me have it at home."

Ray's hand flew to his mouth, and his face slowly colored to match the holly berries on his Christmas tie.

"Oh, Lord. Brian, I didn't mean anything..." He fumbled to put his hand on Brian's arm, jostling his coffee cup. The contents sloshed onto Kevin's desk, and the smell of whiskey filled the office.

"It's OK," Brian said, wishing he could be somewhere—anywhere—else.

"It's just a... it's a joke," Ray sputtered. "I call my wife... I didn't mean anything..."

"He said it's OK," Kevin said, impatient. "Why don't you clean this up and get back to your desk, Ray."

Ray produced a handkerchief and swiped at the booze, then left, still murmuring apologies.

"Forget it. That guy's an idiot," Kevin said, loud enough for Ray to hear out in the hall.

"He's OK," Brian said. "He didn't mean anything."

"Dad should have fired him years ago," Kevin said, leaning back in his chair and stretching his arms over his head. The chair wobbled, and he grabbed his desk.

Brian glanced at Kevin's coffee cup. Kevin caught the look and moved the cup to the other side of the desk.

"Why are you mad at Lynn?"

Kevin blinked at him. "Who said I was mad at Lynn?"

"When I was coming down the hall, I heard you say..." Brian paused, trying to remember. What had Kevin said? He searched his brain but came away with nothing but the idea that Kevin had been complaining about Lynn.

Kevin rescued him. "Oh, you probably heard me talking about this dollhouse Lynn bought Ashley for Christmas. She wants it put together."

A million pieces—now Brian remembered. "And you don't want to?"

Kevin started to lift his coffee cup, then put it back down. "She wants it done Christmas Eve, so we can put it under the tree. I just don't see how I can get it done.

"We have the thing at Mom's, and then there's a party with the neighbors, which is the *only* chance I'm going to have the whole damn month to actually kick back. They do a margarita machine out by the pool—it's a blast. Last year, at the end, we blew off the machine and just did tequila shots. So when am I supposed to put together a dollhouse?"

A grin spread across Kevin's face. "Remember that year we both got bikes and Dad ran out of time to put them together? We came flying into the living room Christmas morning, and there was Dad on the floor in his bathrobe, his tools all around him, still trying to put together those bikes. Mom was *pissed*."

Brian closed his eyes. He could picture the scene. "Yours was blue and mine was green," he said. How could he remember details of a Christmas morning 20 years ago but not what his brother had been saying five minutes earlier?

"I remember, after they were put together, I asked Dad, 'Can we ride them today?' and he said yes, and you must have thought he meant right then." Kevin's shoulders shook with laughter. "You hopped on that bike in your little T-shirt and underpants and started riding around the living room. Funniest damn thing… Do you remember that?"

"Sure," Brian said. "I crashed into the coffee table and scratched it, and then Mom and Dad had a big argument about whether I should get spanked, since it was Christmas."

Kevin's grin disappeared. He reached again for his coffee cup, and again he stopped.

Brian felt like he'd ruined something, again. It was good, remembering stuff that happened when they were kids. "I was in my underwear? I don't remember that. Wouldn't Mom have made us wear PJs?"

"Nothing but your Fruit of the Looms," Kevin said, holding up one hand. "I swear."

"Hey, you know, I could put together the dollhouse for you," Brian said. "I could come over while you're out."

Kevin half-turned away and began to fiddle with some papers on his desk. "You don't have to do that. I wasn't asking you to."

"It would be for Ashley," Brian said. "So she could play with it right away Christmas morning. She'd like that. It would be like a present for her."

"Let me talk to Lynn," Kevin said. He turned again toward Brian. "What are you doing up here, anyway? What did Dad want?"

Brian dropped his eyes to the floor. "I have to leave early, go do a drug test. In fact, I should get going."

"What's that about? Did you mess up?"

"They said it's random," Brian said, turning to leave. "I'm not worried."

5

Brian was worried.

He fretted constantly about tripping up on his parole, and this call out of the blue had him spooked. He'd heard the stories about the guys who got out, committed violations and were right back inside a couple months later.

Brian could not think about going back to prison—if he did, his thoughts inevitably turned to the shotgun locked in his dad's office and a shady spot by a lake where he and Kevin fished as kids.

Brian paused for a minute to calm himself outside the parole office. It was important to appear normal. He didn't want to make anyone suspicious.

Inside, he gave his name and Department of Corrections number to the clerk, who screwed up her mouth at him like she'd just eaten something sour.

"Wait over there," she said, pointing with a pen. "Just so you know, there's a backup and it's going to be a while. Don't be coming up here asking me when they'll get to you. It won't make it go any faster."

All the plastic chairs in the waiting area were occupied, so Brian found an empty stretch of wall to lean against, waiting for his turn to pee in a cup.

A guy across the room stared at the scar on his head. Brian ignored him.

Someone had a radio tuned to one of those stations that played nothing but Christmas music, and "We Wish You A Merry Christmas" was playing. That struck Brian as a cruel joke in a parole office.

For most of his life, Brian hadn't understood how grating it was to be bombarded with unwanted Christmas cheer. Sharlah had tried to explain it to him once, how it felt like there was a party she wasn't invited to and people were rubbing her nose in it, but Brian didn't really get it.

Now he understood exactly what Sharlah meant.

Brian shifted his weight to his other foot and tried to get more comfortable.

It was hard to think about Christmas without feeling ashamed of the way he'd left Sharlah to work at the diner while he spent the day with his family. It was Sharlah's idea, and she talked up the tips, but Brian knew she only did it to make things easier for him. She pretended Christmas didn't matter, and he pretended he believed her.

He'd known even then he was being selfish, but he always figured he'd make it up to her later. It had never occurred to him that he wouldn't get the chance.

Sometimes, Brian still couldn't believe it had been more than four years since Sharlah said goodbye to him in the jail, walked out into a hurricane and disappeared.

s

It took awhile after the storm for anyone to realize that Sharlah was missing.

Hurricane Aileen destroyed a quarter of the buildings in town and flooded whole neighborhoods. Parts of the beach just disappeared. Power was out for weeks.

It was bad enough in Houston that Kevin called an ambulance when Lynn went into labor during the storm. They welcomed baby Ashley in a delivery room lit by an emergency generator. Kevin told people that Lynn was louder than the hurricane, because the epidural guy didn't make it in.

When they restored phone service to the jail and Brian could finally call his folks, his dad told him Sharlah never showed up in Houston after telling Kevin she was on her way.

Mitch thought maybe she didn't get out before the causeway closed, or maybe she got discouraged by the traffic and turned around. He'd tried calling her, but the phone at the house just rang and rang.

Brian thought Sharlah left town like he told her and was holed up in a motel, reading a book, waiting for things to cool down. He pictured her staying someplace decent, maybe with a pool. She had to have found the cash, Brian figured, because how else could she pay for a motel and gas and food?

His one regret was that they hadn't nailed down how she would get back in touch. He'd been too panicked that day at the jail, and Sharlah had been too mad to think clearly. He was confident that she would come up with a good plan. She was smart that way.

Brian had other worries. He was in way over his head, and he knew it even before somebody drove home the message by killing Cliff and Missy and shooting Sharlah.

His lawyer said that even with Cliff dead, he had a chance at probation if he would just give the cops names of other people involved. Before he could do anything, though, Brian needed to make bail so he could have real conversations with no one listening in.

Priority Number One would be explaining everything to Sharlah.

Brian didn't have a lot of practice patching things up with her. They'd had only one big fight before he was arrested, when she found out he'd been betting on football with the guys. It had taken her awhile to get over that, and losing half the rent was nothing compared to hauling a load of marijuana.

While Brian sat helpless in jail, the rest of the world went about its business. After Sharlah had been gone a month, the landlord evicted them, and it fell to Mitch Lowry to clean out the house and deal with the unopened mail.

He discovered the first tangible evidence of trouble: three notices from a company that had towed Sharlah's car from an office park.

That was when Brian got scared, because where could Sharlah go without her car?

The first cop his dad talked to didn't even want to take a missing persons report, so Mitch just kept going up the food chain. He'd taken a rinky-dink boat shop and turned it into a successful business, and Mitch Lowry was not a man to give up.

When the police came to talk to Brian, they started out with easy questions, like what was Sharlah wearing that day at the jail and what did she say about leaving.

Then the questions got more complicated, and Brian began to see just how much of a trap he'd created for himself and for Sharlah.

His dad had given the police Sharlah's bank statement. The cops knew she hadn't touched her account, and they wanted to know how she could be supporting herself. From the way they asked the questions, Brian could tell they suspected that Sharlah took off because she did something wrong.

If the cops found Sharlah with the $20,000, Brian would be in more trouble, but even worse, Sharlah would be in trouble, too. She didn't have parents who would hire a good lawyer. Brian couldn't let that happen to her.

But the other side of the coin was that something might be very wrong, because where could Sharlah have gone without her car? If she was in danger, he wanted the police to help her.

There was another problem: The very first time he'd talked to his dad after the storm, Brian told him Sharlah would be

OK for money because she always kept her tips out in cash. He couldn't very well tell his dad about the $20,000.

He didn't think anything of it at the time. He was used to giving his parents bullshit explanations, covering for himself or Kevin. Half the time, it seemed like his parents weren't even paying attention to what he told them, as long as he told them *something*.

Brian's lawyer had warned him about talking to the police. "Once you tell them something, you're stuck with it," George Ingersoll said.

Mitch Lowry had told the cops what Brian said about Sharlah's tips, which meant Brian was stuck with a lie right out of the gate.

The cops talked to the neighbor across the street and discovered that Sharlah carried her blue suitcase and her purse but nothing else when she left the house.

That worried Brian, too. What about the silver briefcase?

The police asked a bunch of questions Brian found insulting to Sharlah: Did she sunbathe topless? Walk around in front of the windows in skimpy clothes? Flirt with guys at the diner to get bigger tips?

The cop who did most of the asking was an older guy, and Brian didn't like the way he seemed to be judging Sharlah. His mom was the same way—Sharlah wore a lot of makeup, and she waited tables instead of going to school, and she lived with Brian without being married, so she must be trash.

Sharlah wore a lot of makeup because her skin broke out and she thought she needed it. Brian had told her a million times she was pretty without it, but she didn't believe him.

She couldn't get a better job until she got her GED. It wasn't her fault she hadn't finished high school, either, but it wasn't Brian's place to talk about that.

He didn't have to look any further than his own parents to know that he and Sharlah hadn't exactly invented sex before you were married. The idea that Sharlah was some wild party girl, nothing could be more wrong.

Mitch Lowry had to nag the cops and the media to get anything done. When the papers and TV finally did a story, they used Sharlah's driver's license picture, because their photo album was ruined when the storm blew out a window. The picture was so bad that Brian didn't think anyone would recognize her.

A few tips trickled in: Sharlah had been seen at a bowling alley in College Station or a rest stop on I-10 or a convenience store up the road from where they found her car, talking to some guy whose car had Ohio plates.

That meant more questions for Brian. Did Sharlah know anyone in College Station? El Paso? What about Ohio? Brian told them that she didn't and that she wouldn't have climbed in a car with some guy she didn't know.

He never could tell whether they were taking things seriously or whether they were just going through the motions, and he wasn't sure which would be better for Sharlah anyway.

By the time Brian got bail, Sharlah had been gone six weeks. He kept trying to convince himself that everything was OK. The weather had been bad, but she could have walked to the bus station and caught a Greyhound. With the $20,000—assuming she had it—she could have gone to a used car lot and paid cash, even.

Sometimes, though, he woke up in the middle of the night, his gut clenched in fear, terrified that something awful had happened.

His mom was sure Sharlah had run off with some other guy. She said the disappearance proved what she'd known all along, that Sharlah never loved Brian, that she was with him because she thought his family was rich, that once she knew Brian wasn't going to give her the easy life, she'd "found some other sucker."

Brian was better off without her, his mom said.

It wouldn't do any good to argue with her, so Brian just avoided talking to his mother. She was never going to forgive him anyway. She'd resigned from all her church committees out of embarrassment, and she had to find a new grocery store after Missy Burke's mom confronted her in the parking lot one day.

His dad was a different story. His anger was all directed toward the police and the prosecutors. Around Brian, he just seemed sad and bewildered, like he couldn't understand how any of this happened.

They didn't talk about Brian's case. The lawyer had warned them all not to discuss it, which was fine with Brian.

The way Brian saw it, his life was ruined, and there was nothing his parents could do to change that. Why make them suffer more? It was bad enough to listen to them fighting all the time, his mom complaining that his dad was babying him and his dad telling her that they couldn't change the past and she needed to ease up.

Brian knew his dad just wanted to ask one question, and it was the one question Brian could never answer: Why?

❡

Brian's regular parole officer was out, so he had to talk to a different one—a youngish black man with a shaved head, a no-nonsense demeanor and a French last name that Brian couldn't pronounce.

He felt bad about the name. The PO carefully said it for him, but Brian promptly forgot it. It was spelled out on a nameplate attached to his cubicle, but Brian couldn't puzzle it out, not with all those vowels jammed together.

Brian sat in a hard plastic chair next to the desk, bouncing his left leg up and down, as the PO flipped through some pages in his file. Brian didn't even realize he was doing the thing with his leg until the PO pointedly looked at it.

"You seem jumpy. Everything OK?"

Brian stilled his leg. "Surprised to be called down here today, that's all."

"Scheduled *and* random drug tests are a condition of your parole, Brian. Are we going to find something on your drug test?"

"I take an anticonvulsant called…" Brian stopped, searching his brain for the right information. "I can't remember the name, but…"

"I have a list of your prescriptions," the PO said. "Are we going to find anything else, something not on the list? Street drugs? Might as well tell me now."

"No."

The PO went back to the file. "Same address?"

"Yes." Brian was getting more nervous, because the other times he'd been in, no one had really looked at his file or asked him questions. His regular PO hardly talked to him at all, except to tell him how easy it would be to send him back to prison.

The new PO made a note on a form. "Everything OK at home with Mom and Dad?"

"My folks divorced while I was in. I live with my dad," Brian said.

"How you two get along?"

"Fine," Brian said. Then, thinking that wasn't fair to his father, who visited him every week in prison and afterward gave him a job and a place to stay, he amended his answer. "Good."

The PO nodded. "And work? Any problems there?"

Brian hesitated, thinking of the way the woman at Darcy's desk had looked at him. "No problems," he said, finally.

"You sure?"

"I make some of the women nervous," Brian said. "I feel bad about that."

Carmen. The woman with Darcy was named Carmen. He'd said hello to her at the company picnic when he first came back, but she sidled off, and then he'd heard later that she didn't bring her grandkids because she didn't want them exposed to a criminal.

"You talk to anyone there about that? Your boss?"

"My dad's the boss. We don't really talk…" Brian stopped, worried again that he was making his dad look bad. "I mean, we talk. But mostly about sports and…"

Brian tried hard to think of something else he and his dad talked about.

"…educational opportunities?"

Brian looked up at the PO blankly. "I'm sorry, what?"

"This will go faster if you stay with me, Brian. I asked, are you pursuing any educational opportunities? It says here you worked with a dyslexia specialist before your sentencing and went from a fourth-grade reading level to ninth-grade level."

"I had a bad concussion," Brian said. "I have trouble concentrating. Sorry." He realized that he was jiggling his leg again and used both hands to stop it.

"That's in the file," the PO said. He didn't look up, but just the way he said it made Brian sick. A black hole was opening inside him, and he desperately wanted to crawl into it and disappear.

"So, are you taking classes?"

"The thing is, my eye..." Brian's panic flared. Was he supposed to be going to class? His dad had read all the parole paperwork and gone over it with him—how could he have missed that?

"Brian?"

Brian knew the PO had handcuffs—they were right there on his belt. He could be sent straight to the Harris County jail for reassignment to prison.

"Brian." The PO put down his pen. "These are not trick questions."

"Sorry. No, I haven't gone back to the tutor. I'm not in class. Just working."

"What's the story with your eye?"

"The retina detached. There really isn't anything to be done. I wear glasses, but..."

The PO opened a desk drawer and rummaged through it. He found what he was looking for—a brochure—and handed it to Brian.

"There are some support groups that might help you with your adjustment." He nodded toward the brochure. "Give that some thought."

Brian didn't need to look over the brochure to know he wasn't interested. He shook his head. "Thanks, but I don't think so."

"It can help to talk to people who have been there," the PO said.

"I don't want to be in some support group with ex-cons."

Rocking back in his chair, the PO made a steeple of his fingers and stared at Brian.

"It's not like I think I'm too good or anything," Brian added, hurriedly.

"No?"

"I don't want..." Brian paused, trying to think how to explain himself. "I don't want to talk about all that."

Brian took off his glasses and rubbed his eyes. He'd slept poorly the night before, dreading the Lowry Marine Christmas party.

"I just want to forget all that."

＄

It was dark by the time Brian turned onto the street where he lived. He'd been stuck in traffic by the mall and then got lost trying to find a way around it.

Disoriented and furious with himself, he'd pulled into a parking lot and then sat for 10 minutes to calm down. He hated getting upset. It made him feel weak and out of control.

The Lowry house was easy to pick out, even from the end of the block, because everyone else in the neighborhood had Christmas decorations. The only lights at his house were the dim porch bulb and the soft blue glow of the TV through the curtains.

As Brian pulled into the driveway and hit the remote for the garage door, he noticed an unfamiliar sedan at the curb.

His dad hadn't mentioned anything about company, and Brian hoped it wasn't somebody there to talk about his dad's group for prisoners' families. Brian appreciated what his dad was trying to do, but meeting those people made him uncomfortable.

Brian knew they'd all heard his dad's story—how his son had been beaten in the prison laundry, how it was two days before he got word, how unhappy he was with the care in the infirmary. Brian hated the way people looked at him when they heard his father tell it. There was pity, but also, he thought, disgust, because none of it would have happened if he hadn't landed in prison in the first place, right?

Brian's incarceration had turned Mitch Lowry into an activist. Lately, he always seemed to be meeting with other relatives, talking about lobbying Austin for something.

As soon as he walked into the kitchen, though, Brian could tell this was no meeting with a sympathizer—his dad's body language was all wrong. Mitch Lowry was leaning back against the kitchen counter, his arms crossed over his chest, his chin thrust forward.

"Is that the way we do things in America? Drive a load of drugs and you deserve to get beat within an inch of your life? We're not any better than those countries where they cut the thief's hand off, if you ask me."

The driver of the sedan was standing on the other side of the breakfast bar, a briefcase propped on the stool next to him. He did not strike Brian as somebody with a relative in the prison system. His sandy hair was cut unfashionably short, and if he hadn't been in a suit, Brian would have guessed he was military.

"Oh, hey son," Mitch said, turning to Brian. "Everything go OK?"

"Fine," Brian said.

He looked from his father to the visitor, trying to figure out the standoff.

"Brian, this is Detective Zuk from the police," Mitch said. "He says he's got some questions for you. He didn't want to tell me what about."

He was a cop—of course. Although Brian's heart had begun to thud at the word "detective," he crossed the kitchen and stuck out his hand.

"We've met before," Zuk said as they shook.

"I don't remember," Brian said.

"I worked patrol then," Zuk said. He rested one hand on his briefcase. "I wasn't trying to be mysterious about why I'm here; I just thought I ought to wait until you got home."

"Well, he's here now, so let's have it," Mitch said.

Brian shot his father a puzzled glance. His dad had often been short-tempered with him and Kevin growing up, but Brian had never seen him act this way toward a stranger.

Of course, he hadn't seen his father interact with the police much. When Brian was growing up, Mitch Lowry was a law-and-order guy. Now he'd scraped the "Back the Blue" bumper sticker off his truck, and Brian kept expecting one that said "Question Authority" to replace it any day.

The detective seemed flummoxed, too. He kept fiddling with the strap on his briefcase.

"I'm here to talk about the Webb case," he said.

Brian's pulse quickened. There was news of Sharlah? Before he could open his mouth to ask what it was, though, his father spoke up.

"Four years ago I couldn't hardly get you people to take a missing persons report."

Zuk gave a weary nod. "I know you weren't especially happy with how things were handled back then, but I've been taking another look, and..."

"Little late," Mitch said.

"Dad..." Brian tried to break in.

"I just made detective earlier this year," Zuk said. "I got the file out for review, because I've never been comfortable with where we left it."

"Where did you leave it? Been awhile since we heard anything," Mitch said.

Zuk shifted his weight uncomfortably. "It's still officially open. The original detective liked Scott Moreno as a suspect, but…"

"Oh, here we go," Mitch said. "Scott Moreno again."

"Dad, if there's something about Sharlah…"

"Convenient how that all worked out," Mitch said, talking over Brian. "Wasn't but one guy in the whole police department mixed up with drugs, and he went and got himself murdered before anyone could talk to him."

"Mr. Lowry, if we could…" Zuk tried to break in, but Mitch wouldn't be shut down.

"Scott Moreno's the one who killed Cliff, and Scott Moreno's the one who killed Missy. So now you're just going to blame him for Sharlah and that's that, huh? He was a regular one-man crime wave, wasn't he?"

It seemed to Brian that Zuk was irritated but trying hard not to show it. "Moreno had the gun that killed Cliff Knorr," Zuk said evenly. "There's solid ballistics on that. And there are witnesses who saw him talking to Missy Burke at the bar where she worked."

"And Sharlah?"

"That's why I'm here," Zuk said. "I have something I need to show you."

§

The dining room was still unfurnished and it was awkward for all three men to sit at the breakfast bar, so they moved to the living room.

Brian and his father sat side by side on the couch. Mitch picked up the remote and muted the TV.

Zuk took the lone chair and put his briefcase next to the coffee table.

Watching him, Brian had a flash of recognition.

"I met you the day Sharlah found Missy," he said. "You were walking Sharlah down the hall at the station. You uncuffed me so I could hug her."

"Yes," Zuk said.

"Thank you for that," Brian said, ignoring his father's scowl. That one minute in the police station was the last time he ever held Sharlah, and he was grateful for it.

Zuk opened his briefcase and took out a file folder, which he held on his lap. He fussed with some papers inside it, clearly nervous.

"When I pulled the case file, I thought I would try looking at it just like it was strictly a missing persons case, because if you strip everything away, basically what you've got is a 19-year-old girl stranded with car trouble," Zuk said. "One of the new tools we have for missing persons is a nationwide thing called a database, where you can enter a description of a person and the circumstances of the disappearance, and law enforcement all over the country can see it."

"You did that for Sharlah, and someone recognized her?" Brian glanced over at his father, excited by this news. But his dad was pressed back against the cushions, looking like a man expecting a blow.

Zuk took a long time answering. "Not exactly, no. After I entered Sharlah's information in the database, a Texas Ranger called another case to my attention." Zuk pulled a photo out of the folder in his lap and put it on the coffee table. In the photo was a blonde woman in a blue sweater kneeling on a lawn, her arm thrown around a dog.

"Her name is Sabrina Martz. Seven months before Sharlah disappeared, she stopped at a convenience store in Fort Stockton. Her friend went in to buy cigarettes. Sabrina went around the side to use the pay phone. When the friend came back, Sabrina was gone."

Zuk put a second photo on the coffee table—another woman with long blonde hair. She was wearing a purple LSU T-shirt and holding a can of Dixie beer.

"Fort Stockton told me about this one. This is Delia Fontenot, a student in Baton Rouge. Three months after Sharlah disappeared, Delia left her apartment to pick up some things at the grocery store. That's the last anyone's seen of her," Zuk said.

"There's another case over in Port Arthur, about two years ago, that might be related," Zuk said. "She's older—in her 30s—but blonde like these two. All these towns are right on I-10 or just a little jog off the interstate."

Mitch sat forward, his expression grim. "You think there's some Ted Bundy type snatching blonde girls?"

Brian knew this had to be wrong. "Sharlah wouldn't go anywhere with some man she didn't know," he said.

"She had car trouble and the weather was bad," Zuk said. "She might have accepted an offer of help."

"She knows better than to get in a car with somebody," Brian said.

"There could have been a weapon or some type of coercion," Zuk said.

"Sharlah would raise hell. Somebody would have seen something," Brian said. "She's little, but she's strong—stronger than she looks. She wouldn't give up without a fight."

"I know. I saw her handle those heavy trays at the diner," Zuk said. "But even if she resisted with everything she had…" He stopped, searching for the right words before giving up. "I realize this is difficult."

"No, it's easy," Brian said, his voice rising. "Sharlah wouldn't get in some guy's car."

"Brian," Mitch said quietly, putting his hand on Brian's arm.

Brian shook him off. "What? She wouldn't get in some guy's car, Dad. Trust me."

Zuk sat with the folder in his lap, waiting.

Then it occurred to Brian that Zuk had not driven here to tell him about missing women from Fort Stockton and Baton Rouge. How could he be so stupid?

A sick feeling descended on Brian, washing through his veins. He'd had it before—when the cop pulled him over that first morning, when he stood in front of the judge waiting to hear how long his sentence would be. Something bad was coming, and he was powerless to stop it.

Be a man, Brian thought. *Whatever it is, take it like a man.*

He drew a deep breath. "I guess you'd better tell me what else is in the folder."

"I got a call from the sheriff in Luna County, New Mexico. That's west of Las Cruces, along I-10." Zuk spoke slowly and deliberately. "Hikers found a body that matches the general description."

Brian folded his hands in his lap, praying that they wouldn't shake. "Maybe it's one of those other women."

"You described Sharlah as wearing a pink T-shirt the day she left. There's a pink T-shirt with these remains," Zuk said. "I wanted to see whether you could identify it."

He slid a photo across the coffee table to Brian. It showed a stained pink T-shirt stretched out on a white background, a ruler in the foreground.

Brian picked up the photo and held it close to his face. He moved the photo farther away, squinting at it.

He closed his eyes and thought about Sharlah that last day in the jail. He couldn't picture her shirt. Mostly what he remembered was that she had been scared and mad.

"I can't tell," he said, finally. "I'm sorry."

"That's OK," Zuk said. "It was a long shot."

"Show me the rest. I might do better with the shoes or something."

"That's all we have," Zuk said.

"She didn't have any other clothes?"

"Just a T-shirt."

Mitch inhaled sharply. Brian closed his eyes and tried to think about something pleasant, something peaceful.

Nothing came to him.

He picked up the photo again and ran his finger over it, tracing a stain on the shirt. "Is that blood?"

"Dirt," Zuk said. "It's been out in the elements awhile."

"Why is it like that? It almost looks tie-dyed," Brian said.

"The shirt was twisted," Zuk said.

Brian looked up at him.

Zuk cleared his throat. "Around the victim's neck."

"For God's sake," Mitch burst out. "It's two days to Christmas! Is this really necessary?"

"I'm very sorry," Zuk said. "There's no good way to do this, I'm afraid."

Brian stared at the wall above Zuk's head, trying to empty his mind, trying to resist the image forming there.

He exhaled slowly. "It's OK, Dad." Then, to Zuk, he said, "Do you have pictures of the body you want me to look at?"

"It's skeletal remains," Zuk said. "You can't tell anything.

But there are things we can use to make an ID, like dental records. Do you know who Sharlah's dentist was?"

"She didn't go once a year like you're supposed to," Brian said. "She's real self-conscious about her teeth. Her folks never took her to the dentist when she was little. I made her go one time, though, because she had a tooth that was hurting her so bad."

Zuk took a notepad from his shirt pocket and flipped it open. "Do you remember where she went? I've struck out so far."

"Shar called one place, and the lady on the phone wasn't nice when she asked how much it would cost," Brian said. "We came up here, someplace where poor people went. I tried to get her to go to my folks' dentist, but she wouldn't."

"Do you remember the doctor's name, or where the office was?"

"I drove her. I should remember." Brian massaged his forehead. "I think it was... No, I'm getting it confused with something else. Sorry. I do that sometimes."

"Do you remember anything about the doctor or the office? Any detail could help."

Mitch had been quiet since his outburst, but now he spoke up again. "Brian has memory problems," he said, "on account of the beating he took while the guards were looking the other way."

Brian knew his father was just trying to help, but he hated being talked about like he wasn't there.

"Dad, it's OK."

Brian closed his eyes, trying to conjure up that day. He remembered Sharlah leaning her head on his shoulder as they waited. "The doctor's name was Indian or Iranian or something. I know that sounds terrible, but it was... not like Smith, you know?"

"Do you know if she wrote a check?"

"We paid cash," Brian said.

"Can you narrow down the date at all?"

Brian concentrated, trying hard to remember. What had they talked about in the waiting room? Did Sharlah have a coat?

Then something came to him.

"I borrowed money from Kevin so we wouldn't come up short for the rent," Brian said. "It was just after Kevin got married, like maybe a month. He owed me a favor, because I didn't raise hell when Mom didn't want Sharlah at the wedding. They got married..." Brian turned to his father. "What year was that?"

Mitch Lowry provided Kevin and Lynn's wedding date. His voice was shaking.

"That's good," Zuk said. "That could really be helpful. I'll see if I can't track down this dentist and then we'll get the records sent to New Mexico, see if they match."

"It could be some other girl," Brian said.

"It could," Zuk agreed, nodding.

"So you know, I'm not going to believe anything bad until you can prove it to me," Brian said. "I'm going to keep thinking she's out there somewhere, having a good life."

"I understand," Zuk said.

"That would be fair, you know? She doesn't deserve anything bad to happen to her."

"No," Zuk said. "She didn't."

"She's not dead," Brian said.

Mitch patted Brian's arm once and stood.

"Detective Zuk, I'll walk you out."

§

After his dad and Zuk walked outside, Brian slowly unlaced his boots, pulled them off and put them under the coffee table.

He stretched out on the couch. The lamp was shining in his face, but Brian didn't feel like getting up to turn it off. He flung one arm over his eyes to block the light. He could hear his dad and Zuk talking outside, but he couldn't make out the words.

He wondered whether he should have told the cop what happened to Sharlah when she was 15 and took a ride home from a party with a guy she knew from school. He decided it wouldn't make any difference.

Anyway, it wasn't his secret to share. Sharlah only told him because she wanted him to understand why she'd dropped out in 10th grade.

Brian heard the front door open.

"Brian? Are you OK? Are you getting one of your headaches?"

"Tired," Brian said. He swung his legs around and sat up. "I'm going to bed."

"It's not even 8 o'clock!"

His father's voice was loud, and Brian flinched. "I didn't sleep much last night."

"You haven't had any supper," Mitch said, calmer now. "You'll feel better if you eat. How about I call for pizza from that place you like?"

When Brian didn't object, Mitch walked to the kitchen and called in the order.

"Should be about 30 minutes," Mitch said, returning to the living room. He sat next to Brian on the couch. "Do you want to talk about what the detective said?"

"No."

"I think maybe we should. You need to prepare yourself for..."

"She's not dead, Dad. She's not."

"I think maybe this is her, Brian. I think we might finally have an answer."

As he'd been so many times, Brian was tempted to tell his father the truth—the money under the house, all of it. But then he remembered what his lawyer said, that it was selfish to burden family members with knowledge.

"I would know if she was dead," Brian said. "I would feel it—I know I would."

"That doesn't make sense, Brian."

Brian couldn't explain it to his father, but there had been many times when his heart had reached for Sharlah, and he'd never felt a void. She was out there. He believed that. He had to.

Mitch put his hand on Brian's knee. "If she was leaving you, she would have let you know, don't you think?"

Brian shrugged. He had debated this many times in his head and failed to come up with an adequate explanation.

"Brian, I think maybe it's time to get some help with this."

Brian jerked his leg away, dislodging his father's hand. "You mean help believing Sharlah's dead? Why would I want that?"

"You have to move on, son. This isn't right, how you're feeling."

Brian sensed an opening. He turned to look his father in the eye. "It's worse than what you told me, isn't it? I'm brain-damaged or something."

Mitch looked aghast. "No! Of course not!"

"Tell me the truth, Dad. I want to know."

"We've been over this. The neurologist said your symptoms were mostly normal for concussion," Mitch said. "But he also said some of your problems might be psychological. That's why I'm thinking you need to talk to someone."

Brian did not want to have this discussion. He thought about getting up and going to bed, but that seemed rude to his father, who was only trying to help. He wasn't sure what to do—it seemed he never was these days—so he did nothing.

"Brian?" His father put his hand on Brian's arm, and Brian recoiled.

"What are you thinking? It worries me when you drift off like that."

Brian knew this was a problem. He would start shuffling through thoughts in his head like a deck of cards, trying to find the right one to play, and without realizing it he'd go quiet for long stretches. It frightened people.

"Sorry. I'm tired."

"See, that worries me, too," his father said. "Seems like all you do is work and sleep."

"If there's something you need to me to do, just tell me," Brian said. "I don't notice stuff. You have to tell me."

"I'm not talking about chores that need doing. I'm talking about your life, son. Aren't you interested in anything? Why not go back to that tutor for your reading?"

Brian wished he could explain to his father why that idea was hopeless, but he couldn't put into words how his brain worked—actually, didn't work.

"I don't think there's any point," he said.

"You won't know unless you try," Mitch countered. "What about getting some exercise? Why don't you join a gym? Remember how you and Kevin used to shoot hoops in the driveway? You'd switch on the porch light and keep playing in the dark."

Brian understood how his father was able to talk so many people into buying expensive boats—he simply never gave up.

"Gyms cost money," Brian said. "Anyway, my hand-eye coordination is gone."

"Why don't we go out tomorrow and get you a guitar? Wouldn't you like to start playing again?"

Brian started to object—guitars were expensive, the store would be crowded—but his father cut him off. "You can use your bonus, and if you're short I'll front you the rest."

Brian had forgotten about the bonus check. He patted his shirt pocket and was relieved to find it still there.

"Can I borrow your pen?"

Mitch always had a pen in his shirt pocket, at the ready for closing a deal. Puzzled, he pulled it out and clicked it open before handing it to Brian.

Brian endorsed the check and handed the pen and the check back to his father.

"What's this?"

"Put it toward the lawyer's bill."

His father was getting angry now—Brian recognized the signs—but he was trying not to show it.

"How much more are you going to punish yourself, Brian? Seems to me like the state of Texas did more than enough."

"Mom wouldn't agree with you," Brian said. As soon as he said it, he regretted bringing up his mother. It was a sucker punch, and his father didn't deserve that.

Mitch's shoulders sagged. "I know it's hard, but you shouldn't take what she does to heart. A lot of it's got nothing to do with you."

Embarrassed at his loss of control, Brian got up. "The pizza will be here soon. I'd better clean up."

In the bathroom, he washed his hands and face, then paused to study his reflection.

His sister-in-law had helped him choose glasses, and now that his hair was longer, the scar on his head wasn't quite so visible. Anyone who didn't know what he looked like before might not even notice the marks on his face.

Brian had never thought of himself as vain, but he realized that he must have been. As early as sixth grade, girls thought he was cute—not as good-looking as Kevin, maybe, but who was? Sharlah always talked about how she loved his eyes and his smile.

Brian tried a smile for the mirror, just to see.

His father had pulled the living room curtains aside and was staring out the window.

"Still no pizza?"

Mitch turned away from the window and let the curtain fall. "You know what I was just thinking about? The state baseball tournament your junior year."

Brian breathed a sigh of relief. This was safer territory.

"Do you remember that big lefty from San Antonio? You came up to bat, down a run, one on, and you got down two strikes right away," Mitch said. "But you dug in there and you worked the count. Then you smacked that double that tied the game. I was so proud of you, Brian, I thought I was going to bust."

Brian had relived that moment many times. "I remember standing at second and seeing you in the stands," he said. "I didn't know you were coming. But we lost that game, remember? We gave up a homer the next inning."

"Aw, Brian, that's not the point," Mitch said.

"Sure it is," Brian said. "You always told me, 'If you're not out there to win, you're wasting everybody's time.'"

Mitch took a couple strides toward him, and just for an instant, Brian was scared. It was a familiar dynamic—his father angry, him frightened but unwilling to back down.

"Well, if I said that—and I probably did—that was bullshit, Brian." Mitch took a deep breath. "I was wrong. I was wrong about a lot of things," he said.

Mitch's words poured out in a rush. "I shouldn't have let your mother have her way all the time to keep the peace. I look back on all the times I whipped your butt just on her say-so, and I can't believe I did that. I whipped you for getting D's, and I never once asked were you trying your best."

Brian was startled to see tears glittering in his father's eyes. He knew how to deal with his father's anger, but tears were new—and frightening—territory. Brian did not want to explore new territory.

"It's OK, Dad." Brian picked up the TV remote. "Let's see if we can find a game on."

"No," Mitch said. "It's not OK. I need to get this off my chest. Don't think I don't know how much of this is my fault, and your mother's. Not just what happened to you, but to Sharlah, too. We never welcomed that girl in our home, and when she was in trouble, she didn't know where to go or who to trust. I will *always* regret that.

"I know it's late to change, son, but I don't want to be that kind of father anymore. I want things to be different between us." He puffed his cheeks and exhaled. "There. I said my piece. Now it's your turn."

Brian stared at the floor. He didn't know what to say, or where to start.

Mitch sank down on the arm of the couch. "You know why I was so proud that day?"

"You thought I was going to be the hero. But I wasn't."

"No," Mitch said. "It looked for all the world like you were beat, but you hung in there and made something good happen. You can do that again, son."

"It was just a baseball game, Dad."

Mitch turned his head away, and Brian thought he'd finally given up.

But Mitch had had one more sales pitch, and he'd saved his best for last.

"I don't know what became of Sharlah, son, but I do know this: She loved you something fierce. Alive or dead, this is not the life she would want for you."

He got up and walked away then, not waiting for Brian's reply.

Mitch was a salesman. He knew when he'd closed the deal.

EIGHT

ALTHOUGH IT WAS ONLY 9:40, it was hot in the sun, and Brian was beginning to question the wisdom of attending the funeral of a man he'd met only once.

The preacher Brian had hired over the phone was, so far, a no-show.

The funeral director—the only other person in attendance—tried to reassure Brian. "Bert'll be here," he said. "He's always running late. Being the jail chaplain's spoiled him. He's used to a captive audience."

Brian cracked a smile to be a good sport. He'd been out of prison for more than a decade, and it was easier now to let convict jokes roll off him.

He was impatient to get Arvin Webb's ashes prayed over so he could be on his way. He had business he needed to take care of back in Houston, and he had to pick up his niece Ashley at the high school at 2:30. She was grounded, and Lynn had taken away her car.

Brian was starting to regret this good deed, one he'd volunteered for only because Sharlah's brother Rod—the one in the Navy—said he didn't care about a funeral.

Brian wasn't sure Sharlah would care, either. He'd never heard her say a positive word about her father, and Brian hadn't seen anything in his one meeting with Arvin Webb that made him think Sharlah had been unfair.

The call about Arvin's death had caught him by surprise. It had been years since the day he'd visited, and he would have laid odds that the phone number he left had been swallowed up in the trailer's chaos. But no, the deputies found it on the TV, just where Brian had left it.

A dusty brown Oldsmobile pulled into the parking lot, and a banty-rooster type in a Western-cut suit got out and hustled over, a Bible tucked under his arm.

"There's Bert," the funeral director said. "Told you he'd show."

The preacher reached the two men, huffing and puffing from his short jog across the grass. "You must be Brian," he said, extending his sweaty hand. "I sure do apologize for being late. Let's get started. Did Mr. Webb have a favorite Scripture?"

§

Brian's family had no idea where he was on this sweltering September morning. As far as they knew, he'd never been to Sharlah's hometown, had never met her father. Like a lot of things in Brian's life, his silence wasn't planned. It just happened.

Things started to change after the police came to ask about the skeleton in New Mexico. The body turned out to be a California runaway, but it seemed to Brian that it might as well have been Sharlah, the way everyone acted. He hadn't heard from the police again—they seemed to have just given up—and his family started talking about Sharlah like she was dead.

Brian refused to give in at first. He ignored the raised eyebrows when he mentioned Sharlah, and even when Kevin called him "pathetic" to his face, he just shrugged.

Slowly, though, he realized that his unwillingness to concede Sharlah's death pained his father, who saw it as evidence that Brian wasn't "doing better" or "moving on" or any of the other things Mitch desperately wanted his younger son to do.

So Brian went underground with his feelings, quit mentioning Sharlah or letting on that he thought about her every day. He agreed to see a counselor. Within six months, his dad talked about how much better he seemed and how counseling did him a world of good.

The truth was, Brian didn't talk about Sharlah much with the counselor. There was no shortage of messed-up stuff in his life for them to discuss, and he didn't want to hear about the stages of grief and getting closure, anyway.

On Sharlah's 30th birthday, Brian took a road trip. He drove by the diner and their old address, but the house had been torn down, replaced by something bigger and nicer.

Even though it was December, he went to what had been their favorite stretch of beach and sat on the sand, watching the gentle slap of the waves, oblivious to the chill.

Sharlah seemed so far away, and every year that passed just widened the distance. Brian didn't want to lose what little he had of Sharlah. He wanted to hang on.

He had so few memories of her, and the ones he did have had been turned over and over in his mind so many times they were worn smooth by the frequent handling. He wanted more.

There had to be more.

Tracking down Arvin Webb was easy—he was in the phone book. Working up the courage to knock on his door was hard. Brian drove to Sharlah's hometown twice and lost his nerve before the day he finally parked his truck in the weedy yard and climbed the rickety steps to the trailer.

Sharlah had told him that her dad was a mean, miserable drunk, and Arvin did indeed look mean, miserable and drunk when he staggered to the door in response to Brian's repeated knocking. He wore a stained white T-shirt stretched taut over his big belly and work pants that hung loose on his hips. His feet were shoved into bedroom slippers. The top of one shoe was crusted with something rust-colored. Brian suspected vomit.

Arvin didn't say anything, just stood there and glared.

Brian towered over Arvin, and it would have been easy to intimidate him. But Brian had another strategy in mind.

"I want to talk to you about Sharlah," Brian said.

"I already done told them cops, they can't have none of my blood."

Brian had no idea what that meant. "I'm not a cop," he said.

"Who the hell are you, then?"

Brian held up the bottle of Jack Daniel's. "A friend."

Arvin turned back into the trailer, leaving the door open. Brian followed him.

Arvin flopped into a recliner draped in a filthy blue bed sheet. Brian scanned the living room for a place to sit, but the only other pieces of furniture in the room were an end table littered with beer cans and a TV blaring a fishing show.

"Grab you a seat from in there," Arvin said, gesturing with his chin. "You want a glass or is that all for me?"

Brian rounded the corner to the small kitchen, which was even nastier than the living room. He spotted the trailer's back door and gave serious thought to bolting.

Was he really so desperate for any little piece of Sharlah that he'd fish for it at the bottom of Arvin's bottle?

Brian uncapped the Jack Daniel's and took a swig.

"I heard that!" Arvin yelled from the living room.

Brian knocked a bunch of papers off a three-legged stool and carried it back to the living room. He handed Arvin the bottle. "The rest's for you."

"You can cut the TV off," Arvin said. "Use them pliers. Knob's broke."

Grabbing a rusty set of pliers on top of the ancient TV set, Brian turned it off. Then he positioned the stool as far upwind as he could from Arvin and sat down.

Arvin scratched at his unshaven chin. His face was puffy and had an unhealthy yellow cast. He took a long pull on the Jack Daniel's and balanced the bottle on his thigh. He stared at Brian. "Well?"

"Tell me about Sharlah," Brian said. "What was she like when she was a kid?"

Arvin squinted at him. "That's what you want?"

"That's what I want."

Arvin remembered more about Sharlah's childhood than Brian would have suspected.

He learned that when she was little, she called herself "Haha" because she couldn't say Sharlah.

She was good at school, "soaked everything up like a sponge," Arvin said.

Sometimes, Arvin said, he would find Sharlah in her room, writing things down and pretending like she was talking on the phone. "She said she was playing like she was Peggy on *Mannix*. I put a stop to that," Arvin said. "Peggy was colored, you know."

As Arvin got deeper into the bottle, his reminiscences became even uglier. "She quit school, just stopped going. Laid around the house, didn't do nothing but stare at the wall for months on end. Then she run off and left me, just like her goddamn mother. I told her, you walk out that door, don't you never come back."

Arvin had a whole list of people who'd done him wrong: Sharlah's mother, the relatives who wouldn't take the kids off his hands, the county officials who cited him for not cleaning up his lot, the bureaucrats who messed with his disability checks.

Brian could have said his goodbyes and left—Arvin was so far gone that he probably wouldn't have cared. But something in a shoebox on the floor next to the TV had caught Brian's eye, and he didn't want to leave without taking a closer look.

At some point, Arvin was going to need the bathroom or he was going to pass out. Brian could wait. He'd been around guys like this in prison—everything was always somebody else's fault. They just wanted to vent. They didn't care if anyone listened.

He tuned Arvin out and thought instead about his guitar. It hadn't been sounding right, and the old guy at the guitar shop said it was a problem with the bridge plate. He let Brian watch while he repaired it, explaining each step in the process. Brian thought that guy had the coolest job in the world.

Arvin's rant eventually trailed off into a mumble, then a snore.

Brian gave him a few minutes. When he was sure Arvin was out, he snatched the shoebox off the floor and carried it to the kitchen, where the light was better.

The box was mostly junk—rusted bolts, rubber bands and old batteries. At the bottom, he found the thing he'd spotted earlier. He pulled out a frame, a cheap metal one with spots for three photos.

Brian flipped it over. There were school photos in the frame: the Webb children arranged by age from left to right. Towheaded Sharlah couldn't be more than 7. She wore a red plaid dress with a round white collar. One of her front teeth was missing.

Brian licked his thumb and rubbed some of the dust off the glass. Even then she had pretty eyes.

He guessed the photo was taken before their mother left, because the kids looked presentable. Sharlah's hair was up in two pigtails, tied with red ribbons.

Brian turned the frame over and worked the latch with his thumb. He popped out the flimsy cardboard and pulled the photo free.

Arvin snuffled in the living room.

Brian slipped the photo into his shirt pocket and dumped the frame back in the box. He started to carry the box back to the living room, then hesitated.

He grabbed a pencil that was tied to the phone receiver and printed his name and number on the back of an old envelope he'd found in the box.

Brian put the shoebox back on the floor, left the envelope on top of the TV under the pliers, and let himself out of the trailer. That was the last he saw of Arvin Webb.

∫

Back in his truck after Arvin's quickie funeral, Brian shrugged off his coat and tie and turned on his cell phone to check messages.

Brian liked to joke that the invention of the cell phone was a banner day for dyslexics. He didn't have to keep phone numbers straight—they were all stored for him. He didn't have to worry about transposing times for appointments—he just left himself a message or asked the other person to leave one. He relied on his cell phone so much that he didn't even have a home phone; he'd disconnected it as soon as his dad moved out.

Five messages were waiting for him. The first was from a commercial real-estate broker, confirming their appointment to sign a lease at 1 p.m.

The next was from his sister-in-law, Lynn.

"I hate to do this, but Ashley has to have a white dress for this honor society thing tomorrow night, so could you please, please take her to the mall after you pick her up? She just told me about it this morning, and I won't be home before 9. She knows the one she wants, so it shouldn't take very long. Oh, and the honor society thing is tomorrow at 7, if you can come... Well, OK. Sorry to do this to you!"

Lynn knew he'd do anything for Ashley, even go to the mall.

The next message was an update from the man who was designing his website. Brian saved that one for later and went to the next message.

"You bastard, that's my baby! She's MY baby, you ex-con! Loser! You guys got no right, NO right..."

Sighing, Brian hit the delete button.

The next message was from Francine, his stepmother.

"It's Francine. I just talked to Lynn. If you can't take Ashley to the mall, I can figure it out. Also, Tonya called us. It was a 903 area code, so if you see that pop up, let it go to voicemail. She's off the rails again. Love you, honey. Have a good day."

Just the sound of Francine's voice immediately put Brian at ease. She had that effect on everyone. Brian told people that she wasn't just the best thing that ever happened to his dad, she was the best thing that ever happened to him, too.

Francine and Mitch had been married five years, and even though a lot had gone wrong for their family in that time, Brian thought his father had never been so happy. They were one of those couples that made no sense on paper but worked perfectly in real life.

Francine was a doctor's daughter from Atlanta and a graduate of Spelman. Mitch grew up in an Oklahoma oil patch and had two semesters of junior college. She was widowed after a happy marriage. He had been through a contentious divorce. Francine was black, Mitch was white, and both were born in an era when racial lines were sharply drawn.

They met when Mitch gave a presentation to a foundation he hoped would help fund his group for prisoners' families. Francine sat on the foundation's board and also mentored troubled teenagers, many with relatives in the prison system.

They kept in touch after the meeting because their causes overlapped. Over time, they discovered that they enjoyed each other's company.

Brian finally pointed out the obvious to his father: He'd be an idiot not to ask Francine out on a proper date.

Kevin was hostile to Francine from the start. He said that she tried to run everyone's lives, that she was a snob, that she was a gold digger. The last complaint was especially ridiculous—her first husband, a cardiologist, had left her more than comfortable.

The real issue wasn't Francine at all. She just came along at a time when Mitch, worn out by Kevin's cycle of rehab and relapse, had reluctantly taken a harder line.

Brian had been so hopeful the first time Kevin went to rehab—they all were. Kevin seemed genuinely frightened by his drinking and eager to change.

His second and third tries at sobriety were short-lived. When he pulled his truck out of the garage, drunk, and nearly hit Ashley, Lynn filed for divorce. When he got caught having sex with a 24-year-old receptionist in his office, Mitch fired him.

Brian and his father agreed that they had to stop shielding Kevin from the consequences of his actions. No more money, not even if he said he owed someone who was threatening him. No more rides, not even if he was stranded in a bad part of town.

Kevin had to hit bottom, they told themselves. They didn't realize, though, how far he would fall or how hard it would be to watch.

Brian never knew from day to day which feeling about Kevin would prevail, guilt or anger. He'd only wanted to help his brother, but everything he did seemed to make things worse. And yet he felt like he'd given up on Kevin, which—after all they'd been through—sometimes seemed like the worst decision of all.

Kevin's indifference to Ashley infuriated Brian the most. Everyone else had, to some extent, been a willing accomplice—Lynn, Brian, Mitch. But Ashley didn't make any bad choices. She was born into the mess.

Now Kevin had created another innocent victim. He had a 3-month-old daughter, Coco, born to a woman named Tonya.

Brian had watched helplessly over the years as Kevin moved down the food chain of partying companions, from former frat boys who hit it too hard on the weekends through high-functioning employed alcoholics to rock-bottom drunks. Still, Kevin's descent into the world of crackheads like Tonya had been a shock.

Tonya had a family, too, and Brian knew that they must wonder how their lively girl with a wall full of art-show ribbons and fashion-design ambitions got mixed up with an alcoholic twice her age.

She bolted from the hospital right after Coco was born, taking someone else's purse with her. She called occasionally—sometimes sobbing, sometimes abusive—but she made no move to get her daughter back.

Kevin was so lost in his own world that Coco barely registered. Brian arrived at the hospital first, held the baby first.

Despite her parents, Coco was perfect—an absolute miracle. The minute a nurse handed her to him, Brian loved her.

If his life had been different, he would have tried for custody. But his life was what it was, and so he didn't speak up when Francine and his dad took Coco home. They were the obvious choice—they'd raised six kids between them, and Francine's four, at least, had turned out great.

♪

Ashley came sauntering out of school at 2:35, chatting with another girl. She walked up to his truck and stuck her head in the open passenger window. "Hey, Uncle Brian, remember Chelsea?"

Chelsea leaned in the window next to Ashley. "Hey, Uncle Brian," she said, her glossy lips exaggerating every syllable.

Brian wasn't sure whether he remembered Chelsea. Most of Ashley's friends looked the same to him—much older than 17 and barely dressed. He tried not to pay attention.

"Can Chelsea go to the mall with us?"

"You're grounded, right? I think that means you don't get to hang with your friends."

"Oh, c'mon Uncle Brian," Chelsea said, leaning farther into the window. She had breasts, and she wasn't afraid to use them. "We won't tell."

Brian slowly shook his head. "Sorry. We can give you a ride home if you need one."

"Nah, I have my car," Chelsea said, withdrawing with a pout.

Brian waited while the girls stood on the sidewalk making elaborate plans to talk later.

Finally, Ashley opened the door and swung her backpack into the truck.

"What are we listening to today?" Brian asked.

Brian always let Ashley play her CDs in his truck. So far, he had survived Disney soundtracks, Mariah Carey and several boy bands that all sounded the same to him.

"Death Cab For Cutie," Ashley said, producing a case from her backpack.

Ashley cued up the CD, and they rode for a few blocks without talking. Brian thought the music was a little mopey, but he was trying to find something about it he liked, so he and Ashley could talk about it.

"Thanks for doing this, by the way," Ashley said. "I don't know why my mom wouldn't just let me drive. There's, like, no reason to inconvenience other people."

She pulled a tube out of her backpack, flipped down the visor, and began reapplying eye makeup in the mirror.

Ashley had inherited Kevin's blue eyes, which she liked to camouflage under layers of black makeup. Brian was used to these impromptu touch-up sessions.

"Why did you get grounded, anyway?"

"It's soooo stupid," Ashley said. "I told her I was going to Chelsea's, but then we decided to go to Devon's, and when Mom found out she was all, 'The rule is, you have to tell me where you're going and a parent has to be home blah blah blah.' "

"Devon's a guy, I'm guessing," Brian said.

"Like I can just call my friends in advance and find out if any adults are home," Ashley said. "Don't you think that's lame?"

Brian didn't think it was lame at all, because he knew—firsthand—exactly the kind of stuff high school kids did when no adults were around.

"Oh, I think your mom's got a point," he said. "Don't be so hard on her."

Ashley scowled at the mirror. "Right, gotta take it easy on Lynn, because she's had such a rough life, she was married to a drunk." She flipped the visor up and put away her makeup. "And of course being the drunk's kid is soooo much fun. Remember when my dad almost ran over me? That was *awesome.*"

"I remember," Brian said.

Brian didn't believe in sugarcoating anything with Ashley. He worried, though, that she tried to use her family's problems as a license to misbehave, and Brian had no patience with that. Troubled as it was, Ashley's childhood was still a hundred times better than what a lot of kids had, including Sharlah.

"So, since I'm not trusted to be home alone, am I hanging out with you until my mom's done tonight, or what?"

"I'm going to drop you at Dad and Francine's after the mall," Brian said, bracing for Ashley's protest. "I have an appointment later."

"What am I supposed to do there for, like, five hours?"

"Don't you honor society kids have, like, five hours of homework every night?"

"How am I supposed to do homework stuck in a house with a screaming baby?"

"Headphones?"

Brian's joke was met with a scowl.

"This totally sucks," Ashley said.

"You're the one who got grounded," Brian said.

"Her screams are like, fingernails on a chalkboard, but, like, inside my skull."

Brian turned into the mall. "Where's the store you're going to?"

"Other end," Ashley said.

"She can't help it that she cries, Ash. She's a baby. She's not doing it to irritate you."

Ashley sighed elaborately. "Are you sure I can't hang with you?"

"I'm busy," Brian said. "Sorry."

Ashley turned in her seat to study him. "You're dressed nice. Do you have a date?"

"On a Monday afternoon?"

"Why not? Chelsea thinks you're a hottie," Ashley said.

"And that's another reason Chelsea can't come to the mall with us," Brian said.

"You don't think she's hot?"

Brian pulled into a parking spot and shut off the truck. "I think Chelsea should pick on someone her own size."

That, at least, got a laugh out of Ashley. But she wasn't ready to give up. "So, are you, like, never going out with anybody again? You know, everybody's worried that you have no social life now. Francine told my mom she thinks you're lonely."

"I'm pretty busy with other things right now, Ash," Brian said.

"That's a lame excuse."

Brian smiled. "Only one I've got."

He opened the mall door and held it for Ashley. "It would be great if we could wrap this up quick," Brian said. "I could give Francine a break when I drop you off."

"You want to hold Coco. I get it," Ashley said. "I'll hurry."

Brian was abashed that Ashley had seen through him so easily.

"You know," Ashley said, "Coco's not always going to be this adorable little baby. Someday she's going to be a pain in the ass who's pissed at her fucked-up parents."

"I know," Brian said, slinging his arm around Ashley. "And I'll still love her when she's a pain in the ass and uses words she shouldn't, just like I do you."

𝓈

Brian took one look at the store where Ashley wanted to shop—full of teenage girls chattering like a flock of birds—and told her she could find him at the French pastry place when she was done.

He got an overpriced cup of coffee and sat down with his cell phone to catch up.

He called his web designer and went over some changes. Brian didn't spend much time online—all that type made his head swim—but everyone told him he needed a business website, so he was getting a business website.

He checked in with Lynn and Francine. He listened to a message from his 4:30 appointment, calling to confirm.

Thinking about that meeting gave Brian a little bit of a rush, although he'd promised himself that he wouldn't get his hopes up.

How long did it take to buy a dress that was already picked out? Brian craned his head down the mall, looking for Ashley.

There was no sign of his niece, but he did see a familiar figure making her way through the café's serving line.

Kristen Worth had been Brian's only serious relationship since Sharlah, and it had lasted more than two years.

Kristen was an occupational therapist, helping people who'd had strokes or head injuries learn to button their shirts and brush their teeth again. Her sister, who worked in Accounting at Lowry Marine, had introduced them.

Kristen was patient and gentle and accepting of people's limitations, all of which appealed to Brian.

Brian was never sure what Kristen saw in him. He suspected she was drawn to him because she was comfortable with broken people.

They'd mostly been happy, at least at first, and Brian had been surprised to discover he could love someone who wasn't Sharlah. But as time passed, he started to feel the weight of Kristen's unspoken expectations, and he spent the last six months of their relationship trying to psyche himself up to propose.

After he'd let several self-imposed deadlines go by—her birthday, Christmas, Valentine's Day—Brian decided he was being unfair to Kristen and ended things. She wanted to get married and have kids, and Brian didn't want to hold her back.

Kristen hadn't spotted him, and Brian considered ducking around the corner to avoid her, even though he knew she'd be pleasant if he said hello. Kristen's life was turning out great, everything she wanted, and she never seemed anything but happy when he saw her.

Seeing her was hard, that was all. He was sure he'd made the right decision—well, pretty sure, anyway—but sometimes he missed her.

Any thought of taking the coward's way out vanished when he saw how much trouble she was having negotiating the cafeteria-style line with a stroller. Brian got up and walked to the cash register, where Kristen was trying to retrieve money from her wallet one-handed while she used the other to balance her son on her shoulder.

"Kristen," he said. "Hi. Need a hand—or two?"

She glanced up, startled. "Oh! You surprised me."

She seemed pale, and the dark circles under her eyes worried Brian a little. He helped her pay, then guided the stroller to a table. He urged Kristen to sit and went back to pick up the tray with her salad and drink.

Kristen smiled gratefully as he put the food down in front of her. "Thank you," she said. "I'm not having the best day. It's 3:30 and I'm just getting lunch. I had a zillion errands to run." She boosted the baby higher and tried, one-handed, to pry the lid off her salad dressing. "He's doing this thing today where he screams when I put him in the stroller."

Brian had his coffee in his hand, ready to bolt. He could wait for Ashley on a bench outside the store.

"Want me to hold him while you eat?"

Brian couldn't quite believe he'd said that, and he expected Kristen to say no. But she didn't hesitate.

"Would you? My arm's about to fall off."

Brian put down his coffee and reached for the baby. "Come here, buddy," he said. Kristen's sister had told him the baby's name, but Brian had forgotten it.

"Just make sure you..." Kristen watched Brian nestle the baby against his shoulder. "Never mind. Looks like you know what you're doing."

"I'm used to holding my niece," Brian said. He eased into the chair opposite Kristen. "But this little guy's a lot heavier than she is."

"How is she? April said she was in and out of the hospital a lot," Kristen said. She forked up a bite of her salad, which was disappearing fast.

"She's doing better," Brian said. "She's gaining weight now. She's really fussy, though, which is normal for babies born with drugs in their systems, so you have to ..."

Brian had been about to tell Kristen about the methods the neonatal nurses taught him for calming Coco, but he stopped. She wouldn't want to hear all that.

Kristen seemed not to notice. "How's Kevin?"

There had been a time when Brian would shade the truth about his brother, but lately, he had given up the habit. It was pointless to lie to Kristen, anyway. She'd seen enough.

"He's pretty bad," Brian said. "Worse than ever, really."

"Oh, Brian. I'm so sorry. That's so hard." Kristen looked up at him, her eyes filled with concern, and Brian felt the tug of regret. Kristen had always been a good listener.

"Thanks." Brian shifted the baby and patted his back. "I keep thinking that something's going to happen to turn things around, but it hasn't happened yet. In the meantime, you know, I just have to keep living my life."

"April told me you're quitting Lowry Marine and starting your guitar shop." Kristen beamed at him. "That's so great!"

Brian allowed himself to feel proud, if only for a minute. "I just signed the lease today, a place in The Heights. I'll open next month."

He told Kristen about the space, and how he'd chosen the location in one of Houston's older, eclectic neighborhoods.

"It sounds great," Kristen said. "But won't that be a long commute?"

"I'll move at some point," Brian said. "Don't want to rent from my dad forever."

Brian knew he had miles to go before anyone would give him a mortgage. He didn't have the credit history to get any kind of loan. He was starting his business with his savings and a matching amount—to be paid back ASAP—from Francine and his father.

"Uncle Brian?"

Ashley had walked up unnoticed while Brian and Kristen were talking. Brian saw that she didn't have a shopping bag and sneaked a glance at his watch.

"Hey, Ash. What's up?"

"Hi, Ashley," Kristen said.

Ashley tried—mostly successfully, Brian thought—not to seem surprised that he and his former girlfriend were chatting while he held her son. "Hi, Kristen. Uncle Brian, could I borrow a twenty? I found earrings that go with my dress. I can pay you back."

Grinning, Brian pulled out his wallet and handed it to Ashley. "Tell you what—I'll buy, and then I don't have to figure out what to get you for making honor society."

Ashley opened the wallet, and Brian immediately regretted handing it to her. He could tell by Kristen's face that she'd noticed the photo opposite his driver's license.

Ashley took out a twenty, handed Brian his wallet and paused to stroke the baby's foot. "He's cute," she said. "I'll be back in, like, five minutes."

Kristen watched Ashley walk away. "Wow. She's grown up since I saw her last."

"Yeah," Brian said. "Just one more year of high school."

Maybe he was wrong. Maybe Kristen hadn't seen the photo.

"How is she about having a baby sister?"

"Furious," Brian said. "She really hates her dad right now. Not that you can blame her."

"She's lucky to have such a great uncle."

"Oh, I don't know about that," Brian said.

"I do," Kristen said. Then she took her purse from the bottom of the stroller and fished out her car keys. "Well, I'd better get the munchkin home before he decides to do his screaming trick again," she said. "Thanks for holding him. I seriously needed a hand."

"Sure," Brian said. "It was good seeing you."

"You too," she said. "Good luck with the business. I'm really excited for you."

Brian handed Kristen the baby. She hesitated, obviously debating something.

"Has there been anything new? About Sharlah?"

Brian was embarrassed, though he couldn't really say why. Kristen knew he had Sharlah's first-grade photo; he'd kept it in his dresser drawer while they were together. Kristen had always been generous when it came to Sharlah.

"Nothing new," Brian said. He thought about the meeting at 4:30. "But I hope..." He stopped himself. Better not to talk about it.

Kristen shifted the baby on her shoulder. "You hope... what?"

"Nothing," Brian said. "I just hope. That's all."

ƒ

Coco was asleep when Brian dropped Ashley off at her grand-parents' house. He knew this was a good thing—Coco was getting needed rest and Francine was having a few minutes of peace—but he couldn't help feeling a little disappointed.

He got home earlier than he'd planned, which left him time to get nervous about the meeting.

When Brian first had the idea to hire a private detective, he pictured a gruff middle-aged guy.

He called his old lawyer for advice. Brian had no problem believing George when he said Susan Davila was the best, but he was taken aback the first time he met her. She was tiny—maybe 5 feet tall. George said she was ex-military, and it was true that she looked strong and wiry. Her dark hair always seemed to be in a ponytail, and the times Brian had seen her, she was dressed more like a college kid than somebody with a concealed weapon permit.

Brian had developed a bit of a crush on her, which he had absolutely no intention of pursuing.

At 4:25, Susan strode up his walk wearing running shoes, jeans and a black T-shirt. She was balancing two thick three-ring binders in one arm.

Brian opened the door and moved to take the binders from her, because they looked heavy. "Hi, Susan."

"Hello, Brian." Susan let him take the binders and stepped inside.

"You want coffee or anything?" Brian asked.

"I'm fine, thanks," Susan said. "I know you said you didn't need a written report, but I put those together just in case you wanted to refer to something later."

Her cell phone buzzed on her hip, and she checked the phone's display.

"I need to step out on the porch and take this," she said. "I apologize. Should only be a couple minutes."

Brian put the binders on the coffee table and eyed them warily. He couldn't imagine trying to get through them—at the rate he read, it would take him a year, at least.

George had told him that Susan would take every scrap of information he gave her and pursue it as far as she could.

After a lot of soul-searching, Brian told her some of the things he'd always held back—about the briefcase and its contents and that he wasn't sure whether Sharlah had found it, despite his hints.

Of course, Susan wanted to know right away what the name was on Sharlah's ID, and Brian confessed the truth that had tormented him for years: He'd never even looked.

Susan wasn't very encouraging, but Brian told her it was OK, he didn't expect miracles. All he wanted was for someone to take a hard look and give him straight answers to the questions that kept him up at night.

He'd never really understood why the police seemed to give up after the body in New Mexico wasn't Sharlah's.

Brian knew some of it was his fault.

He'd been seriously depressed in those first years after prison, and there had been a long stretch when it was all he could do to get out of bed and go to work. Badgering the police required energy he simply didn't have.

It was more than that, though. He'd not asked questions because he was afraid of the answers. And he'd spent years avoiding decisions, because every time he'd tried to make something happen, the results had been disastrous—for him, for Sharlah, for his family. It seemed safer not to do anything at all.

Brian wasn't sure what made him decide to change. Maybe it was his 40th birthday on the horizon; maybe it was seeing his father take a risk and end up happy.

Whatever the reason, Brian was ready for something different.

§

Once she finished her phone call, Susan Davila came inside, took a seat and got right down to business.

"When you signed me up, Brian, I told you I didn't think I

could do much with a 17-year-old case," she said. "I'm afraid that's pretty much proved true."

Brian reminded himself that he had been prepared for this outcome and that he shouldn't be disappointed. He smiled ruefully. "I guess I was hoping there was some new technique now that they didn't have back in the '80s."

A wisp of hair had escaped her ponytail, and Susan pushed it back behind her ear, which struck Brian as a strangely girl-like gesture.

"Well, a lot *has* changed. It was weird looking at the case and thinking about how different things would be now," she said. "We could ping her cell phone and track her debit card. And it's hard to believe a pretty white girl went missing and it wasn't a big deal. Now cable news would be all over it, and you'd have a website that would get a million hits the first week."

"So there's nothing new that can help us?" Brian asked.

"Detective Zuk has tried everything I can think of," Susan said. "Sharlah's in the national database. He's got dental records and even DNA—he got a sample from the brother in the Navy, all the way over in the Persian Gulf, because the dad and the brother in prison turned him down. Given the case he inherited, he's done the best he could, I think."

One of the things that had always bothered Brian was the idea that critical information was lost early on because the police didn't think Sharlah was important, and the reason they didn't think she was important was that her boyfriend was a drug dealer.

"Did they blow it off in the beginning? I've always been afraid they ignored her because of me," Brian said.

Susan picked up one of the binders and leafed through it until she found a spot marked with a blue tab. She placed her palm over the page.

"I know your father got the impression they weren't doing anything," she said, "but I think there was more action on the case than he realized. The big mistake early on, in my opinion, was that they got very focused on a suspect and pursued him to the exclusion of other ideas."

"A suspect? No one ever told me that!"

Susan slid the binder over to him. "Recognize this guy?"

The binder was open to a mug shot of a man with long gray hair and a beard. He held a card that gave the date—July 10, 1983—and his name: Percival Wellington.

Brian suddenly had a vivid memory of having his own mug shot taken—at the police department, and again when he was processed at prison. He took a deep breath, trying to dispel the anxiety bubbling inside him, and focused on the photo.

The man looked vaguely familiar, but Brian couldn't place him. He looked up at Susan and shook his head. "Percival Wellington? Never heard of him."

"He was your neighbor," Susan said.

Brian looked again. "Well? The hippie across the street? How come we never knew about this?"

"I think in the beginning the police didn't tell you because they didn't trust you," Susan said. "They thought you were covering something up." She looked up at Brian, her eyes frank. "Which you were, of course."

It seemed more a statement of fact than an accusation, so Brian let it go.

"They got interested in him because he had this Peeping Tom arrest"—Susan patted the binder—"and they found his thumbprint inside Sharlah's trunk. He was seen skulking around your house the night she was shot; he admitted he was there later, to board up the broken window. But he went to a hurricane party the day she disappeared, and they eventually decided he didn't have quite enough time to do anything to Sharlah and dispose of a body."

Brian realized then that the police must have thought from the very beginning that Sharlah was dead.

"Here's the basic problem: It doesn't matter how hard you work a case if you don't have leads," Susan said. "From the very beginning, there just wasn't much to work with. And on a case this old, there's usually only two ways to get new information: Somebody who's always known something decides to clear his conscience, or somebody suddenly realizes the importance of something he's known all along."

She flipped to another page in the binder, this one marked by a yellow tab. "There's only been one new piece of evidence since the first few weeks of the investigation."

Susan handed him the binder, which was open to an evidence photo of a book. Brian looked up at her, confused. A book?

"I don't know if you knew this, but Sharlah had this book checked out of the library when she went missing. It's *Sophie's Choice.*"

Brian didn't know, but it didn't surprise him. Sharlah always had a book out.

"Where did they find it?"

"Seven years ago, it was mailed to the library in a plain manila envelope. No note."

"Seven years ago?" Brian was on his feet, sending the binder clattering to the floor. "Why didn't anyone…"

Susan retrieved the binder and held up a hand to calm him. "The librarian remembered Sharlah and called the police right away, which was lucky. But it was another dead end. They didn't pick up any usable prints or DNA. They traced it to a mailbox at a strip mall in suburban Mobile. The trail ended there."

Brian's mind was racing. He couldn't believe no one had told him about the book.

"It might have been mailed by someone who found it, saw the library nameplate and thought they were being a good citizen," Susan said.

Brian stared at her, incredulous. "That's what the police think?"

"They don't know. Now, the fact that Mobile is on I-10, is that a coincidence? It arrived 10 years after she disappeared. There's some thought it could be a taunt."

"From Sharlah? Why would she do that?"

"From the perpetrator," Susan said quietly. "That would fit the serial killer angle."

Brian sat down hard on the couch. He'd been so sure that Zuk's I-10 theory was wrong.

"So they just decided to keep it from me? I don't get it," Brian said.

Susan leaned toward him. "At the time you were asked to identify the pink T-shirt, Zuk had a conversation with your father in which he asked that the police not contact you again unless they had something definitive."

"My dad *what*?"

"He told Zuk he didn't want your hopes or fears raised about leads that might not pan out. He was worried about your emotional state. He's apparently very persuasive."

"I can't believe he would do that," Brian said. "All I wanted was to know what happened to Sharlah. Why would he shut that down?"

But even as he said the words, Brian knew exactly why his father had done it. It was the same reason he'd bailed Kevin out of jam after jam. He felt guilty about the father he'd been when they were kids, and even though they were adults now, he wanted to shield them as much as he could.

"People make all kinds of misguided decisions trying to protect loved ones," Susan said with a shrug. "I see it all the time."

Brian only half-heard her—suddenly the last place he wanted to be was in this room with Susan Davila. "I need a minute," he said, heading for the kitchen. "Excuse me."

"Sure. Take your time," Susan called after him.

In the kitchen, he drank cold water straight from the tap and splashed some on his face.

He felt like an idiot, the way he'd been looking forward to this meeting. Hadn't he known there wouldn't be anything new? All he'd learned was that his father had kept him in the dark, which actually made perfect sense by Lowry family logic.

He stopped by his desk to grab his checkbook. Susan was standing when he returned to the living room.

"Are you OK?"

"I'm fine," Brian said. He slowly wrote a check for the balance he owed, triple-checked that he had the numbers right, and tore it off, handing it to Susan.

"I'm really sorry. I wish I could have done more," she said. "As hard as it is to accept, you're probably never going to know what happened."

Brian thought about the amount on the check and all the overtime at Lowry Marine it represented. He wanted more to show for it.

"You must have an opinion." He pointed to the binders on the coffee table. "You can't have put all that together and not have an opinion."

"My opinion? The police have considered a lot of scenarios," Susan said, "and I can find fault with all of them."

"So do that for me," Brian said.

"OK," Susan said. "Start with the I-10 Killer: What was a serial killer doing out in that weather? Random crime actually goes down during natural disasters. And it just doesn't *feel* right—it makes more sense for it to be linked to you and Missy and Cliff."

"Did they ever find any of those women?" Brian closed his eyes, trying to remember their names. "Sabrina from Fort Stockton, and… who were the other two?"

"Sabrina Martz and Delia Fontenot have never turned up," Susan said. "The other case, from Port Arthur, wasn't related. It turned out to be the married boyfriend. He buried her on some land his family owned."

Even though Brian knew almost nothing about the woman from Port Arthur, this news saddened him. He tried to imagine what the people who loved her felt when she went from "missing" to "murdered." Were they crushed? Or was even the worst possible news better than no news at all?

"So," Susan said, commanding his attention again. "We've got the I-10 scenario." She held up one finger. "We've got Moreno." She held up another finger. "When did this guy—who strikes me as someone in over his head and panicking, by the way—find time to track down Sharlah while on duty in the middle of a hurricane? Or am I supposed to believe he just ran into her? What are the odds?"

She held up a third finger. "I could make a pretty good case it was somebody else altogether, some suspect they haven't come up with yet."

Brian waited, but Susan seemed to have finished her recitation.

"She could be alive, couldn't she?"

"Where could she go without her car, Brian?"

"She could have taken the bus, or..."

"Zuk followed up with Greyhound," she said. "They suspended service because of the storm. The timeline doesn't work—she would have missed the last bus. And even if she'd caught that bus, don't you think she would have called?"

"She was really mad at me that day," Brian said. "Maybe she decided she didn't love me and so she just left."

"I listened to the recording of your last conversation at the jail, Brian." She pointed to the binders. "The transcript is there. She started out mad, but she wasn't at the end. One of the last things she says is that she doesn't want to leave you."

"But..." Brian began.

But what? He'd asked Susan for her opinion, and she'd given it to him. And yet he waited, willing her to say something that would feed his hope, no matter how slim it was.

Susan usually radiated a restless energy, but suddenly she seemed very still to Brian.

She looked out the window for a long time and took a deep breath. "In my experience, when people go missing and never get in touch with their loved ones..."

She met Brian's eyes. "In my experience, those people are dead."

PART THREE

Elizabeth

NINE

ELIZABETH ELLSWORTH hated to fly.

And yet here she was, early on a September morning, trundling her carry-on and laptop bag through the Tallahassee airport, her boarding pass and driver's license clutched in her free hand.

Elizabeth was traveling to a conference in San Diego, filling in at the last minute for a co-worker whose father had died. As soon as she heard about the death, Elizabeth knew she would be asked to make the trip. She knew, too, that she would not be able to refuse. It was an important conference; grant money was at stake.

She had stayed up late the night before, obsessively reading websites so she would know exactly what to expect at the airport. Elizabeth had flown only a handful of times, and she had not flown at all since Sept. 11, 2001.

Her outfit had been chosen with special care. She wore a black pantsuit and black shoes, low-heeled but still fashionable—the official uniform of professional women of a certain age. The lavender of her blouse played off her blue eyes and blonde hair, which she wore shoulder length and simply styled. Her earrings were small silver hoops, unlikely to set off the metal detector. She wore no other jewelry—no watch, no bracelets, no rings. She had skipped a belt and had decided, after much deliberation, to forgo an underwire bra.

She had purged her makeup bag of anything that might cause alarm, even the round-tipped nail scissors that everyone online agreed were permissible.

Elizabeth had arrived early at the airport, her boarding pass already printed, to give herself plenty of time to clear security. Rushing sometimes caused her face to flush, and Elizabeth wanted to project an image of serene calm, no matter how hard her heart was hammering in her chest.

Because she was filling in for a colleague, her flight had been booked in the last 24 hours. Elizabeth knew passengers ticketed at the last minute tended to raise red flags.

Elizabeth worked very hard not to raise red flags.

$\textit{5}$

To casual observers, to airport security screeners, even to co-workers who saw her every day, there was nothing particularly unusual about Elizabeth Ellsworth.

She was 39 years old and in her tenth year as a librarian at the university. She had come to Tallahassee from a small college library in Tennessee, her first job out of grad school.

She'd lived in the same apartment for a decade, a one-bedroom in a 12-unit garden complex favored by retirees with modest pensions and entry-level employees of the state government. She could afford something better on her salary, and had anyone ever asked, she was prepared to say that she loved the location and hated moving.

She drove a 10-year-old Honda, purchased used in a cash transaction. Her driving record was clean.

She had one credit card, which she used sparingly and

paid off each month. Her credit rating was excellent, in part because she had no debts.

She lived frugally, bringing her lunch to work every day. She ate at her desk, working the *New York Times* crossword between bites.

Elizabeth's colleagues liked her well enough. She was enthusiastic about her work and generous with her time and expertise. She had an aura of reserve that they found a bit puzzling, though. She never socialized outside the office. If asked about her weekend or vacation, she'd say where she'd gone and what she'd done, but there never seemed to be any people in Elizabeth's stories.

Her boss, Naomi Tate, had seen Elizabeth's résumé and knew that she had a GED rather than a high school diploma. From this, and from Elizabeth's vagueness about her family, Naomi surmised that Elizabeth came from a hardscrabble background and yet had managed to propel herself to a bachelor's degree and then a master's.

Naomi admired this presumed triumph over adversity. That, combined with Elizabeth's excellent work and willingness to take on unpopular tasks, made Naomi more forgiving of Elizabeth's social deficits.

Bronwyn Rubio, whose desk was nearest Elizabeth's and who was secretly writing a novel set in a university library, had her own theories. She observed Elizabeth's frugality and evasiveness and concluded that Elizabeth was hiding a gambling addiction, or a heroin habit, or a lesbian lover who liked to be kept in high style.

In truth, Elizabeth Ellsworth's co-workers knew very little about her.

They didn't even know her real name.

❧

As a drenched 19-year-old standing in a convenience store parking lot, Sharlah Webb had only dimly perceived the law of unintended consequences.

Elizabeth Ellsworth understood the concept all too well. It had ruled her life for 20 years.

She could not vote or apply for a mortgage without committing a federal crime. She cringed every time she was asked to show ID. She read newspaper stories about identity theft and couldn't sleep afterward, dreading the knock on the door.

It was pointless, she knew, to look back and wonder "what if?" And yet, when she was depressed about the narrow confines of her world and all the things she'd unwittingly given up, she often rewound her life to that convenience store and thought about what she would change, if she had the chance.

As she waited to use the pay phone that day, she'd made up her mind to call the diner and ask one of the girls to come get her. She would ride out the storm at home.

Then a police car rolled by, and she thought about Brian's panic when she told him about the cop who kept turning up.

The girl monopolizing the phone was Vicky, and she'd driven down with her friends to spend a week at her grandparents' condo before starting the fall semester at Iowa. For the price of a tank of gas, she was willing to provide a ride to Houston.

Vicky introduced the hitchhiker to the other girls as Sharon, and Sharlah didn't bother to correct her. The three Iowa girls immediately plunged back into an argument that had clearly been running awhile, something about a boy.

The new passenger wasn't expected to contribute to the conversation. Sharlah, still suffering the effects of a gunshot wound and a painkiller, leaned back against the seat and went to sleep.

When she woke up, they were barely a quarter of the way over the causeway, and the chatter in the car had died away. Vicky was completely focused on the road. The other girls were looking nervously at the roiling bay. They were Midwesterners, unfazed by blizzards and tornadoes, but a hurricane was something else altogether.

For hours, they rode in silence, the car creeping forward 5 or 10 feet at a time, then coming to a standstill.

It was past 8 when they finally reached Houston. Vicky took the first exit off the highway and dropped Sharlah at a chain motel, the first open business they saw.

Inside, Sharlah had to fight her way past a group of 20 or so people all demanding information from one beleaguered clerk. She found another long line at the pay phone.

She waited her turn, eavesdropping on the conversations around her. The motel had no more rooms. The clerk had called places nearby but hadn't found any vacancies. People were getting nervous. The weather was worsening, and it was too late to drive to San Antonio or Austin or other points farther inland.

When it was her turn at the phone, Sharlah dialed Kevin Lowry's home number and waited, dismayed, as it rang and rang and rang. Where could Kevin and Lynn be?

She let it ring while she contemplated her options. She did not want to give up the phone until she had a plan.

Should she call Brian's parents? Renee had told her not to call the house again, but it was an emergency. Mitch would be home from the office, and Sharlah believed he would not leave her stranded. Still, her pride balked at the idea of appealing to Brian's parents.

While she was debating, a man poked his head into the

corridor and announced, "The Red Cross has a shelter open at a school around the corner."

Her decision made, Sharlah hung up the phone. She rode out the storm perched on a cot in a dank gym, drinking bad coffee and keeping a nervous watch on her suitcase. While the hurricane roared, she thought about what to do next. Her arm was throbbing, a sobering reminder of the danger she faced.

The scene at the motel had given her an idea. She had money. She could keep herself safe, just like Brian said, without any help from his family. They wanted nothing to do with her? Fine. She'd have nothing to do with them.

In the morning, when the storm had passed, she asked a volunteer for a ride to the bus station.

🌀

Elizabeth Ellsworth apparently sounded no alarms with airport security, because the screener waved her through after only a cursory look at her ID.

She breathed a little easier after clearing that hurdle, but she knew it was only the first one. She still had to make a connection in Dallas. Elizabeth had successfully avoided Texas for 20 years, and the thought of going back, even to change planes, made her queasy.

She found a seat in the terminal and got out her laptop to work on the presentation for the conference. Her co-worker had put it together, and although it was good, Elizabeth thought it could be improved.

Soon she was engrossed in rearranging pages and tweaking copy. Some good statistics were buried, and Elizabeth wanted to make sure they got the attention they deserved.

As she fiddled with the presentation, her anxiety began to

ebb. Her work was the one thing that always made her feel centered and in control.

Sometimes when Elizabeth told people what she did for a living, she detected pity in their reactions, and she could tell what they were thinking: "What a dull job." Men, in particular, were prone to make jokes about boring librarians, and they seemed especially likely to do so when they were trying to pick her up.

Despite all that had gone wrong in her life, Elizabeth believed she had the best job in the world.

Yes, there were days when her co-workers' personal questions put her on edge, but she could always immerse herself in a research project or wander out onto the library floor and find someone to help.

Some colleagues were perplexed that Elizabeth voluntarily looked for people who needed assistance. The younger librarians spent as much time at their computers as possible. Bronwyn made no secret of the fact that she hated interacting with people, and she often told mean-spirited (but funny, Elizabeth had to admit) stories about clueless students on wildly misguided hunts for information.

Elizabeth enjoyed the students, even the clueless ones—maybe even especially the clueless ones. She volunteered to lead the orientation tours each semester, long considered a thankless task, and she lobbied hard to take over the training of the students who worked part-time in the library.

Naomi had talked to her once or twice about pursuing her doctorate so she could teach library science, but Elizabeth had no interest in that.

She had found her niche, and it made her happy.

❧

As the plane began its descent into DFW Airport, Elizabeth stared out her window at a skyline, trying to decide whether she was looking at Dallas or Fort Worth.

She'd seen Dallas only once before, from the window of a Greyhound bus rolling north on Interstate 35.

When the Red Cross volunteer dropped her off, two buses were leaving Houston within the next 15 minutes. One was headed to Memphis, the other to Kansas City.

Without giving it much thought, she'd chosen Kansas City. She had the vague idea that Kansas City was closer—it wasn't—and that the people there would be nice, because she'd waited on a family from Kansas once who'd over-tipped her.

The trip took 16 hours, during which Sharlah slept and read and tried to keep her arm from being jostled.

It ended at a bus station in a rough neighborhood. Suddenly she wasn't so sure of her plan. She hadn't expected to arrive in the middle of the night, and she didn't know how to find a motel.

She tried the phone book, but it was huge—three times the size of the one back home, even with the white and yellow pages in separate volumes.

Finally, she approached the lone bus company employee onsite, a matronly woman whose name tag said "Deena."

"Excuse me, is there someplace around here I can get a room, someplace clean and safe and not too expensive?"

Deena looked her over. "You got money for cab fare?"

Sharlah nodded.

"You want Johnson County, on the Kansas side," Deena said.

After a long cab ride to the suburbs, Sharlah checked into a motel along a busy commercial strip lined with restaurants and shopping centers.

For the first few days, she stayed in the room, reading and watching TV, leaving only to grab fast food. She felt trapped by the money—afraid to leave it in the room for any length of time, afraid she'd be conspicuous walking around with her suitcase.

Once she'd finished *Sophie's Choice*, she started to get restless. She and Brian hadn't talked about how long she should stay away, but she'd settled on three weeks.

Sharlah found a blank pad of paper in the nightstand drawer and worked out a budget. Then she called around until she found a motel with by-the-week rates and kitchenettes.

Once she'd moved up the road to the new place, she ventured out to a discount store and bought a big shoulder bag so she could take the money with her when she left the room. She stocked the fridge with bread and milk and peanut butter.

The next day, she walked up to a big mall and saw a Tom Cruise movie to kill an afternoon. When she left the mall, she got turned around and walked the wrong direction, which was how she discovered she was staying less than a mile from a library.

She started going there every day. At first she just read magazines and newspapers. But then she felt bold one afternoon and looked for *Cinnamon Skin*, the John D. MacDonald book that had always been checked out back home. When she found it on the shelf, she carried it back to a table and read it in one sitting.

Another day, she noticed a summer reading list for high school students taped to the end of a shelf. From it, she chose *An American Tragedy*. That was more book than she could finish in an afternoon, so she wrote down her page number at the end of each day and put the book back, hoping that no one would check it out.

Sharlah felt guilty sometimes, like she'd gone on vacation with Brian's money while he sat in jail. She worried about him all the time, but especially at night, alone in her motel room. She couldn't wait to go back to him.

She knew, though, that she shouldn't show up until she'd checked with Brian first to make sure she'd be safe. The trouble was, she wasn't sure how to do that.

She couldn't call him at the jail—no incoming calls were allowed. She considered sending him a letter, but she thought the police might read the mail.

What she needed to do, she decided, was get a message to Brian. She spent several days formulating a plan.

To make the call, she used the pay phone at the library, which was tucked down a hallway by the restrooms. It was quiet there.

Years later, she could still vividly remember that library hallway—the faint smell of a lemon-scented cleaning product and the air-conditioned quiet as she listened to the words that would set her life on a different path.

It's not safe for you here. It will never be safe.

Brian won't cooperate because he's protecting you. If he talks, your life is in danger. But if he doesn't talk, he'll go to prison. The only way to help him is to stay away so they can't find you.

Suddenly everything made sense. Brian had wanted her to find the money so she could go away and he could do what he needed to do.

He's willing to go to prison. He would make that sacrifice for you, to keep you safe.

But if no one could find her, then no one could hurt her, and Brian could cooperate with the police. It was his only chance at saving himself.

Will you stay away? Will you make that sacrifice for him?

She begged for one last chance to see Brian, to talk to him on the phone—anything. But it was too dangerous. Cliff and Missy were dead, and someone had tried to kill her.

It has to be this way. Don't ever come back. Forget about Brian. Start a new life.

After the call, Sharlah locked herself in a bathroom stall at the library and cried for so long that someone told a librarian, who came to check on her.

She lied and told the librarian that her boyfriend had died. It didn't feel like a lie, though.

She stayed in bed the next day, turning the maid away at the door and not bothering to eat or shower.

The day after that, she got up early, put on her makeup and curled her hair. Then she walked up and down the commercial strip, putting in applications at every restaurant.

The first line of each application was the same.

NAME: Elizabeth Ellsworth.

🌀

At the airport in San Diego, Elizabeth was sorely tempted to rent a car. She'd glimpsed the ocean as the plane descended, and she'd been seized by a desire to drive up the coast with the window rolled down, the breeze in her hair. She'd never seen the Pacific before and probably never would again. She had a whole afternoon to kill before the conference's opening reception that evening.

Elizabeth reminded herself of the reasons a car was a bad idea. She'd have to use her credit card—that was one. She'd end up in another database—that was two. Weighed against the risks, the pleasure of driving the coast wasn't worth it.

She marched past the rental counters and out to the curb to find the hotel shuttle. San Diego probably had a perfectly adequate bus system if she wanted to see the ocean.

Still, she couldn't help sighing a little as she climbed into the dingy shuttle van.

Elizabeth's life had been full of these calculations, something she hadn't anticipated the day she cut up Sharlah Webb's driver's license.

Those first few weeks as Elizabeth Ellsworth went by in a blur. She talked her way into a job waiting tables—even though she couldn't list references—and found a furnished studio apartment. She got a Kansas driver's license and paid $1,200 cash for a used car.

Whenever her courage started to falter—and it did, often—she reminded herself that this was what Brian wanted for her. She'd started over from scratch when she left her hometown, too. She could do this.

The money was both a gift and a burden. It gave her security she'd never had, but she worried constantly that she'd get caught with it. Even after she paid for a car and rented an apartment, she still had nearly $17,000.

Eventually, she hit on a plan she thought was perfect. She paid as many as bills as she could with cash, which helped whittle down the stacks of twenties. She also added extra money to her tips every week and deposited it all in the bank. She wanted to declare as much of the money as income as she could and pay taxes on it.

This was her life: She worked as many shifts as she could get, and she went back to her tiny apartment and read. No matter how many shifts she worked, though, or how many books she read, she missed Brian.

She couldn't imagine a whole life of nothing but waiting tables and reading and missing Brian, but she couldn't imagine anything else, either.

One day she noticed a stack of brochures in the library lobby for a GED program. Impulsively, she took one.

Cold weather moved in, colder than anything she'd ever

experienced. The holidays almost crushed her. On her 20th birthday—her *real* birthday, not her new one—she got in her car, determined to drive to Texas, danger to herself or to Brian be damned. She got as far as Wichita before she turned around.

A month later, she signed up to get her GED.

She had forgotten how much she loved school when she was a kid, back before her brother killed a boy from a well-liked, churchgoing family and her last name became an unbearable burden in her hometown.

Her GED teacher, impressed by how well she'd done, encouraged her to try community college. "One class," he said. "Just try."

She took freshman English and aced it.

Brian always told her she was smart enough for college, but she'd never quite believed him. Now she did. Emboldened by her success, she took three classes the next semester and set her sights on transferring to a four-year school.

At 21, she moved 40 miles down the road to Lawrence and enrolled in the university as an English major.

Her adviser, concerned about a 21-year-old freshman, encouraged her to give up waiting tables. He thought an on-campus job would ease her transition.

Elizabeth found a part-time job in the library, a beautiful old building right in the center of campus. She spent hours there, even when she wasn't working, studying in front of the big windows that overlooked the football stadium and the valley beyond.

She tried dating, but Brian was never far from her thoughts.

Sometimes she wondered whether it was really necessary for her to stay away from him forever. If Brian testified against the people who were threatening her and helped put them in prison, how could they hurt her?

She began to think about getting in touch with him, maybe after she'd graduated. Part of her motivation was selfish—she knew that. She wanted Brian's parents to see how wrong they'd been about her. She also desperately wanted someone to be proud of her, and she thought no one would be prouder than Brian.

Elizabeth discovered that the library had back copies of one of the Houston papers on microfilm, and she spent one rainy weekend going through the archives, searching for news of a big drug trial. Every time she saw a headline that looked promising, she'd stop the machine and read the article all the way through to the end.

While she was scanning for Brian's name, she got an education about drug cases.

When she first read the term "money laundering," Elizabeth envisioned cash swirling round and round in a washing machine. She knew that the police used drug-sniffing dogs, and she had the vague idea that dealers' cash might be tainted by telltale scents.

Eventually, she realized that the term couldn't be literal— no one was loading up a Kenmore with cash. Laughing at her own naïveté, her curiosity piqued, she went to the reference section and pulled the big legal dictionary off the shelf.

Money laundering, she discovered, involved taking the profits from illegal activities and passing them through legit- imate channels, like bank accounts. That, of course, exactly described what Elizabeth had done with the $20,000.

The legal dictionary didn't offer any clue what the punish- ment might be, so Elizabeth dashed across campus to the law library, her heart pounding.

There, she discovered she'd committed a federal offense punishable by 20 years in prison.

Elizabeth had always known the money was dirty. But

she'd convinced herself that spending it was OK—because she didn't know about the drugs, because she was putting herself through school, because she'd paid taxes.

She saw herself as an innocent victim who made the best of a bad situation. But the law wouldn't see it that way, and Elizabeth knew she had only one person to blame for that. And just like that, she never wanted to see Brian again.

9

Elizabeth's hotel room wasn't ready, so she got some information from the clerk about San Diego's bus and trolley system and left her bags at the bell desk, thinking she'd do a little sightseeing.

But she changed her plans when she spotted the hotel's business center.

People indulge in all kinds of secret habits when traveling—drinking too much, committing adultery, ordering X-rated in-room movies.

Elizabeth had a different habit: searching the Internet for information about Brian.

Her anger toward him had softened over the years. The first step in the process was a messy love affair in grad school. She realized that she was doing exactly what Brian had done to her: deceiving someone she cared about not out of malice but because she couldn't find the words to tell the truth. The lies just kept adding up until it became impossible to find a way back to the truth.

She ended the relationship and vowed never to fall in love again.

As the years went on, she thought more and more about Brian. She often wondered how his life had turned out, and sometimes she indulged her curiosity.

The Internet was a terrific tool for tracking people down, and Elizabeth was very adept at using it. But she also knew that Internet searches left tracks, and she hadn't gotten away with being someone else for all this time by being sloppy.

To avoid leaving a trail, she only used computers where someone else was logged on. Elizabeth was always on the prowl for such opportunities, no matter how brief, and she wasn't above telling a white lie or two to get them. Her one rule was that she never used a university computer—it seemed both too risky and ethically questionable.

Elizabeth always told herself that if she could get just one hit on Brian's name, she'd quit. So far, in her haphazard searching, she hadn't. She didn't expect him to have a blog, but she was a little puzzled that he never popped up at all. Sometimes she wondered if he'd ended up in a witness protection program.

The hotel business center was empty except for one 50-something businessman tapping away, his suitcase and briefcase propped against the desk next to him.

He looked up when Elizabeth walked in, and she gave him her warmest smile. "Hello," she said, allowing herself to sound a little more Southern than she usually did.

He returned her smile.

Elizabeth went to the computer opposite him. At the login prompt, she typed in a made-up room number and the name of one of her favorite college professors as a password. "Shoot!" she said under her breath.

She moved to the next computer and repeated the maneuver, then sighed in frustration. "Excuse me," she said to the businessman. "Is the login they gave you working?"

"Yep," he said. A printer against the wall whirred to life. "That's my boarding pass printing right now."

It was working out exactly as Elizabeth had hoped.

"I bet it's because I'm not officially checked in yet," she said. "They didn't have my room ready." She smiled at him.

"I hate to ask, but if you're leaving, could you stay signed on and let me use that computer? I just have to check my email." She lowered her eyes, then looked up at the man again. "I promise not to visit any NSFW sites."

The man laughed as he got up. "Be my guest," he said, holding out the chair for her.

Elizabeth slid into the chair. "Thanks so much."

She clicked around harmlessly for a bit just to make sure he wasn't coming back. After 5 minutes of checking weather and headlines, she called up a search engine.

She always searched the same way. First she tried Brian's full name—Brian Joseph Lowry. Next, she'd try Brian Lowry and Houston.

Nothing useful came up when she tried Brian's full name, so she moved on.

When she typed in "Brian Lowry" and "Houston," a link popped up. It appeared to be a headline from the Houston paper.

Slain Woman's Mom Looks To DNA For Closure

Elizabeth clinked on the link and got a "file not found" error.

A story about a dead woman that hit with Brian's name had to be about Missy. Elizabeth called up the search engine again and typed in "Missy Burke" and "Houston."

The first link was the same newspaper headline she'd just seen, and clicking on it produced the same error message.

The second link was intriguing. The top line said "Missy Burke" and under that was a squib of text: *finds Missy Burke dead in her apartment*

Elizabeth clicked on the link and waited for the page to load. The first thing that appeared on her screen was a bold headline:

WHAT HAPPENED TO SHARLAH WEBB?

Gasping, Elizabeth glanced over her shoulder, but no one in the lobby was watching.

She scrolled down to read the text.

Sharlah Marie Webb disappeared when she was 19-years-old, after her boyfriend Brian Lowry was arrested in a drug case and two of their friends were murdered. The night before she disappeared, Sharlah was shot in the arm.

The day she disappeared, she was wearing a pink tee shirt, blue jeans and sneakers. She carried a blue suitcase and a brown purse. The last known person to talk to her was a neighbor who helped her load her suitcase in her car around 2 p.m. Her car was abandoned in a parking lot near the Galveston Causeway.

Sharlah is 5 foot 3 and weighs 110 pounds. She has blonde hair and blue eyes and may have a scar on her right upper arm.

Instinctively, Elizabeth's hand flew to her right bicep.

Below the bloc of text was a photo that caused Elizabeth to gasp again.

She remembered that red dress from first grade.

After the photo came a timeline listing the events of that week—Brian's arrest, Cliff's murder, Missy's murder, Sharlah's disappearance.

At the bottom was one last line:

If you have information about Sharlah, click here.

Elizabeth's first impulse was to shut down the computer, collect her luggage from the bell desk and flee, but she forced herself to remain in her chair, to think.

She whirled her chair around and grabbed a blank piece of paper from the printer against the wall. Back in front of the computer monitor, she took a pen from her purse.

Who?

Elizabeth tapped her pen under the word she'd written, thinking. Halfway down the sheet, she wrote another word.

Why?

Elizabeth scrolled up and down the website again, looking for clues.

The site was basic—just text in a box, really. The URL gave it away as a site built from a simple online template and hosted by a discount company.

At the bottom of the page, Elizabeth hesitated and then hit the "click here" link, curious to see where it led.

The businessman had left himself signed in to his email account—lucky for Elizabeth, but he really should have been more careful. An empty email prompt came up with the "to" field filled in as *findsharlah.* The service provider offered no clue; it was one of the free web-based email services.

Elizabeth closed the email program and went back to the website.

Who?

Who might want to know where Sharlah Webb was? Elizabeth wrote down the first two answers that came to mind—the police, someone from the drug ring. Who else? Brian? Elizabeth wrote down his name, put a question mark behind it.

A gray-haired woman dressed like a tourist—stretch jeans, T-shirt with whales on it, tennis shoes—paused in the doorway of the business center. Elizabeth quickly clicked on another icon to bring something up in front of the website.

"Can anybody use these computers?"

"Hotel guests. You can get the password at the main desk," Elizabeth said, trying to sound brisk and businesslike.

"Oh, OK," the woman said, turning away. Elizabeth watched as she meandered across the lobby.

Elizabeth called the web page back up and hit the print menu. She couldn't just sit out in the open and stare at the screen—it was too risky.

She grabbed the paper off the printer and moved to the corner of the room, where she could sit facing the lobby.

Police. Drug dealers. Brian?

Elizabeth went to her second question. *Why?*

The police—that was obvious. She was a money launderer and an identity thief. But wouldn't the police department have put its phone number on the website?

Elizabeth couldn't fathom why drug dealers would be looking for her, not after all this time. Twenty years was a long time to wait for revenge.

Brian? Brian might be curious about her life, just as she was about his. But Brian knew perfectly well what happened to her. She left town because he told her to, with the money and the false papers that he directed her to, and she stayed away because...

Something about the website had been nagging at her, and suddenly Elizabeth realized what it was. She read the text again.

The last known person to talk to her was a neighbor who helped her load her suitcase in her car around 2 p.m.

That wasn't true, and Brian knew it.

Elizabeth drew a line through Brian's name. It had been a little foolish to consider him, she realized. A man who could barely read creating a website? Not likely. And where would Brian have found her first-grade photo?

For that matter, where would drug dealers have found her first-grade photo?

She drew a line through *drug dealers* on her list.

That left the police, unless she could come up with someone else who would care what happened to her. Not her father and certainly not her brother Wayne. Her brother Rod? He'd given her his car when he shipped out to basic training, but he'd never written, and the last thing he said before he left was, "You're on your own."

Rod?

She wrote his name underneath where she'd scratched out Brian's.

Elizabeth read over the text yet another time, straining for ideas.

It didn't read to her like something a police officer would have produced. She thought back to the time she'd spent in the police station, answering questions about Missy.

Sharlah was shot in the arm.

The cops she'd met would have said something like, *an unknown assailant fired on her, striking her in the arm.*

Most of the sentences were subject-verb-object, very simple. There were a few errors, too. The phrase 19-years-old didn't need hyphens, and the writer missed the appositive commas to set off Brian's name. Tee shirt should have been T-shirt.

She was evaluating the site like an English major. Elizabeth laughed at the absurdity.

And what about the photo? Certainly the police could have obtained it from her school, but why on earth would they choose something so old? The first-grade photo was useless to identify her.

Elizabeth's eye was drawn back to the photo. She and her mother had made a special shopping trip to Lufkin for a dress, and they'd gone from store to store to store, her mother carrying piles of things into the dressing rooms for her to try. Once they'd found the dress, there had been the hunt for the perfect red knee socks to match, and then a trip to the shoe store for new Mary Janes, and finally, the fabric store for hair ribbons.

When she was younger, she had cherished that memory as proof that her mother loved her, no matter what she'd done later. As an adult, Elizabeth was able to see the desperate, manic quality of her mother's actions that day.

Turning over the paper, she prepared to start a new list on the back.

Exposure

Would anyone connect librarian Elizabeth Ellsworth of Florida with Sharlah Webb, drug dealer's girlfriend in Texas?

When people asked where she was from, she always answered, "I was born in Louisiana."

Blonde hair, blue eyes, 5 foot 3—that description wasn't specific enough to give her away. But the scar on her arm was another story.

Elizabeth tried to think of who might have noticed the scar on her arm, which she generally kept covered.

Any man she'd slept with might have noticed it. That was not a list she wanted to contemplate, but she knew this was not a time to go easy on herself.

There were a couple drunken hookups in college, but Elizabeth doubted either guy had noticed her arm.

Eamon, her lover in grad school, had asked about the scar. She invented a story about falling into a broken fence when she was a kid, an explanation she'd stuck with since.

She'd sworn off dating for a couple years after Eamon. When she started again, it was with a strict set of rules. It was a given that no relationship could have a future, so she kept it casual. She never dated anyone associated with her work, and she didn't date anyone for longer than three months. Any man who seemed too curious about her past or the inner workings of her soul didn't last even that long.

She ran through the list in her head: the environmental lobbyist, the urban planner, the man who managed his family's landscape business. He'd asked about her arm, and after she told him the story, he wanted to know what kind of fence she'd tangled with.

Elizabeth glanced again at the printout of the website and realized, suddenly, how silly this mining of her romantic past was. The chance that any of those men would have seen this site was astronomically small. No one was going to stumble across it accidentally.

Elizabeth was surprised she hadn't found the site sooner. It should have come up all the times she'd searched for "Brian Lowry" and "Houston." Maybe the site was new. How long had it been since she last searched? It was a year at least, maybe longer.

So, she had a site put up in the last year or so devoted to a 20-year-old case, a site that was practically impossible to find unless...

Elizabeth froze.

What if the site was a trap, one designed to snare anyone who searched online for Sharlah Webb? She'd read about the police setting up websites to trap child molesters. Surely they could adapt that tactic to other uses.

Elizabeth quickly folded the papers on the desk and shoved them in her purse. She got up and started to walk toward the hotel exit. Then she forced herself to overrule her panic, to stop and think.

If the website was a trap, what had it just captured? It recorded a hit from a hotel in San Diego and the email address—maybe—of some unsuspecting businessman who was getting ready to board a flight to Phoenix or Des Moines or Raleigh.

It would take time to find him, to ask questions, to search the registered guests, to look at the hotel's surveillance video.

Elizabeth always suspected her luck would run out someday—no one could escape detection forever. She had dreaded it but also planned for it.

Hidden in her apartment was a stash of cash she'd amassed over the years. She'd lived well below her means since she'd finished grad school.

She would call her boss and plead some kind of emergency, leave the conference and catch the first available flight back to Florida.

Elizabeth headed back toward the check-in desk, hopeful that her room was ready. She had some work to do.

$$\mathbf{\textit{5}}$$

Up in her room, Elizabeth left her suitcase, still packed, standing against the bed and got out her laptop so she could start checking flights.

When she turned it on, the presentation that she'd been working on popped up.

Elizabeth slammed the laptop closed, overwhelmed with guilt.

Suddenly exhausted, she stretched out on the bed, not bothering to kick her shoes off.

She closed her eyes and pondered her options, hoping she'd hit on some magic solution she'd previously overlooked.

She wished there were someone she could run things by, but there was no one.

As Elizabeth, she had things Sharlah could only dream of—an education, a job she loved, enough money to live comfortably.

As far as she'd come, though, some things hadn't changed: When she faced a big decision, she faced it alone.

Elizabeth felt herself sliding into the warm embrace of self-pity and willed herself to stop.

Opening Door A meant closing Door B. Just because she hadn't realized she was giving up the chance to share her life with someone, hadn't realized at 19 that she'd desperately want a baby later, well, that didn't make it unfair. That was just how life worked. There were tradeoffs.

She would not feel sorry for herself, and she would not shirk her responsibilities.

She would paste on her best smile and go network at the opening reception. She would give her presentation in the morning, and she would knock it out of the damn park.

TEN

ELIZABETH WAS UP at 4 a.m. Her body was still on East Coast time, and her mind was stuck in the past.

She'd dreamed about Missy, something that hadn't happened in years.

In the dream, she was standing outside Missy's condo staring at Missy's lifeless form on a stretcher, the body bag unzipped just enough to reveal her bruised face and blood-matted hair.

But then the bag began to rustle, and she realized that Missy was trying to unzip it the rest of the way from the inside.

Elizabeth woke with a start, her heart pounding.

She got out of bed and made herself a cup of weak in-room coffee. She was too awake to go back to bed, but it was too early to think about venturing out.

Elizabeth got out her laptop, thinking she'd give her presentation one final run-through. As soon as she opened it, though, Elizabeth realized that she was sick of it. She'd been through it a dozen times already; more tinkering wasn't going to accomplish anything and she might even sound bored when the time came to deliver it.

She walked over to the window and pushed the curtains aside, but there wasn't anything to see. It was still dark out.

She found herself thinking about Missy and wondering about the story behind the newspaper headline she'd spotted before she stumbled on the website that changed everything.

Elizabeth sat down at the desk. There had to be a way to get that newspaper article despite the broken link online, some way that wouldn't be traced to her.

She had one idea. Unfortunately, it would violate the bright line she had always drawn keeping her professional life and her past separate. It also involved lying and appropriating someone else's identity, although Elizabeth had to admit it was probably a little late to be squeamish about that.

She had always believed that whoever killed Missy was the same person who shot her. Wouldn't that be useful information to have? It might even provide a clue about who was behind the website. She rationalized that a little deception might be OK.

Her mind made up, Elizabeth set about creating a new email identity.

☯

Because she thought it might be the last good thing she ever did for her employer, Elizabeth put everything she had into the presentation.

The audience was sleepy at first, probably still hung over from the opening cocktail reception. People began to perk up after the first few minutes, though, and she got a nice round of applause when she finished.

Several people came to her during the break between sessions asking for more information. She worked through the crowd as quickly as she could without seeming rude, handing out copies of the fact sheet.

Finally, Elizabeth was able to slip away to a pay phone.

She called her boss in Tallahassee first. Elizabeth led with the good news, telling Naomi about the enthusiastic reception for the presentation. Then Elizabeth explained, rather hurriedly, that she had a "personal matter" that required her attention and that she needed to leave the conference early. She would, of course, pay the necessary fees for changing the plane ticket.

Naomi didn't object, which was fortunate, because Elizabeth had already booked herself on a flight leaving at 1 p.m.

After she talked to Naomi, Elizabeth dialed the number she'd looked up that morning for the newspaper in Houston, and asked for the paper's reference library.

When she had a librarian on the line, she introduced herself as Leslie Rosen from Florida.

"I'm helping a student track down an article," Elizabeth began, reciting the speech she'd worked out that morning. "The link online was broken. The headline read 'Slain Woman's Mom Looks To DNA For Closure.' "

Elizabeth could hear the librarian in Houston typing. This was a simple request, quickly fulfilled, and she was hoping the woman would commit this act of professional courtesy and then quickly forget it.

"I've got it," the woman in Houston said. "Shall I email it to you?"

"That would be great," Elizabeth said. Then she paused, just as she'd rehearsed. "But the tech geniuses changed our filters and a lot of our attachments aren't getting through. Why don't you send it to my personal email? I'd hate to have to bother you again."

Elizabeth rattled off the email address she'd created just that morning. She thanked the Houston librarian and hung up.

She hoped Les Rosen wouldn't haunt her for borrowing his name. He'd been her boss once—a sweet man with a sly sense of humor and a whole file of correspondence addressed to "Ms. Leslie Rosen" that he liked to show off.

Her next stop was the bell desk, where she collected the luggage she'd deposited first thing in the morning, after she'd checked out. From there, she went to the reception desk. Just as she'd hoped, the same clerk who'd handled her checkout was working.

"Hello," she said to the young woman. "I need to get online and print my boarding pass. I already checked out. Can I get some kind of temporary ID and password?"

"The one we gave you at check-in still works," the clerk said. "They don't get disabled until after lunch."

Elizabeth made a show of frowning. "Well, I can't get it to work. Maybe you could walk over to the business center and help me?" She did her best to appear befuddled by all this newfangled technology.

"I can't leave the desk," the clerk said. She scribbled something on a piece of paper and handed it to Elizabeth. "Here's the master ID. It should work."

"Thanks so much," Elizabeth said. "You're a lifesaver."

In the business center, she got online using the hotel's untraceable master ID. She accessed the Leslie Rosen email address she'd created that morning and printed out the article from Houston that was waiting there.

The question has haunted Audrey Burke for nearly 20 years: Who killed her daughter?

Police have long maintained that Missy Burke was killed by one of their own—Scott Moreno, a young patrolman caught up in a drug ring with Missy's boyfriend and a clandestine romantic entanglement with Missy.

Audrey Burke has her doubts. The truth, she believes, is trapped in the fabric of a pair of blue satin panties edged with white lace and a white T-shirt, men's extra large, emblazoned with the image of a Three Musketeers candy bar.

Elizabeth stopped reading. Scott Moreno? She knew that name, but she couldn't place it. He wasn't the cop who'd kept popping up everywhere she went. That cop's name was Zuk, rhymes with book. She hadn't forgotten him.

She glanced at her watch and realized she needed to hurry to catch the airport shuttle. Elizabeth stuck the article in her computer bag and walked out of the hotel.

❧

Elizabeth managed to sleep on the last leg of her flight, even though her mind was whirring, trying to process all the information in the article about Missy.

Halfway through the article, she'd remembered Moreno. He'd been one of the two officers at her house after the shooting—Zuk and Moreno.

According to the story, police had linked Moreno to Cliff's murder using ballistics tests on a gun found at his home. When they started asking around, they found people who had seen Moreno talking to Missy several times at the bar where she worked. From that, they concluded he was the man Missy was seeing on the side.

Missy's mother didn't believe her daughter was involved with Moreno; reading between the lines, it was clear she didn't think Missy would date someone Hispanic. Ever since DNA profiling had become available, she'd been asking the police to test the clothes Missy was wearing when she died.

But Moreno was dead—shot in the head and dumped by a road just a few months after Missy died—and the cops didn't seem to be in a hurry to verify their theory.

Brian was mentioned in only one sentence. It said that Cliff became involved in running drugs with his buddy Brian Lowry, and that the two of them, along with Brian's brother, had called themselves the Three Musketeers in high school.

Elizabeth bristled a little, because she thought the story made it seem like Brian got Cliff involved when anyone who knew them knew that Cliff was the schemer, not Brian. Brian was Mr. Go-along-to-get-along.

It was after midnight when Elizabeth wheeled her suitcase into her apartment. She hurriedly unpacked and changed into her pajamas.

Before she could collapse into bed, though, she had one more thing she wanted to do.

After making sure the front door was locked and the deadbolt was on, Elizabeth went to the laundry room off her kitchen.

She nudged the dryer away from the wall and retrieved a metal box wedged into the space behind the washer. Then she locked herself into the bathroom and sat on the floor.

The sight of the money comforted her, as it always did.

The cash was in hundreds, neatly bound with rubber bands. She carefully thumbed through the stacks, counting until she reached $14,800.

Once all the cash was out of the box, all that remained was the gun, wedged in the corner and still wrapped in the same old shirt.

Elizabeth hated the gun, had always hated the gun. It was an unwanted relic of her old, downwardly mobile life, like her bad teeth and country accent.

She'd consciously muted her accent over the years, and 20 months of orthodontia in her early 30s had fixed her teeth, but the gun wasn't so easily shed.

She'd been carrying it around, moving it from apartment to apartment, but she'd never even unwrapped it. Maybe it was time, finally, to do something about it.

Elizabeth lifted the bundle, taking care to keep the barrel pointed away from her, and unwrapped the gun.

And just like that, she realized that all the answers were right there. They'd always been right there.

§

Elizabeth did not approve of all-nighters. She'd found them useless when she was in college, and she always advised students against trying to cram half a semester's work into one night.

At the moment, though, she was grateful that college students were procrastinators and that the library was open round-the-clock on weekdays to accommodate them.

Sitting on her bathroom floor, realizing how wrong she'd been about everything, she'd come to one overwhelming conclusion: She had to find Brian.

Once she'd resolved to do that, Elizabeth wanted to make up for 20 years of inaction as quickly as possible.

She considered simply sending an email to the link on the website she'd found but rejected the idea as cowardly. If her theory was correct, she was about to detonate a bomb in

Brian's life. She needed to find the most humane way to do it, and email wasn't it.

A grad student named Chloe was on duty at the library's main desk, and she did a double take as Elizabeth pushed through the main doors.

Affecting an aura of calm, Elizabeth greeted her. "Good morning, Chloe. How's it going?"

"Wow, it really is you," Chloe said. "I didn't recognize you. The schedule said you weren't back until Monday."

Elizabeth always dressed more conservatively than anyone else on the staff, but for the first time ever, she'd come to the library in capris, a T-shirt and flip-flops.

"I've been in San Diego and I'm still on Pacific time, I guess," Elizabeth said.

That was not true. It felt very much like the middle of the night to her, especially because she hadn't slept well in two days. "I thought I'd get some paperwork done at my desk, see if that puts me to sleep," she said.

Elizabeth took the stairs up to the staff offices and let herself in. The area was dark. Chloe was the only person on duty at this hour, and she had to stay at the main desk.

Elizabeth logged in at her computer using her regular ID and password.

She sifted through the papers stacked on her desk and found a project she'd started before she left for San Diego. She called up a database and initiated a search.

If anyone checked later, they would find that Elizabeth Ellsworth had logged in at her desktop and worked on one of her assigned projects.

Elizabeth locked her purse in her desk drawer and left the staff office.

Up on the next floor were computers that any student or university employee could access with a school ID. The staff had posted signs reminding users to log off when they'd completed their sessions, but people invariably left themselves logged in. Elizabeth was banking on someone's forgetfulness.

Only one cubicle was occupied, by a student who appeared to be asleep.

Elizabeth made her way down the row, checking each computer. For once, students had followed directions. Everyone had logged out. She'd have to go with Plan B.

She sat down at the last cubicle, the one farthest from the sleeping student.

Because she ran the training for part-time student employees, Elizabeth had access to a generic ID and password. At least twenty people used the account, so the trail would not lead directly to her, not right away. Before this night, she'd always resisted the temptation to exploit it for personal reasons.

Elizabeth called up the prompt and entered the user name, then the password. She was proud of the password—it was Melvil, for the man (nee Melville Louis Kossuth Dewey) who invented the Dewey Decimal system.

On the drive from her apartment to the library, Elizabeth had puzzled over why Brian never showed up in any of the searches she'd tried.

She'd decided that she had to deal with the most obvious explanation first. Brian had been involved with dangerous people. Both Missy and Cliff ended up dead.

She called up the Social Security death index and typed in Brian's full name.

No hits.

Elizabeth breathed a sigh of relief.

Then her professional training kicked in. She knew she'd made her search too restrictive. If Brian's name were there without his middle name, or middle initial, or misspelled as Bryan, she'd missed him.

She hit "new search" and typed in "Lowry, Br" and then a symbol for a wild card. That would give her all the Lowrys whose first names started with the letters Br.

That search yielded hundreds of hits. Elizabeth paged slowly through them. Brandon, Brant, several Brendas, Brennan.

Then she saw it: *Brian.* Her heart lurched.

She clicked on the record and discovered that the birth date didn't match. Elizabeth exhaled.

The next name on the list caught her eye.

Lowry, Bridget

Last benefits paid out in Oklahoma. Born in 1920.

This was Brian's grandmother, the woman he called "Gramma." She'd met Gramma once, at Kevin and Lynn's housewarming. Gramma was fat and loud and sat in a lawn chair in the back yard knocking back beers with the young people. She had loved Gramma, in part because Brian's mother was so obviously horrified by her.

It only took a few minutes to find Bridget Lowry's obituary online.

> *Mrs. Lowry is survived by her sons, Mitchell of Houston and Roger of Tulsa, OK; five grandchildren, Lisa Burns of Dallas, Jerald Lowry of Broken Bow, OK, Mark Lowry of Olney, MD, Kevin Lowry and Brian Lowry of Houston; thirteen great-grandchildren and one great-great grandchild.*

Elizabeth recognized all those people from Brian's stories, even though she hadn't met them—Uncle Rog, Jerry and Mark, Lisa, the only girl among the cousins, the princess who tattled when the boys got into trouble.

Because she'd never found Brian in phone databases before, Elizabeth decided not to bother with them. The obit said Brian lived in Houston; she'd start with property tax records.

As she waited for the search to finish, she thought about those 13 great-grandchildren. At least one, she knew, was Kevin and Lynn's. How many were Brian's?

Her hunch about tax records paid off. She discovered that Brian owned a house, purchased the year before for a price that seemed very low. His name was the only one listed. She was surprised; she expected Brian to be married. The tax filing didn't mean he didn't have a wife, of course, only that her name wasn't on the deed.

Elizabeth tried to picture what Brian might be like in his 40s. He liked to work with his hands. Given his reading difficulties, it was unlikely he had a white-collar job.

Lots of jobs required state licensing. Elizabeth clicked over to the official Texas state website to see what sort of databases were available. She found him in the business licenses, the sole proprietor of something called Come Monday.

A few clicks later, she found the Come Monday website. Brian was in the business of repairing guitars—"making them right," the website said.

Unbidden, a memory came to her of Brian at the Laundromat, singing for her.

Elizabeth dug the heels of her hands into her eyes. She needed to stay focused.

Why had she never found this website when she searched for Brian? She clicked quickly through the site and discovered that Brian's name wasn't listed anywhere.

She mapped Brian's house and business. Total distance from Tallahassee: 721 miles. Total traveling time: 11 hours and 18 minutes. Elizabeth checked the clock. It was just past 2 a.m.

She would have to wait a day. Houston was too far, and she'd had too little sleep the past two nights.

Elizabeth logged out and headed home to get some rest. She needed to be sharp when she saw Brian.

ELEVEN

ELIZABETH PULLED OUT of her apartment complex at 4:49 a.m.

She'd managed to sleep for a couple of hours, but then she'd bolted awake. *Now,* her brain said. *Go now.*

As her Honda glided down the hushed streets toward the highway, she thought about all the times she'd done this—hit the road with nothing but an audio book or her thoughts to keep her company. She'd driven to the beaches of South Carolina and the mountains of North Carolina, all the way to Washington to see the museums and monuments.

For a while, she'd made regular trips every month or so to Athens, Georgia. She dated someone there—Wyatt, a man she'd met on a trip to Savannah. She'd liked him so much that she'd let him stay in her life past the three-month mark, rationalizing that the distance between them would keep things in check. But then Wyatt started talking about missing her and wanting to see her more, and she'd had to cut him loose.

She'd enjoyed those drives. She'd savored the idea of Wyatt with a glass of wine, listening to music, keeping an eye on the clock. When she pulled into his driveway, he would always walk out onto his porch, smiling, glad she was finally there.

235

She didn't know what kind of welcome she would get from Brian, but she refused to dwell on that. She set her cruise control and kept the car pointed west.

It was a perfect day for driving, nothing but sunny skies and dry roads. She stopped for coffee and a muffin in Pensacola, and again in Baton Rouge for gas and a sandwich. Gaining an hour as she drove west, she hit Houston at 3 p.m..

Brian's house and business were only a couple miles apart, much closer to downtown than the suburb where he'd grown up. She didn't recognize the neighborhood on the map, but then, she'd never really known her way around Houston. She'd relied on Brian.

Elizabeth had debated whether she should approach Brian at home or at work. There was no good way to do what she was about to do, but she'd decided that going to his business was the least disruptive.

She wanted to drive by his house first, though, just to check it out. When she'd looked at the property records and seen how little Brian paid for his house, Elizabeth worried that he lived in a bad part of town.

She was surprised and relieved, then, to find herself in a charming neighborhood full of Victorians, bungalows and small shops.

Brian's street was on the edge of the neighborhood, a mile or so from the grander homes. The houses were smaller here, mostly well maintained, although a few had peeling paint and sagging roofs.

Elizabeth rolled slowly down the block, ticking off the address numbers. When she got to Brian's house, she fought the impulse to slam on the brakes in the middle of the street. Instead, she went to the corner and looped around so she could park opposite the house.

Brian's bungalow was painted a grayish-blue with white trim. A wide wooden porch spanned the front of the house—crying out, Elizabeth thought, for a swing.

The paint job looked new and the house seemed to be in good repair. The yard was patchy, though. Flower beds had been dug along the foundation, but they were bare except for a new layer of mulch.

There were no potted geraniums that spoke of a woman's touch, no toys or bikes strewn around. It was impossible to tell anything from the blank façade of the house.

A driveway ran alongside the house toward a detached garage at the back of the property. The drive was empty; the garage door was down.

The front of the house had one big window, set to the left of the door, and another small one to the right. Elizabeth could see something white poking out of the top of the mailbox, which gave her an idea.

Elizabeth rolled down the car window and listened. The neighborhood was quiet except for the whirr of air-conditioners and the hum of traffic on a nearby road.

She propped the printout of the map and directions on her steering wheel and pretended to study them. She waited five minutes, then ten. A dog began to bark somewhere in the neighborhood, then stopped.

Elizabeth checked the map one more time, noting the name of the next street over. If anyone asked, she'd pretend she was lost.

She got out of the car, crossed the street, climbed the three steps to the porch and knocked on the front door. She stepped back and waited, glancing at the envelope poking out of the mailbox. It was addressed to Brian. That didn't help her at all.

Elizabeth knocked again, then peered into the big window, shading her eyes with her hand.

A brown sofa backed up against the wall under the window. In front of it was a coffee table, its surface bare. The light was too dim to see much else.

She did not see anything that seemed especially feminine. But the room seemed clean and uncluttered, which worried her, because Brian had always been such a slob.

The blinds were down on the other window, so there'd be no snooping there.

Elizabeth realized that she'd looked long enough.

🌀

Come Monday was a couple blocks off the neighborhood's main drag, in a narrow storefront flanked by a Tae Kwon Do studio and some kind of computer business. The name was spelled out on a sign—simple font, no logo—that hung above a display window about 6 feet wide. The entire shop looked to be no more than 10 feet wide.

The block did not look prosperous, but it didn't look down-at-the-heels, either. Most of the storefronts were occupied, although one lot sat vacant and weedy.

Elizabeth found a parking place at the opposite end of the block, next to a bar.

She'd imagined, a thousand times, what it would be like to see Brian again. But now that it was almost upon her, she couldn't envision what would happen. She'd walk into his shop and Brian would… what?

The bar was open. For a millisecond, she thought about having a drink.

Instead, Elizabeth walked purposefully down the block to Come Monday. As she came even with the door, though, she saw that there was a customer. A pony-tailed man in shorts and a tie-dyed shirt was standing at the counter with one hand resting on an open guitar case, talking, though Elizabeth couldn't see Brian or anyone else.

She hurried past the door and tucked under the awning of the business next door, where she had a good view through Come Monday's display window. She pulled her cell phone from her purse and put it to her ear, pretending to take a call.

After a few seconds, a man came out of the back of the shop and walked to the counter with what looked like a catalog in his hand.

The way he walked, the set of his shoulders, the tilt of his head—they were all instantly familiar to Elizabeth, all unmistakably Brian.

She had steeled herself for the possibility that Brian had not aged well. It was a bit of a jolt, then, to find him still fit and good-looking, if a little gray at the temples and in need, apparently, of glasses.

Brian put the catalog on the counter and spun it toward the customer. As the man studied the page, Brian lifted the guitar from its case and inspected it. He plucked a string and bent his head, listening. He said something to the customer. The customer replied, and Brian laughed. She remembered that smile.

Out of the corner of her eye, Elizabeth noticed a police car crawling down the street. She turned her head away, pretending to be engrossed in her call.

At the corner, the car made a U-turn and came back, gliding to the curb near Brian's door.

Suddenly, everything felt wrong. She'd been so certain she had everything figured out, but now she had doubts. Could the website be a trap after all?

She put her phone in her purse and headed back down the block, toward her car, eyes front, not daring to look at the cop or Brian's shop.

She needed a different plan.

♪

Three people—they had the look of regulars—were clustered at one end of the bar when Elizabeth walked in. She sat at the other end and asked for a club soda with lime. The bartender nodded, then asked if she wanted a double. She forced a laugh.

Elizabeth loved bars. She could be completely anonymous in a bar, but at the same time, there was always the tantalizing possibility of easy camaraderie if she chose it.

As much as she loved bars, though, she had always done her serious drinking at home. Sometimes it was just one glass of wine, but often it was four or six or however many it took to soften the hard edges and make the bad things recede.

She never drove drunk, never missed a day of work, never embarrassed herself in public. The worst she ever did was wake up on her couch with a headache and the TV still on and an empty wine bottle on the coffee table.

She hadn't really meant to give up drinking, not entirely, not at first. She'd only meant to quit keeping wine in the house, removing the temptation to kill a bottle when she was feeling low. But then she felt awful—anxious, nauseated, unable to sleep—for the first few days she didn't drink, which scared her. So she quit altogether.

She didn't really miss it. Of all the things she'd given up in her life, alcohol was the one she regretted the least, which allowed her to sit in a bar and plan her next move without even a twinge.

The police car had spooked her. Maybe it would make more sense to try to catch Brian at home. Of course, the reason that she'd gone to his business in the first place was that she wasn't sure he lived alone.

A week's worth of insomnia seemed to catch up with her all at once, and it occurred to her that she'd walked to the wrong end of the street. She should have gone to the espresso place she'd spotted at the other end of the block. She'd slept, by her count, about 12 hours in the past three days.

She thought about finding a hotel room and getting a good night's sleep, trying Brian at home in the morning.

There was only one problem with that idea: She'd never get a good night's sleep until this was done. Procrastinating was only going to prolong her misery.

She checked her watch; it was 5:10.

The sign in Brian's window said he closed at 6.

Elizabeth caught the bartender's eye and signaled for a refill.

𝄢

After two club sodas, Elizabeth drove to Brian's street and found a parking spot five houses down from his place. If he took the route she expected, she'd see him in her rear-view as soon as he rounded the corner. If he came from the other direction, she had a clear view of his driveway.

At 6:20, Elizabeth caught sight of a blue pickup truck in her mirror, Brian driving. He was alone, the window down, his hand tapping out a rhythm on the steering wheel.

Brian had always liked to sing along with the radio.

He was wearing sunglasses and starting straight ahead, but Elizabeth instinctively turned away as he drove by.

He parked in his driveway and got out. He opened the rear

door of the truck's cab and pulled out a backpack and a guitar case. Elizabeth opened her car door and got out.

She hoped to catch him outside, just in case someone else had come home since she checked earlier. But he was up the walk and inside too quickly for her. She'd have to knock on the door.

She walked past the truck in the driveway and up the steps to the porch.

Somehow, she'd known Brian would still drive a truck. The only thing that had changed was that this one was bigger than the one he'd driven when he was younger, with a little back seat so he could carry more than one passenger.

Her heart was pounding. Elizabeth took a deep breath and then another. She raised her fist, exhaled again and knocked.

As soon as she knocked, the realization of what she'd just seen hit her.

She whirled around to check. Yes. Brian had a child's car seat in his truck.

Elizabeth backed away, preparing to leave, but the door opened almost as soon as she knocked.

Brian must have been just inside. He was in the middle of taking off his sunglasses, one earpiece clenched in his teeth, a case holding regular glasses in his hand.

Elizabeth started to say his name, but her mouth was too dry. She swallowed hard and looked into Brian's eyes.

They were just as blue as she remembered them, friendly and... puzzled.

Brian didn't recognize her.

Thank God. I can still salvage this.

"Can I help you?"

She half-turned toward the street and shook her head.

"I must have the wrong street," she mumbled. "Sorry to bother you."

Brian smiled at her, that slow, lazy grin she'd always loved. "Where you headed? Maybe I can help."

He put on his glasses and turned to put the case on a table just inside the door.

Then he turned back to face Elizabeth, and his smile began to fade.

Elizabeth knew she should leave, but she felt pinned there by Brian's eyes.

"Oh God," he said. He took a step back, caught his heel on a rug, staggered a little.

"I'm sorry," Elizabeth said. "I've made a mistake."

Brian's voice was barely a whisper. "Is it really you?"

"This is a mistake."

A car went speeding down the street, and Elizabeth turned to look. It was a police car. She felt exposed, standing on Brian's front porch like this, but there was nowhere to go.

Brian looked over her head at the car whizzing down the street, then back at her.

Without a word, Brian grabbed her wrist, pulled her inside and pushed the door shut behind her.

"I shouldn't be here," Elizabeth said. "I didn't realize…"

"Everybody said you were dead." Brian's voice broke, and he threw his arms around her, pulling her into a hug so tight she could hardly move. Elizabeth could feel Brian's breath coming shallow and ragged.

"Brian."

There. She'd said it.

He exhaled once, hard, when she said his name, but he didn't let go.

She tried again. "Brian. Please. I can't breathe."

Brian relaxed his grip and backed off half a step. "It really is you."

"I shouldn't have come. I didn't realize... I didn't know about your kid. I don't want to disrupt your life, I just need..."

Brian frowned, shook his head. "My kid?"

"Maybe you could meet me somewhere, if you could get away and..."

"What kid? Where did you come from?"

Elizabeth stopped mid-sentence. They were carrying on parallel conversations, talking over each other, neither getting answers.

"There's a car seat in your truck," she said. "You're a dad, right?"

"It's for my niece," Brian said, dismissing the question. "I can't believe I opened my door, and here you are. After all this time, you're just..." He opened his arms wide. "Here."

Elizabeth let her purse fall from her hand and walked into Brian's open arms. She rested her head on his shoulder. They fit together, the way they'd always fit together. She turned her face into Brian's neck and inhaled. He even smelled the same.

She knew she should step back and explain herself, but she didn't. She just stood there letting her breathing settle into a rhythm with his.

The first kiss was tentative, a question—Brian's hand under her chin, his lips barely brushing hers.

The vehemence of her answer surprised them both.

Then Brian was pulling her deeper into the house. Or maybe she was pushing him.

She banged her shin on a table as Brian led her down the hall. "Ow!"

"Sorry," he murmured, reaching behind him to open a door.

Those were the only words either spoke for a long time.

❧

With her eyes closed, Elizabeth could almost will herself to believe that 20 years hadn't passed. She and Brian might be back in their little shotgun house, before the drugs, before Cliff and Missy died, before the hurricane, before everything that went wrong.

Later, Brian sprawled on the bed next to her, his mouth close to her ear, and whispered the one word that brought her back to reality.

"Sharlah."

Elizabeth kept her eyes pressed shut, not wanting the spell to be broken. She just wanted to linger here, savoring the heat of Brian's hand on her stomach.

"I can't believe this is happening," Brian said.

This is a disaster, Elizabeth thought.

She couldn't even explain to herself why this had happened. Because Brian's eyes were still blue and he still had the smile that melted her heart when she was 17? Because she was lonely and scared, and Brian had always been able to make those feelings go away?

She'd expected questions. She had not been ready for *this*. It was, she realized with a start, exactly the kind of thing Sharlah would have done.

Well, she wasn't Sharlah. Not anymore.

Brian was stroking her hair, his breath warm on her neck. She put her hand on his shoulder and gently pushed him away.

"Brian, please stop."

He drew back. "What's wrong?"

Elizabeth took a deep breath and summoned her strongest, hardest self, the one who had said no to Eamon, who had dispatched Wyatt—over the phone, no less—when he seemed to be falling in love.

"This was a mistake," Elizabeth said. "I shouldn't have let it happen. I didn't mean…"

She felt her resolve slip away. "God. What have I done?"

Brian's eyes grew wide, and he groped for her left hand under the sheet. "Are you married?"

"No."

"Me neither," Brian said. "So we're legal."

"I only wanted to talk to you."

Brian rose on one elbow and propped a pillow under his head. "Let's talk, then."

"Not like this," Elizabeth said. "We should get dressed."

After a long pause, Brian rolled to the far side of the bed. He sat for a moment, his back to her, hands resting on his knees. Then he stood, pulled on his boxers and T-shirt, and put on his glasses.

He picked up clothes from the floor, putting them on the bed. When he picked up her blouse, something seemed to register.

"You walked by my shop today," he said. "I remember this blue shirt. I saw you, but from the back. Why didn't you come in?"

"There was a police car parked outside."

"What kind of…" Brian started, then stopped.

He looked down at her for a few beats. Finally, he said, "Whatever trouble you're in, that wasn't about you. I asked him to come take a look at my security because there've been some break-ins on the street."

He folded her shirt and put it on the bed.

They stared at each other, Elizabeth clutching the sheet to her chest, Brian standing at the foot of the bed.

"Hang on," he said.

He walked out of the bedroom and reappeared with a bathrobe. "Here," he said, draping it across the bed.

"Thanks," Elizabeth said. "Would it be OK if I had a quick shower?"

"First door on your left," he said, pointing. "Do you want a drink?"

"Water would be good. Could you bring me my bag? I left it in the living room."

As soon as Brian closed the bedroom door behind him, Elizabeth threw back the covers and shrugged into the robe. She gathered up her clothes, wincing at the sight of the condom wrapper on the bedside table.

I am a weak, horrible person.

Brian knocked when he came back, which only made her feel worse. He was obviously bewildered but trying hard to do the right thing.

He walked a couple steps into the room and dropped her bag on the bed. She fished out an elastic band and pulled her hair into a ponytail. "I'm sorry about this," she said. "Just give me a minute and then we can talk."

"I'm not going anywhere," Brian said.

❡

Elizabeth cranked the shower as hot as she could stand it and stood there in the scalding spray trying to figure out what the hell she was doing.

It had been a long, long time since she'd fallen into bed with someone when she wasn't intending to. Elizabeth still couldn't quite believe it had happened.

But it had, and now she had to figure out how to deal with it.

As she stepped out of the shower and began to towel off, Elizabeth took note, for the first time, of her surroundings.

The bathroom was small, but the tile and fixtures looked new. It was spotless—a far cry from the first bathroom she'd shared with Brian.

She realized she needed to stop these endless comparisons with the past—Brian was more this or less that than he'd been when they were together. It was nothing but a distraction. Those people no longer existed.

Elizabeth finished dressing and stepped into the hall. "Brian?"

"Back here," he said.

Brian had dressed and made the bed while she was in the shower. The condom wrapper was gone from the bedside table, replaced by a glass of water.

"I brought you water," Brian said. He picked up his shoes from the floor by the bed and put them in the closet, then stood, expectantly, like he wasn't sure what to do next.

"Thanks," Elizabeth said. She sat down on the bed and pulled one leg up under her.

Taking the cue, Brian sat down, too, carefully positioning himself a few feet from her.

"I've got to be honest," Brian said, "I don't understand what's going on. I feel like maybe I should apologize for earlier? I guess I got carried away. I thought you..."

"Brian, it's OK," Elizabeth said. "You didn't do anything wrong. It was my mistake."

"Where did you come from? How did you get here? I didn't see a car out front."

Elizabeth decided to take the easiest question first. "I left it down the block, in front of the yellow house," she said.

"If you need to get it off the street, you can put it in the garage," Brian said. "It's best if I don't know what's going on with the police, but I'll try to help you if I can."

Elizabeth's heart sank a little. Brian was still loyal, even if it might be to his own detriment.

"I think it's OK," Elizabeth said. "But thanks. That's very generous. You've been really..."

Brian interrupted her. "I went through your purse while you were in the shower, before you get too far down the road on how generous I am. I'm sorry. I got paranoid."

Elizabeth's perception of Brian shifted again. Perhaps he wasn't as trusting as he used to be. She was surprised, but not angry. "OK," she said, shrugging. "I don't blame you."

"So you're Elizabeth Ellsworth now? And you live in Florida? I saw your license, and a badge for the university."

"Yes." This was not really the path Elizabeth wanted to take. She had not planned to tell Brian about her life. But he knew now, and maybe it would be easier to let him get his questions out of the way. "I work there," she said, "in the library."

An unexpected grin broke across Brian's face. "The library? Really?"

Elizabeth couldn't help smiling herself. "Really."

"Have you been in Florida the whole time?"

Elizabeth shook her head. "The last ten years or so."

A silence stretched between them, and Brian's face slowly clouded over.

"This is so weird, because I've thought so many times about seeing you again and now you're here and I don't know what to say."

"I'm sorry to show up like this," Elizabeth said. "I know it's a shock."

"Yeah," Brian said, nodding. "You could say that."

Elizabeth waited, giving Brian time to gather his thoughts.

"I guess the thing I really want to say is, I don't blame you for leaving me. I screwed up pretty bad. The part I don't understand is why you never called or anything."

Here was the opening Elizabeth needed.

"I called."

Brian leaned away, surprised and perhaps a little angry.

"When? When did you ever call?"

"Three weeks after I left."

"I was still in jail," Brian said. "What did you do? Try the house once and give up?"

Elizabeth took a deep breath, knowing that what she said next would change everything. "I called the house first, but when no one answered, I called Kevin."

"Kevin? But he never..."

"He told me my life was in danger," Elizabeth said, remembering the pay phone in Kansas City, the quiet of the library hallway. "He said the only way you could cooperate was if I stayed away so you'd know I was safe. He said if I came back, you'd have to choose between helping yourself and protecting me, and you would choose me."

Brian's initial reaction was shock—Elizabeth could tell—followed swiftly by a recognition that he worked hard to mask.

Elizabeth waited to see what Brian would say next, sure now that she was right.

"That doesn't make sense."

Did he genuinely not understand? Or was he still covering up? Elizabeth couldn't tell.

"I think it does," Elizabeth said. "You just have to turn it around."

"Turn it around?"

"Kevin wanted me to stay away, not to free you up to cooperate, but because he thought it was the best shot at *keeping* you from cooperating. He wasn't worried about me, or you. He was worried about himself."

Brian stared straight ahead, refusing to look at her.

"Am I right, Brian?"

Elizabeth could see a muscle in Brian's jaw twitching. "You can tell me, Brian," she said. "It's OK."

She waited, staring at Brian's profile. There were lines around his eyes now, and a scar in his eyebrow that she didn't remember, but she recognized the stubborn set of his jaw.

When a few minutes passed and Brian still hadn't answered, she tried again.

"For a long time, I thought it was Cliff who talked you into the drug deal," Elizabeth said, "but then I realized that Kevin made so much more sense."

Brian still said nothing, and Elizabeth felt her composure begin to slip.

"What I don't understand is why, Brian. We were poor, but we had a plan. I thought we were happy." She hated the ache in her voice, but she pushed on. "Weren't you happy?"

That, finally, broke through to Brian. He turned to her. "Those two years with you, that was the happiest part of my life."

"Then why?"

Brian took a deep breath and let it out. "Kevin needed money. He was in over his head with a bookie." Another sigh. "I guess nothing about Kevin should surprise me anymore, but he could have told me you called. He could have said, 'Sharlah's fine, but she thinks you're a loser and she's leaving you.' He didn't have to make me suffer for 20 years, not knowing. Why do that?"

Elizabeth had known the things she came to tell Brian would hurt him, but that didn't make his pain any easier to witness.

"I didn't want to leave you, Brian," Elizabeth said. "I know that doesn't help, but I planned to come back. I'm sorry— sorry that I believed him then. And sorry to be the one to tell you now."

"It's not your fault," Brian said. "Kevin could be pretty convincing."

Kevin had seemed reasonable and compassionate on the phone that day, someone who genuinely regretted the bad news he had to deliver. From a distance of 20 years, it was easy for Elizabeth to see how he'd manipulated her. Kevin had played on her worst fears: that she wasn't good enough for Brian and that he'd be better off without her.

Brian gave Elizabeth a tired smile. "I turned him down the first time he asked me. I told him, 'Tell Dad. He'll chew your ass, and you might never hear the end of it, but he'll give you the money.'"

"He wouldn't take no for an answer?"

"He didn't want to bring Mom and Dad into it. He was trying to keep it from Lynn. This was right when they found out she was pregnant, and I don't know if you remember, but she was really sick. Kevin was worried she'd lose the baby."

Elizabeth sat quietly, listening. Now that the dam had been broken, Brian's words were tumbling out.

"And I think he just didn't want them to know, because he was used to being the one they were proud of," Brian said. "He didn't want to be a disappointment like me.

"I knew it was wrong, but I felt like I owed it to him. My whole life, Kevin looked out for me, doing my homework, running interference with Mom and Dad, beating up kids who called me stupid.

"It was just supposed to be one time, and Kevin and Cliff both said these guys were cool, it would be fine.

"It wasn't fine. One of them pulled a gun on me." Brian pointed to the center of his forehead. "He put the barrel right here, and he said, 'We're going to call you next week, and you'd better be here, and the week after, and the week after.'"

Brian held his hands out. They were shaking. "Look at that. Twenty years later..."

"Here, have some water." Elizabeth handed him the glass. "You must have been so scared, Brian."

"Scared and pissed," he said, taking a big gulp of water before passing the glass back to her. "I kept telling Kevin, 'Man, you have to get me out of this,' and he just kept saying he was working on it. We argued about it all that spring. You knew something was up. I kept expecting you to ask me, and I knew I wouldn't be able to lie to your face."

"I knew something was up, but I guess I was afraid to ask, in case you were looking for an opening to break up with me," Elizabeth said.

"Never," Brian said. "Coming home to you was the best part of my day, every day."

Elizabeth remembered those days, how she'd sit in her chair reading, waiting for the sound of Brian's truck. He'd come home dirty and sweaty, and she'd lean against the bathroom sink and talk to him while he showered. Seeing his smile when he walked through the door always made her forget whatever bad thing had happened that day.

"I finally decided I had to get myself out of it," Brian said. "So I asked around—there were always guys working construction who weren't legal and had fake papers. I got everything ready, but then I chickened out whenever I tried to tell you."

Brian spread his arms wide. "Anyway, that's how it went down."

He let his hands drop into his lap. "I didn't know anything to tell the cops. All I did was drive from Point A to Point B. Before I got bail, I kept thinking they'd catch somebody who would put them onto Kevin, and he'd cut a deal for us both."

"But they never caught anyone else?"

"Nobody but me," Brian said. "Once I got out on bail, I thought Kevin would tell me something I could use to get a deal."

"Did he?"

"He said I'd have to decide for myself what to do, that he had to do what was best for his own family. When I saw him with his baby, it was hard to argue with that. So I kept quiet."

Familiar emotions stirred in Elizabeth—indignation at the way Brian's family treated him and sympathy for how much it hurt him. "That must have been so hard," Elizabeth said. "You looked up to him so much."

"It sounds weird, but sometimes I think I did him more harm than good," Brian said. "I never bring it up, but sometimes he does, and he always says he never asked me to do it, that I decided for myself. And that's true, I guess. But the guilt has eaten him up anyway. It doesn't matter what I say—he can't forgive himself."

Elizabeth knew this was her opportunity to tell Brian the rest, but she hesitated. In a lifetime of hard things, what she needed to do next was the hardest.

Brian was staring at her, wary. "There's something else, isn't there?"

"There's no good way to tell you this," Elizabeth began.

"I've heard that more times than you can imagine," Brian said. "Whatever it is, just tell me. I'll deal."

Elizabeth reached out to take Brian's hand, and he let her. She took a deep breath.

"I think Kevin killed Missy."

Brian jerked his hand away. "No." He shook his head. "A cop named Moreno killed Missy. That's the guy she was seeing behind Cliff's back."

"Her mother doesn't believe that," Elizabeth said. "I read an article online where she said Missy wouldn't have been involved with him."

"That's because he was Hispanic, and Missy's mom is racist."

"Missy was too," Elizabeth said. "Do you really think Missy would have been involved with him, the way she was?"

Brian waved her question away. "Why would Kevin hurt Missy? She was his friend."

"I think they were more than friends," Elizabeth said. "The police said that she hinted at work that there was something off-limits about whoever she was seeing on the side. Being married would make Kevin pretty off-limits."

"No," Brian said, not budging. "No. I can see why you'd think Kevin is the worst person in the world. But you're wrong. What happened to Missy—Kevin couldn't do that. He wouldn't do that."

Elizabeth tried to keep her voice steady. "I'm pretty sure he did, Brian."

Brian leapt up from the bed and whirled to face Elizabeth. She held her ground, even though a part of her wanted to shrink back.

"The back of her head was bashed in! I saw the pictures. It was horrible!" Brian said. "How can you think Kevin would do that? Missy was his friend!"

"The story I read said the police still have her underwear and a Three Musketeers T-shirt she was wearing when she died," Elizabeth said, fighting to stay calm. "Her mom wants it all tested for DNA."

"Yeah? So what?"

"That's Kevin's shirt."

"It's Cliff's! Cliff had a shirt too, remember? Three Musketeers—Kevin, Cliff, me." Brian thumped his hand against his chest for emphasis.

Elizabeth pressed ahead. "Remember that last night we saw Cliff and Missy? Missy got sick all over our porch and all over Cliff. He put his shirt in the trash at our house. That was Cliff's Three Musketeers shirt."

"The one she was wearing must be mine, then," Brian said. "She must have borrowed it, or maybe I wore it to the beach with them and it ended up with their stuff."

He was grasping at straws, and Elizabeth's heart ached for him.

"Brian, no," Elizabeth said gently. "I have your shirt. I wrapped the gun in it."

"You're mixed up," Brian said. "You took a different shirt."

"No, Brian. It was your Three Musketeers shirt. It's in the trunk of my car right now," Elizabeth said.

"My Three Musketeers shirt? You're sure?"

Elizabeth nodded. "The gun, too—both in my trunk. I think Kevin and Missy slept together, and then Missy got out of bed and put on Kevin's shirt. It has to be Kevin."

Brian dropped back onto the bed—hard—and stared at Elizabeth with such pain that it frightened her.

Then he buried his head in his hands. "Oh, Kevin," he whispered. "What did you do?"

❡

Brian sat for a long time with his head bowed. Elizabeth waited, watching the numbers on the clock next to the bed slowly turn. Five minutes passed, then ten.

Finally, Brian looked up at her.

"This is my fault. You know that, right? If I'd told the police about Kevin right away, he'd have been locked up, and Missy would still be alive."

Elizabeth couldn't let Brian blame himself. "How could you have known? Kevin's responsible for what he did, not you."

"I should have figured it out. Missy always had a thing for him. Kevin slept with her once in high school," Brian said. "Missy was all set to dump Cliff. I had to tell her that Kevin didn't want to be her boyfriend. He wasn't going to say anything."

He took off his glasses and rubbed his face. "I didn't tell Cliff, because he would have been mad at Missy and Kevin, and Missy and Kevin would have been mad at me. I wish to God I'd told. Everybody would have stopped speaking to each other back in high school, and none of this would have happened."

"Brian, this isn't your fault."

He put his glasses back on and focused on Elizabeth. "How long have you known?"

"What's today? Friday? I've known since about 12:45 last night, I guess," she said. "I saw a website about me, and I got worried the police were looking for me. I was going through old stuff and unwrapped the gun, and saw the shirt, and it all came together."

"So you saw my website," he said. "I wondered whether you would ever... Wait, how long does it take to drive here from Tallahassee?"

"Eleven hours and 18 minutes, according to the Internet," Elizabeth said.

"You drove all that today?"

"Once I figured it out, I just wanted to find you and tell you," Elizabeth said. "You know, when you have to do something horrible, you just want to get it over with."

"So now you've told me," Brian said. "And you want me to do... what?"

"Well, I don't think he should get away with it," Elizabeth said. "Do you think Kevin would turn himself in?"

"I haven't talked to Kevin in three years," Brian said. "He's an alcoholic and a drug addict. I had to cut off contact with him. Trying to save him wasn't helping either of us."

Brian grew quiet, and again Elizabeth waited.

"I always thought it was guilt about me that messed him up, but I guess it was Missy. Jesus." Brian ran his hands through his hair. "I can't believe my brother did that, killed her in cold blood like that."

"Maybe they argued, she pushed him, he pushed her, she hit her head—something like that," Elizabeth said. "Maybe he was drunk."

Elizabeth realized that she was just trying to make things easier for Brian, but a part of her hoped she was right, that Kevin had acted in the heat of the moment.

"Maybe she threatened to tell. Missy knew about the drugs, right?"

"She wasn't supposed to," Brian said. "We all agreed we'd leave the girls out of it." He turned to Elizabeth. "I'm sorry I left you in the dark. I thought I was protecting you."

After another long, uncomfortable silence, Elizabeth tried to steer the conversation back to their next step. "Do you think you could talk to Kevin, or..."

"I have to make up my mind right now?"

Brian hadn't raised his voice, but there was no mistaking the edge there.

"This is a lot to take in, you realize that, right?"

"I'm sorry," Elizabeth said. It seemed inadequate, but what else could she say? Brian felt boxed in—of course he was angry. She understood that feeling all too well.

"You could have just called the police and told them," Brian said. "Why didn't you?"

"I thought I owed it to you to tell you first," Elizabeth said. "And I'd rather not deal with the police, obviously. I took $20,000 in drug money—that's money-laundering. And I'm living under a fake name."

When Brian didn't respond, she stood and picked up her purse. She didn't blame him for being angry, but she was starting to feel uneasy—he knew too much about her now. "I'll give you some time to think about it."

Brian reached for her arm. "Wait. Where are you going?"

"I'm tired. I'm going to go find a hotel and something to eat. I have the number for your shop. I'll call you after you've had some time to think."

"You just got here," Brian said. "Don't go yet. I can fix us something to eat."

๑

"Just so you know, the kitchen is the worst room in the house," Brian said as he led her into the hall.

Elizabeth hadn't paid much attention to the house once she was inside, but it was obvious now that Brian was in the middle of renovating. The baseboard was pried off in the hallway, and three different colors had been painted in wide swaths on the wall.

Brian pushed open a door and waved her through. "Don't say I didn't warn you."

The kitchen was square and ugly—peeling yellow linoleum, avocado green stove and refrigerator, cabinets stained a weird brownish-orange. The wall opposite the hall was missing entirely, replaced by a curtain of plastic.

A card table was marooned in the middle of the room, two metal folding chairs pulled up to it at right angles.

"The house was trashed when I bought it. It had been a rental and got really run down. It's been kind of a slow process," Brian said. He pointed to the plastic sheet. "I took out the wall there. I'm going to do a breakfast bar, but the guy who's making the cabinets is behind schedule."

Brian opened the refrigerator, which was covered with photos and papers held up by magnets. "I was going to grill a steak for dinner. It's big—we can split it."

He seemed determined to switch to small talk, and Elizabeth decided to play along. "Isn't that a lot of trouble to go to this late?"

"The stove doesn't work," Brian said. "I've got the grill or the microwave. Your other choice is a frozen burrito."

"In that case," Elizabeth said, "steak sounds good. Can I do anything?"

"You could put together a salad while I start the charcoal," Brian said, opening a door that led to the back yard.

Elizabeth grasped the refrigerator door and then got distracted by the collection of photos. She recognized Brian's father in a few. Mitch Lowry's hair had gone silver, but otherwise, he looked the same. She would have known those eyes anywhere.

In one photo, his arm was thrown around a teenage girl in a cap and gown. She had startling blue eyes ringed in layers of black eyeliner.

In another photo, he wore a dark suit and posed with his arm around an African-American woman in a silver cocktail dress. She was nearly as tall as he was. She had gray hair, worn very short, and a warm smile. They appeared to be at some kind of party.

The same woman popped up in another photo. This time, she and Mitch Lowry were dressed casually. The woman held a girl, maybe a year old, with big hazel eyes and café au lait skin. The girl was reaching out toward Mitch, and all three of them were laughing.

Elizabeth turned around as Brian came back in. "Your dad looks great. Who's this?" Elizabeth pointed to the graduation photo.

"That's Ashley," Brian said.

Elizabeth gave him a blank look.

"Kevin and Lynn's daughter," Brian said. "She was born the night of the hurricane. She's in college now."

"Who's the woman with your dad in these other photos?" Elizabeth asked.

"That's Francine," Brian said. "My stepmom."

"Oh," Elizabeth said, startled. "I didn't realize… did your mom pass away?"

"She lives in Arizona with her third husband," Brian said. "We don't really talk much."

"Is this Francine's granddaughter? She's adorable."

"That's Coco," Brian said. "She's Kevin's, too." He rummaged in a pile of papers on the counter. "That's an old photo. I took a bunch down the other day to clean and didn't put them all back up. Hang on, I'll show you some new ones."

"Here," Brian said, handing her a photo. Coco devoured a cupcake, smiling wide through the icing smeared on her face.

Elizabeth laughed. "Oh, she's cute! How old is she?"

"She's three," Brian said. "And she's doing great, which is a miracle, considering her mom was using while she was pregnant. She can count to three—not just say the numbers, really count. She can sing the ABC song, and she knows Brian starts with B and Coco starts with C.

"The one in her Easter dress is here somewhere." Brian, animated now, pawed through the papers. "She's in a funny stage. Everything is why, why, why?"

He found what he was looking for and handed Elizabeth another photo. Coco stood on a sidewalk in a frilly lavender dress. Brian squatted next to her, holding an Easter basket.

Studying the photo, and the pure joy on Brian's face, Elizabeth felt a twinge of sadness. "That's her car seat in your truck?"

"Yeah, it's easier than switching one from car to car, you know? Dad and Francine have custody, but I get to spend a lot of time with her," Brian said.

Elizabeth handed him the photo. "She's beautiful, Brian."

Brian's animation waned and a wistful note crept into his voice. "Kevin's made such a total mess of his life, and yet he's got these two amazing girls. Somehow it seems..."

"Not fair," Elizabeth said.

Brian nodded slowly. "Yeah," he said. He tacked the photo up in a prominent position. "The charcoal's going to need some time. You can sit. I'll make the salad."

He got lettuce from the refrigerator and a tomato from the windowsill over the sink. "You're going to like this tomato—I remember how much you complained about the ones at the grocery store," he said. "One of my customers has a huge garden, and if he needs something little done, I let him pay me with food."

Brian crossed back to the refrigerator and pulled out a bottle of Shiner. "Want one?"

"No thanks."

"Something else? There's white wine from the last time Lynn was over to help me pick paint."

"I'll stick with water," Elizabeth said. Feeling bolder, she added, "I don't drink anymore. It seemed like it was starting to be a problem, so I quit."

Brian took that in, a little surprised, and moved to put his beer back in the refrigerator.

"Please don't put that away on my account," Elizabeth said.

"Are you sure? I don't mind."

"I'm sure."

Brian fixed her a glass of ice water and opened his beer. "I don't drink like I did when we were together. One beer is pretty much it," he said.

"I guess Kevin's situation would make anyone think twice."

Brian tore lettuce and sliced the tomato, his back to Elizabeth. She'd thought he was starting to relax, but suddenly he seemed tense again.

"Even before Kevin got so bad we couldn't ignore it anymore, I had a stretch where I didn't drink at all," he said.

He put the salads on the table and, sighing, pulled out a chair. "You know I was in prison, right? Then I was on medication for a few years, so I couldn't drink."

Elizabeth's heart began to pound. She wasn't sure what to say.

"I was sentenced to four years and did thirteen months," Brian said. "I took a beating my first month there."

He pushed his hair aside, revealing a long scar above his ear. "That took twenty stitches." He pointed to his left eyebrow, then his nose. "Eight here and six here. I lost some vision in my left eye because my retina detached. I had a really bad concussion, a head injury, really. I had to take anticonvulsants so I wouldn't have seizures."

"Brian, that's awful."

"It's a different world in there. You can't help anybody, ever. You just have to look the other way. And if somebody wants to fight, you have to fight," he said. "I knew that going in, but... it's hard to explain what it's like."

He moved his beer bottle in a slow circle on the table. "I was in pretty rough shape when I got out. I saw a counselor for a couple years. She said I had post-traumatic stress. I took meds for that, too."

Elizabeth wasn't sure what to say. Brian stared at the table.

"I'd better see if the charcoal is ready," he said. Before Elizabeth could reply, he got up and walked outside.

When he came back in, Elizabeth sensed some kind of change in him, as if he'd debated with himself and reached a decision.

"It'll be ready in a couple more minutes," he said, sitting again.

"There were all these things I swore I was going to tell you if I ever saw you again," Brian said. "And now I'm losing my nerve."

Elizabeth smiled what she hoped was a reassuring smile. "I understand if you're angry. I left you at a really bad time. It's OK to be mad. I was mad at you for a long time, too."

Brian's face crumpled a little. "I was never mad at you. It's not like that." He took a deep breath. "One of the things I always wanted to say was, I'm amazed at how brave you were, telling me what happened when you were 15, about the rape. I'm so glad you told me."

Elizabeth tried to keep her face blank, a mask.

She had tried for more than two decades—sometimes successfully, often not—to keep that memory at bay. She'd never told anyone but Brian, and they'd never spoken of it after that first conversation. She realized that she hoped he'd forgotten it over time, which was ridiculous. Of course he hadn't. What ever made her think he could?

"I'm sorry," Brian said. "I didn't mean to upset you. Are you OK?"

She shrugged, feigning more calm than she felt. "It's an ugly word, that's all."

"But it's the right word," Brian said, his eyes never wavering from hers.

"I've never been able to bring myself to say it, not even in my head," Elizabeth said. "I know that doesn't make sense."

"I understand," Brian said quietly. "It's hard to say 'I was raped.' It was for me, too."

The trajectory of the conversation suddenly became clear to Elizabeth, and she cursed herself for not seeing it.

"Oh, Brian. I didn't realize…"

"When things were really bad for me afterward, I thought about how you kept going, how you didn't let it destroy you," Brian said. "You have no idea how much that helped. I might have been one of those guys who hangs himself in his cell if not for that."

"Brian, I'm so sorry."

Elizabeth reached for Brian's hand and squeezed it. She wanted to say something more, but too many emotions were too close to the surface, and she didn't trust her voice.

"I remember those nightmares you used to have," Brian said. "Did they go away?"

"That's why I drank," Elizabeth said. "So I could sleep."

"Did you get help? Talk to somebody?"

"About the drinking?" Elizabeth shook her head. "No, I just quit. And the other… I couldn't bring myself to drag it all out again. I just want to forget, you know?"

Brian looked at her for a long time, like he wanted to say more, but he didn't.

"Why don't you come outside and talk to me while I cook," he said, finally. Seeing her hesitate, he added, "Nobody can see into the back yard. You're safe."

5

Brian's back yard was enclosed by a new-looking fence, but everything else was scruffy. The small concrete patio was cracked and the yard beyond was patchy, more weeds and bare spots than grass. The patio held a charcoal grill, two cheap plastic lawn chairs and an old-fashioned metal glider pocked by rust.

"It's kind of a mess back here." Brian put the steak on the grill. "When I have time, I'm going to jackhammer this patio and fix everything up nice."

He nudged one of the plastic chairs toward Elizabeth with his foot. "I just cleaned that one off this morning so I could have my coffee out here."

Brian inspected the other plastic chair, which was covered in bird droppings, before settling on the metal glider. It groaned in protest.

"Somebody put this out at the curb," Brian said. "It just needs the rust sanded off and some paint and WD-40 and it'll be fine. Another project on my to-do list, after the kitchen, and the patio. Oh, and I want to finish the attic, too, put a bedroom up there."

"That's a long list," Elizabeth said.

"I can't believe I'm sitting here talking to you about my to-do list," he said. "This is unreal, Shar."

Shar. Brian had been the first to call her that. Cliff and Missy eventually picked it up, but she would always think of it as Brian's name for her.

"It's been a long time since anyone's called me that," she said.

"What do your friends call you now?"

"Everybody calls me Elizabeth," she said, skirting the issue of friends.

"Elizabeth." Brian frowned.

"What, you don't like it?" Elizabeth tried to sound playful, but she wasn't sure she succeeded.

Brian, to her relief, smiled. "It's a classic, I guess," he said. "It just seems kind of standoffish. You were never that way."

Elizabeth had never been called standoffish—not to her face—but its synonyms had received a workout from jilted lovers and exasperated co-workers: reserved, distant, cold.

"I think I probably am now," she said, and then, because she didn't want to talk about her life: "Your yard is huge."

Brian let her change the subject. "When I bought this place, I was thinking I'd get a dog, you know, for company. But Coco's afraid of them right now, so I'm holding off until she's older and until I know I'll have plenty of time to train it."

He got up to check the steak and turned it.

"I want to convert the garage and put my workshop there," he said. "Then I can run the business from home and I'll be here to deal with a dog."

"That sounds like a good plan," Elizabeth said.

"I just have to get the money together," Brian said. "The business would be in good shape if I didn't have to rent space. But I don't have the money to do the garage because I have to pay rent. Catch-22, right? You probably read that book."

"I did," Elizabeth said. "My bachelor's is in English lit."

"You went to college?" Brian face lit up, and Elizabeth felt something inside her give way. Thinking about how proud Brian would be had buoyed her through many lonely days in college.

"I have a master's, too," she said. "Library science. That's how I used the money."

"That's good," Brian said, nodding. "Really good. I'm glad."

When the steak was done, they went inside, and Brian showed Elizabeth where to find plates.

"One of my stepsisters redecorated and decided those didn't go anymore. So I got nice dishes and her daughter gets free guitar lessons," Brian said.

"Seems fair," Elizabeth said.

"Not really," Brian laughed. "But it's not worth trying to argue with her. She's the bossy one in the family—a lawyer."

It wasn't until she took the first bite that Elizabeth realized how hungry she was. In the past few days, she'd eaten almost as little as she'd slept.

"Have you ever talked to a lawyer about your situation?"

Her mouth full, Elizabeth merely shook her head.

"It might not be as bad as you think," Brian said. "The cops never knew about the money. They assumed I was a sucker who didn't even get paid his share."

"But Kevin knew you got paid," Elizabeth said. "Do you remember that last night before the storm, you called me from the jail? Kevin ransacked the bedroom while I was on the phone. He said he was looking for your good clothes for your next court appearance, but he pulled everything out of the dresser."

"You think he was looking for the money?"

"Maybe," she said. "Or maybe he was going to take your Three Musketeers shirt, to replace the one on Missy."

It was clear from Brian's expression that he didn't want to discuss Kevin and Missy. Elizabeth decided not to force the issue.

"The money may not even matter anymore," Brian said. "I bet the statute of limitations has expired."

Elizabeth had researched this question. "The statute of limitations for money laundering is five years," she said. "But they can charge you with conspiracy on the original crime, which can change the equation about a million different ways. And the identity theft laws are practically impossible to figure out. Believe me, I've tried."

"That's why you need a lawyer," Brian said. "It's not like you stole someone's information and used it to rip people off. This is a victimless crime."

This was another issue Elizabeth had researched. "Not exactly. There was a real Elizabeth Ellsworth from Louisiana," she said. "She drowned when she was four. Her family probably wouldn't be very happy to know someone is impersonating her."

"A lawyer could..."

Elizabeth was out of patience. Why wouldn't Brian leave it alone?

"I'd lose my job, Brian. I could go to prison."

"Maybe not. You could get your life back."

"My job is my life," Elizabeth said. "There's nothing else—nothing to get back."

Elizabeth was suddenly, overwhelmingly tired, so tired that she thought she could put her head down on the table and sleep right there. Instead, she pushed her empty plate away and stood up.

"I'm too tired to talk about this," Elizabeth said. "I'm going to go. I'll call you, I don't know, next week or something."

Brian stood too. "Stay here," he said. "You shouldn't drive. You're too tired."

"I don't think I should stay," she said. "What happened before, that was a mistake."

"There's a futon in the other bedroom," Brian said. He carried their plates to the sink. "It's not deluxe or anything, but it sleeps OK."

Elizabeth watched Brian wash the dishes, sorely tempted by his offer. Somehow the thought of getting in her car, finding a hotel and checking in seemed overwhelming.

Brian stacked the plates in a dish drainer. "Where are your keys? I'll move my truck and put your car in the garage," he said.

$$\mathscr{S}$$

Elizabeth dried the dishes and put them away while Brian was outside.

He was back a few minutes later. "I brought your bag," he said, hoisting Elizabeth's overnight bag. "If the gun's in here, you need to take it back to your car. I'm a felon—I can't have it in my house."

"It's behind the spare in my trunk," Elizabeth said. "I shouldn't have brought it, but I wasn't thinking very clearly this morning. I had this idea that I'd have to prove everything to you."

"Have you ever cleaned it or anything? It was a cheap piece of crap 20 years ago," Brian said. "You need to be careful with it."

"I hadn't even unwrapped it from the shirt until last night," Elizabeth said. "I only have it because I haven't been able to figure out how to get rid of it. It's not like I can take it to Goodwill."

"No, I guess not," Brian said. He pointed down the hall. "This way."

The guest room was at the front of the house with a window that looked out onto the porch. It obviously served as an office, music room and playroom.

The futon was shoved against one wall. Next to it were guitar cases. A desk across the room held a laptop and neat stacks of folders and papers. All the cables—computer, printer, cell-phone charger—were tidily banded together.

Under the window stood a tiny easel with a pad of paper.

Elizabeth bent down to look at the child's drawing propped there, a blue square with some squiggles next to it.

"Did Coco draw this? Is it your house?"

"Drawing is her favorite thing," Brian said. "She gets that from her mother. Tonya wanted to be a fashion designer. That's where Coco got her name—like Coco Chanel."

Elizabeth wandered to the desk. She picked up a framed photo of Brian holding a baby who looked impossibly tiny in his arms. His face was turned away from the camera—all of his attention was focused on Coco.

He would have been a good father.

The thought sped out of nowhere, sideswiping Elizabeth. Tears stung her eyes, and she blinked them back, not wanting Brian to see.

He crossed the room and was at her elbow. "She's not even an hour old there. I was the first one to hold her. I hurried up there because we wanted to get the ball rolling with social services, so Tonya wouldn't leave the hospital with the baby. But the nurse asked me if I wanted to hold Coco, and the minute they handed her to me..."

Brian noticed Elizabeth's distress and put his hand on her shoulder. "Hey," he said softly. "Are you OK?"

Elizabeth nodded furiously, dabbing her eyes. "I'm fine."

"What's wrong?"

"Sorry," she said, laughing a little. "That's just my biological clock going off. It does that sometimes—a lot, actually. Just ignore it."

Brian squeezed her shoulder. "When Tonya was pregnant, I kept having this dream about this beautiful teenager coming up to me in different places—the grocery store, a club. She'd start talking to me, and I'd not understand why, and then I'd realize she was my daughter—*our* daughter."

"Oh, Brian," was all Elizabeth could manage.

"I know," Brian said. "I used to wake up and think, 'Brian, that's just pathetic.' "

Elizabeth turned to face Brian. "Don't be so hard on yourself," she said. "Nobody can control what they dream about. God knows I've tried."

Brian leaned against the desk. "I think about that time we were worried you were pregnant and I wonder, what was I so scared of? That I'd end up working for my dad until I was 40? I did that anyway, and it wasn't so bad. If we'd been married and had a kid, I would have told Kevin no. Everybody would have been better off."

It was tempting to fantasize about the life she might have had with Brian, but Elizabeth resisted. She always resisted.

"I don't know, Brian. Would I have gone to school if I'd had a baby at 18? I would have been a totally different person."

Brian's eyes slid toward the floor. "Yeah, you're probably right. Who knows?" Obviously deflated, he started for the door. "I'll just get the sheets. They're in the hall closet."

Elizabeth regretted hurting his feelings, but she believed it was important to be honest. There was no point indulging in what might have been.

She did another circuit of the room while he was gone, exhausted but jittery. "How many guitars do you have, anyway? I count five cases," she called out to the hall.

"Only four are really mine," Brian answered. "The other one, a customer was shipping out with his Guard unit for Iraq, and he asked me to take care of it."

"That's nice of you, to keep it until he comes back," Elizabeth said.

Brian returned to the room. "He died over there," he said. "I asked his ex-wife if she wanted the guitar, but she doesn't.

I keep thinking some kid will come into the shop with a really crappy guitar one day, and I'll just give it to him."

"You have such a good heart. That was always one of the things…"

Elizabeth checked herself. She'd been about to say "I loved about you."

It was true—she'd always loved Brian's generosity. But it seemed wrong to say that out loud.

"It was always one of my favorite things about you," she said, instead.

Brian dumped the sheets onto the futon and began to fiddle with the mechanism to fold it out flat. "I think the pillow's in the closet there—would you look?"

Elizabeth opened the closet and found the pillow. As she reached for it, something else on the shelf caught her eye—two black binders marked WEBB INVESTIGATION.

She backed out of the closet. "Brian?"

"Is the shelf too high for you?" Brian grinned. "I'll get it."

"The shelf isn't too high. What are these notebooks that say 'Webb investigation?' "

The grin disappeared. "I hired a private detective a few years ago." Brian reached past her and pulled down the pillow.

A private detective? Investigating her? Elizabeth found the idea disquieting. She waited for a further explanation, but none came. Brian seemed embarrassed.

"Why?"

"Why?" Brian busied himself putting a pillowcase on the pillow. "Because I wanted to find out what happened to you. I thought she could tell me something the police couldn't or wouldn't."

"It's weird to think of myself as being investigated," she said. "What did she find?"

"You can read the report if you want," Brian said. "There were all kinds of theories and suspects, but never anything definite. About four years after you left, they thought they'd found your body in New Mexico and they asked me to ID the shirt they found, but it turned out to be some other girl."

"My God, Brian. I had no idea."

He tossed the pillow on the futon and returned to the closet, pulling down the two binders.

"Nobody could figure out how you left without your car. Even after my dad put up a reward, there was nothing," Brian said. He held the binders out. "Here," he said. "You can look. Maybe it will seem funny or something now."

"Your dad put up a reward?" Elizabeth gaped at Brian. "I would think your parents were happy to see me gone. Hell, your mom would have paid to make me disappear."

Seeing that she wasn't taking the binders, Brian put them on the floor. "My mom is just a really unhappy person. A lot of what she does, it isn't personal."

"And your dad? He didn't exactly welcome me with open arms, either."

"My dad let her have her way because that was easier than fighting. When I got arrested, that's when the whole house of cards came down. He's different now. He's my best friend. He feels a lot of guilt about you. If he knew you were alive, he'd..."

Brian's cell phone rang, and he walked over to the desk to check the display.

"How weird. It's my dad." His brow furrowed. "He doesn't usually call this late. I'd better take it."

"You can't tell him about me!"

"It's OK. I won't," Brian said, signaling for her to sit down or stay calm—she couldn't tell which. "I'll put it on speaker. You can listen."

"You can't…"

"I won't." Brian pushed a button on his phone. "Hey, Dad."

"Hey, son." Mitch Lowry's voice boomed across the room. "Wasn't sure I'd catch you," Mitch said. "Thought you might be out hearing some music tonight."

"I decided to stay in," Brian said. He crossed the room and sat, balancing the phone on his knee. Elizabeth sat next to him.

"You painting that hallway? Lynn said she picked the color for you."

"No, just… not doing much of anything," Brian said. "What's up with you?"

"I'm waiting at the pharmacy," Mitch said. "Coco's got another of her ear infections, so the doc called in something."

Elizabeth felt Brian tense next to her. "Is her fever bad?"

"She's fine, Brian, don't worry. She's hardly even fussing, especially after Frannie gave her a Popsicle."

"You'll call me if you have to take her to the ER again, right?"

"We will, but I don't think you need to worry," Mitch said. "You OK, son? You having a bad night?"

Brian's shoulders slumped, and he hung his head. "OK, I guess. Just tired."

"Well, the main reason I called is Francine's going to keep Coco home from church Sunday," Mitch said. "I know you were planning to come see the preschoolers do their program. Francine says you should still come for Sunday dinner. We'll get Coco to sing her little song for you—that'll make her just as happy as doing it in church. She's been practicing all week, and oh my gosh, is she precious."

Elizabeth found herself charmed by Mitch as he prattled on about his granddaughter, but Brian was staring at the floor, his shoulders hunched, clearly miserable.

"Francine said I'm supposed to find out do you want pot roast or chicken on Sunday, because if it's pot roast I've got to get carrots and if it's chicken I'm supposed to get... shoot! Something. Where'd I put that piece of paper?"

A rustle came over the phone, the sound of Mitch searching his pockets.

"Either's fine," Brian said. "You probably put the grocery list in your wallet."

There was a pause and more scuffling sounds. "Right you are, it's here in my wallet. Well, if you don't care, I'm going to tell her you said chicken." Mitch's tone was calm, but concern bobbed below the surface. "You sure you're OK, son?"

"Yeah," Brian said. He ran a hand through his hair. "I've been thinking about Kevin. When's the last time you heard from him?"

"Kevin?" Mitch seemed momentarily stunned, but he recovered quickly. "What brought this on, Brian? Have *you* heard from him?"

"No," Brian said quietly.

Mitch sighed. "I do know he called your mother awhile back with some story about how he had a spot at a rehab place in California and would she wire him money for the plane. But she didn't fall for it. You know he pulled the same stunt with your cousin Lisa."

"How's Mom?" Brian's voice was so soft Elizabeth could hardly hear him.

"I didn't talk to her," Mitch said. "It was her husband who called. Apparently her golf game's coming along."

Brian was quiet. His back rose and fell with his breathing.

"Don't do this to yourself, Brian. It's enough that Kevin's wasting his own life. Don't let him waste yours, too," Mitch said. "We've talked about this."

Brian exhaled, hard, and Elizabeth instinctively put her hand on his back.

"I'm sorry, Dad. Sorry for everything that…"

"You have nothing to apologize *for*, son. You know that," Mitch said. "Tell you what—why don't you come on over to the house? You can check on Coco yourself and then we'll find a late ballgame to watch. You can stay over in the guest room."

Brian slowly shook his head. "I think I'm just going to go to bed. It's late."

"Oh, c'mon. I'll sneak into the kitchen and put on a pot of real coffee—not that decaf crap Frannie makes me drink," Mitch said.

"I'd better pass," Brian said, his voice stronger. "Thanks, Dad."

"Well, if you change your mind, call me," Mitch said. "I'll be up awhile once I get home."

"OK," Brian said. "Give Coco a kiss for me."

"Oh, the pharmacy fella's calling me," Mitch said. "I love you, son. You get some rest. Tomorrow's going to be better."

❧

"It's hard talking to him, knowing what I know now about Kevin," Brian said after he hung up. "I hate lying to him."

"You're not responsible for this," Elizabeth said. "Kevin is."

"I'm responsible for lying to him," Brian said.

Elizabeth looked around—at the guitars, Coco's drawing, Brian's neat desk. Brian had gutted his life and rebuilt it, just as sure as he was rebuilding his house. Now she'd come along to expose a section of rot he'd overlooked. Elizabeth was flooded with regret.

"I shouldn't have come here," she said. "I should have found another way to do this. You've put together a good life, and I've ruined it."

"You didn't ruin it," Brian said. "Knowing you're alive, that's the thing I've wanted most for 20 years. It's just... it's just typical of my life, you know? The best possible news comes with the worst possible news."

Elizabeth winced. "I'm sorry."

"If my dad finds out what Kevin did, it's going to destroy him," Brian said. "And what about Ashley, finding out her dad killed someone? She's only 20."

"Missy was only 20," Elizabeth said, then immediately regretted it when she saw Brian's expression.

She tried to think of something to comfort him, but she knew there was nothing. What she was asking of him was difficult. She would not pretend otherwise.

"Everybody's going to think I knew this all along and let Kevin get away with murder," Brian said. "What am I going to say? I was just sitting in my shop and thought, 'Oh, you know, I bet that's Kevin's shirt that Missy had on when she died.'"

"Maybe you can persuade Kevin to confess," Elizabeth said.

"I can't remember the last time Kevin did the right thing."

He put his hands on his knees and made to get up. "Well, it is what it is. Whatever people think, whatever happens to me—it's not like I'm an innocent victim."

He motioned for her to get up and began to wrestle with the futon. Brian finally hit the hinge right, and the bed dropped flat with a loud crack.

Elizabeth flinched at the sound. "Brian, I'm so sorry. You deserved better."

Brian unfolded the sheets and began to make up the futon, his actions quick and rough. "Oh, I think I got what I deserved."

He stopped and looked at Elizabeth. "The thing that scares me is, ever since I got out, I've been able to count on my dad. And now... I just hope he can forgive me. Again."

TWELVE

ELIZABETH HAD INTENDED to sleep in the guest room, but then Brian asked her—almost shyly—if she would sleep in his bed.

"It doesn't have to be anything else," he said. "I just don't want to feel alone right now."

Elizabeth knew exactly what he meant. Sometimes she thought she'd taken lovers just for the simple comfort of sharing a bed, the reassurance of another's weight and heat and breath next to her in the dark.

Elizabeth changed into her pajamas in the bathroom and brushed her teeth while Brian turned off lights and locked doors. When she got into bed, she instinctively chose the side she'd always taken with Brian, ever since that night when she'd walked into his room and told him she was cold.

She'd often cringed at the way her relationship with Brian started. Naïve! Stupid! When she was feeling especially down on herself, she'd tell herself that any relationship so poorly considered was destined to bring trouble.

But she found, to her surprise, that a few hours in Brian's company left her feeling vindicated. Although she'd been 17 and lonely and desperate, her judgment on Brian hadn't been so bad. He'd trusted the wrong people, but he was a good, decent man.

She had not been wrong to love him.

✪

After a few hours, a nightmare woke her—rough hands pushing her down as she kicked and pleaded.

Elizabeth sat up, gasping.

It was always the same: the terror and the anger. And the guilt—always the guilt.

Brian quieted her, as he had so many times before. "You're OK, Shar," he repeated over and over, until she came fully awake and aware of her surroundings.

Only then did he touch her, putting his hand gently on her shoulder, urging her to lie back down. He'd learned the hard way—he'd reached for her too soon the very first time, and she'd fought him as though her life depended on it.

Elizabeth put her head on Brian's chest and let him put his arms around her. She listened to the slow thud of his heartbeat and waited. Brian had always been able to pull her from the strong, swift current where she thrashed into calm, peaceful water.

He didn't ask what the dream was about; he never had. He'd hold her and breathe and follow her lead.

In the old days, she would occasionally drift easily back to sleep after a nightmare. Other times, she'd want to talk. The topic was never anything important—a book she was reading or whatever had happened that day at the diner. The point was to put something harmless at the center of her mind and crowd the bad thoughts into the corners.

Sometimes talking wasn't enough. Sometimes she needed to push back against the ugliness, to be reassured that she wasn't worthless, that the damage could be mended or at least overlooked.

Twenty years had gone by, but Brian knew. Maybe it was a change in her breath or a subtle shift of her weight against him, but he knew.

Not that. This.

Again, Elizabeth had the sensation of closing her eyes and willing away the last 20 years.

Afterward, wide awake despite the hour, they talked.

"Right now, it feels like nothing ever changed between us," Brian said, propping himself up on one elbow and looking down at her. "Is that weird?"

Elizabeth smiled, because she'd just been thinking the same thing. "It's like hearing an old song on the radio, and before you know it you're singing along, even though you would have sworn you didn't remember the words."

Brian stroked her cheek. "Your smile is even prettier than I remembered."

"That's because I had my teeth straightened," Elizabeth said, laughing.

Brian turned serious. "There's really not anyone in your life? How is that possible?"

Elizabeth told him then about Eamon, who had loved her, and Wyatt, who might have if she'd let him.

Brian told her about Kristen, and how he'd never been able to overcome his doubts and marry her. Then, once he'd let her go, he worried about whether he'd done the right thing.

"That's my whole life, right there," Brian said. "Other people seem to know for sure what's right for them, but I never have. It's like when I was a kid, and everyone else could read and I couldn't, and I didn't know what was wrong with me. I just knew something was wrong."

"Other people are less sure than you think," she said. "Most of them are faking it."

"You were always sure," Brian said, "even when you were 17."

Elizabeth studied his face in the dark, searching for some sign he was teasing. She found none. "Did I seem that way? I think mostly I was sure what I *didn't* want. I just wanted something different, and I had no idea exactly what it was or how to get it."

"But you have it now," Brian said. "Right?"

"I love my job," Elizabeth said.

"And you're good at it, aren't you?"

"I am," Elizabeth said, knowing that with Brian there was no need to demur. "But it wasn't just that I wanted a good job so I wouldn't be poor. I could stand being poor. What I couldn't stand was not being *respectable*."

"I knew you'd be pissed about the drugs," Brian said. "That's why I was afraid to tell you."

"And now it turns out you're the one living the respectable life," Elizabeth said, "and I'm the one who's a criminal."

❡

When Elizabeth woke again, the sun was slanting through the blinds and Brian's side of the bed was cold.

She squinted at the bedside clock: 7 a.m.

8 a.m. in Florida, she thought involuntarily.

From down the hall, she heard the faint sound of a guitar. As she listened, the music stopped, then began again, a sequence repeated.

Elizabeth thought about calling out to Brian. She could picture the scene: He'd amble down the hall and appear in the doorway, still a little disheveled from sleep, that grin on his face. They could spend the morning lazing in bed, just as they'd done 20 years earlier.

She'd always had a weakness for Brian when he was disheveled, and she allowed herself to linger on that thought, but only for a minute or two. There would be no calling Brian back to bed.

Elizabeth no longer believed that it had been a mistake to sleep with Brian, not exactly. But it could not happen again, she was sure of that. She would go back to her life and Brian would go back to his. He understood that, or would soon. He had to.

By the time she'd finished showering and dressing, the music had stopped. She found Brian in the kitchen, staring out the window over the sink.

"Hey," she said softly, worried that she'd startle him.

Brian turned, a smile on his face. He took in Elizabeth's packed overnight bag at her feet and the smile slipped, just for a second.

"I guess you're hitting the road," he said.

"I have to be at work Monday morning," Elizabeth said. "It's a long drive."

"At your desk at 9 a.m. sharp, I guess." His tone was breezy, but Elizabeth could see the effort behind it.

"I usually get there at 8:45. I like to have time to get organized."

Brian chuckled. "Remember Joan, your old boss at the diner?"

"Joan. Wow. There's somebody I hadn't thought of in a long time."

"She told the private detective you were the best worker she ever had, always on time. She felt terrible about firing you. She held onto your last check for a long time, hoping you'd come back for it."

Brian turned away and opened a cupboard. "Coffee will be ready in a second. You want some breakfast before you go? I have cereal. It's cornflakes, though, not that one you like. Captain Crunch, isn't it?"

"Captain Crunch—wow. There's another thing I haven't thought of in a long time," Elizabeth said.

Brian took down two coffee cups. "I could make you some eggs."

"Two meals in a row cooked by you?" Elizabeth laughed. "That rates another 'wow.'"

She could tell immediately by the set of Brian's shoulders that she'd said the wrong thing.

"I'm sorry I was so useless when we were together, Shar." Brian turned to face her, and the hurt in his eyes made Elizabeth want to look away. "I look back at the way I just sat around watching TV while you cooked and cleaned and did every-thing for me, and I can't believe I did that. Every other stupid thing I did, at least I had a reason. But there was no reason for that. I was just lazy. You must have been so pissed at me."

"Really, I wasn't," Elizabeth said.

That wasn't entirely true. There had been a period in college when she'd been very angry with Brian, and not just because he'd made a money launderer out of her. She'd seethed about the inequality in their relationship.

Over time, though, she realized that she'd taken on all those tasks and never asked for help. It would have been nice if Brian had done his share without being asked, but it wasn't entirely fair to blame him. She could have spoken up.

"I liked having our own little place," she said. "And I actually liked cleaning. I was happy I didn't have to live in chaos. Please don't feel bad about that."

Brian poured a cup of coffee and handed it to her. "So, what's it going to be? I make pretty good scrambled eggs. I can do bacon, toast..."

"You really don't need to cook," Elizabeth said. "I should get going."

Seeing Brian's disappointment, she added hastily. "Toast would be good."

It felt strange to be having an awkward conversation about the breakfast menu after she and Brian had been so honest with each other in the night.

The problem, Elizabeth realized, was not Brian, but her. She could have left the packed bag in the bedroom. She'd wanted to send a clear message that there would be no lingering, but she'd overdone it, and Brian was hurt.

She sat down at the table, to show that she wasn't planning to grab her toast and bolt out of the house.

Brian loaded bread in an ancient-looking toaster.

"That toaster is quite something," Elizabeth said, trying to make conversation.

"I got it at a yard sale for a quarter," Brian said. "It's amazing how much perfectly usable stuff people are willing to junk because it's got a scratch or something. As long as it's not going to electrocute you, who cares what your toaster looks like?"

Elizabeth could think of nothing to say in response.

Brian got strawberry jam from the refrigerator and put it on the table. "I know you like peanut butter on your toast, but I'm out," Brian said. "I had Coco one afternoon last week and I used the last of it in her PBJ."

Elizabeth hadn't eaten peanut butter on her toast in a long time.

Brian was bustling around, avoiding her eyes. She tried to think of a way to put him at ease.

"I heard you playing this morning. It made me think of that summer you were learning 'Jack and Diane.' I thought you were going to wear the album out."

"Picking up something by ear is slow going," Brian said, grabbing the toast as it popped up. "I'm a lot faster now that I can read music."

"You read music?" Elizabeth hoped she sounded impressed rather than incredulous.

Brian put a plate on the table in front of her with two pieces of toast. "Some people with dyslexia can't ever get the hang of it, but I did."

Elizabeth thought he was going to fix his own breakfast then, but instead he pulled out a chair and sat.

"I know you want to get on the road, so I'll get to the point. You don't have to worry about this situation," Brian said. "I'll handle it. Right now, I'm leaning toward giving Kevin a chance to do the right thing before I go to the police. But that's something I want to discuss with my dad first."

Elizabeth was taken aback. She'd expected he'd want more time to think about it.

"How will you explain to your dad about suspecting Kevin killed Missy?"

"I don't know," Brian said. "I don't want to lie to him again, ever. But I won't drag you into it, I promise. You can leave the gun, too. Just put it on the shelf in the garage before you pull your car out."

"I thought you could get in a lot of trouble for being a felon with a gun?"

"I'll figure out some way to get rid of it," Brian said.

"I don't want you to be in trouble, Brian."

Brian shrugged. "I'm responsible for this mess, not you. Don't worry—I'll be careful."

Elizabeth felt guilty, as though she'd unfairly dumped everything in Brian's lap.

"You can go back to Florida and be Elizabeth Ellsworth knowing nobody's looking for you and you don't ever have to think of this again, if that's what you want," Brian said.

He looked at her, those blue eyes holding steady. "Is that what you want?"

Was that what she wanted? Elizabeth, who was used to being very sure about things, was suddenly less sure about everything.

"Would you like to see me again?" Brian's voice was softer now. "Because I would like to see you again." He smiled. "I could be the new what's-his-name—the guy in Georgia. What's halfway between here and Tallahassee? New Orleans? Biloxi? We could meet."

Elizabeth allowed herself a moment with the idea. It would be wonderful to recapture that feeling she'd had with Wyatt, those hours spent in her car on Friday nights, knowing that at the end of her trip someone was waiting for her.

She savored the possibility, then she let it go. "I don't think that's a good idea, Brian."

Brian wasn't ready to give up. "I'm willing to drive to Mississippi a few times to find out."

"It's not fair to you."

"I guess I can decide that for myself," he said.

Brian hadn't showered yet, and his cowlick was sticking up at the back of his head. She'd always thought his cowlick made him seem boyish. She felt tender toward Brian. She didn't want to hurt him.

"It's just that there's..." Elizabeth faltered.

"No future for the librarian and the felon?"

"That's not it, Brian. You know that's not how I think of you."

"What is it, then?"

"There's no future for Brian Lowry and *Elizabeth Ellsworth*."

Brian sat with that a minute, fiddling with his coffee cup.

"And there's no chance you would ever want to be..."

"Sharlah Webb again? I could go to prison, Brian. I don't have a family that would give me a place to stay and a job when I got out. I'd have nothing, and no one."

"You would have me," Brian said. He gestured around his half-done kitchen. "Obviously, I'm basically broke, but anything I could do for you, I would."

"I can't ask that of you."

"You didn't ask. I'm offering."

When Elizabeth didn't answer, he pushed back a little from the table. He seemed to accept that the conversation was over. "Offer's good any time," he said.

"Thank you. That means a lot."

"Can I ask a favor?"

Part of Elizabeth wanted to say yes, of course, but she was wary. "What is it?"

"Can I have a picture of you?"

"A picture?"

"All of the pictures of you were ruined in the hurricane," Brian said. "The only thing I have is your school picture from first grade."

"I saw that on the website. Where on earth did you get that?"

"From your dad."

"My *dad*?"

Brian picked up her empty plate, and Elizabeth slid her cup toward him. Brian carried the dishes to the sink. "I went to see him once."

The idea that Brian met her father filled Elizabeth with shame, which surprised her.

"Oh, Brian. Why?"

"I guess the best way to put it is, I felt like you were slipping away from me, and I didn't want that. I wanted to hold on to whatever little piece of you I could find."

"But my dad? He's so awful."

Or was he? She hadn't seen her father since she was 17. Perhaps he'd changed.

"He *was* awful," Brian said. He turned on the water and scrubbed the dishes. "It wasn't a great idea, but at least I got the photo out of it. He's dead now. Three years ago."

Elizabeth thought she should feel something, but she didn't.

Brian turned to face her. "Will you let me take a photo? I swear to you that no one else will ever see it."

"Yes," Elizabeth said. "It's OK."

"Let me get my camera from my desk," Brian said. "Be right back."

He squeezed her shoulder as he passed out into the hall.

❡

Seconds after he walked out of the kitchen, Brian was back, a stricken look on his face.

"My dad's here. He's parked at the curb and walking up the sidewalk."

"What?" Elizabeth stood so quickly that her chair nearly toppled over. "Did you tell him?"

"Of course not! You heard everything." Brian grabbed the back of the chair to steady it. "I don't know why he's here—he never drops in. He always calls first."

"Should I..."

"What if it's Coco?" Brian said. "If her fever spiked, there's a risk of..."

There was a knock at the front door, and they both jumped.

"I'll go back to the bedroom," Elizabeth said.

Brian shook his head. "He can see down the hall from the front porch. Stay here in the kitchen. I'll see what he wants."

Brian stepped into the hallway and pulled the kitchen door firmly closed. His footsteps echoed down the hall.

Elizabeth sat at the table feeling vaguely embarrassed and guilty, like she had the time Renee Lowry found her and Brian kissing in the hall after Thanksgiving dinner.

She heard the front door open.

"Good morning, son," Mitch boomed. "How are you this morning?"

"What's going on, Dad? Is Coco OK?"

Brian's voice had a note of panic in it, and Elizabeth cringed.

"Aw, shoot, I didn't mean to worry you showing up like this," Mitch said. "Coco's fine. She was up and down all night, but she's OK."

The voices had not progressed any closer, and Elizabeth imagined that Brian was standing in the doorway, keeping his father on the porch.

"I thought maybe I could talk you out of a cup of real coffee," Mitch said.

"Sure," Brian said, sounding perfectly calm now. "I've got some made. Why don't I bring it out and we can sit on the porch?"

"I can tell you ain't been out yet today," Mitch said. "It's hot as blazes. I'm sweating just standing here."

Brian laughed. "You're right; I haven't been up very long. C'mon in. Have a seat. I'll just get the coffee."

Elizabeth looked around her, frantic. Only a sheet of plastic separated the kitchen from the dining room, which was open to the living room. Mitch might easily spot her. She considered heading out the back door, toward the garage, but the dining room had a window that looked out over the patio and back yard.

Brian's footsteps came toward the kitchen, and his voice seemed louder than necessary. "Why don't you turn on SportsCenter, Dad?"

"Aw, that's all right," Mitch said. "I don't need to watch TV."

His voice was getting closer. He was following Brian down the hall.

Elizabeth's eyes fell on the door to the attic. She crept across the kitchen as quietly as she could and opened the door, hoping the hinges wouldn't squeak.

"Have you had breakfast?" Judging by Brian's voice, he was right outside the kitchen. "We could go out, if you wanted. There's that place over on Heights Boulevard—their coffee is better than mine."

Elizabeth pulled the attic door partway closed and then realized, in a flash, that her overnight bag was still sitting in the middle of the kitchen.

She calculated the odds, then scuttled back across the kitchen and grabbed it.

"You're not even dressed, son," Mitch said. "I don't mean to roust you. I just thought we could have some coffee and talk a little."

Elizabeth was halfway to the attic door.

"The kitchen's pretty much a mess," Brian said.

Elizabeth heard the kitchen door scrape on the floor behind her. She pulled open the attic door and climbed up two steps, pulling the door half-closed behind her.

Mitch laughed. "When has it ever not been a mess? It was a worse mess when you bought the place."

He was in the kitchen now. Elizabeth didn't dare close the attic door the rest of the way. Carefully, quietly, she put her bag down and lowered herself to sit on the steps.

She heard the clatter of the cups as Brian pulled them down from the cupboard and the slosh of the coffee as he filled them.

Mitch sighed. She imagined he'd just taken a chair.

"What's this about, Dad? It's not like you to just show up."

"I apologize for busting in on you like this, Brian. But you didn't sound right last night, and I was sitting up with Coco and you know how everything seems worse in the middle of the night? I just got so worried. I wanted to check on you."

"I'm OK," Brian said. "Yesterday was a long day, that's all. I wish you wouldn't worry so much."

"It's not just me," Mitch said. "Frannie said you seemed down the other day when she picked up Coco."

"I'm always sad when Coco goes home."

Brian was trying to be funny, but Elizabeth mostly heard wistfulness.

"Frannie thought maybe you were worried about the business. Is that it? I thought you were feeling better after we went over the numbers last week."

"Yeah, that helped," Brian said.

"I sure wish you'd let me loan you the money to do the garage," Mitch said. "I think that's a real smart move. Every business needs credit now and then—sometimes you have to spend money to make money."

Brian mumbled something Elizabeth couldn't make out.

There was a long silence then, broken only by the clink of a spoon in a coffee cup.

"What's new with that gal you've been seeing?"

What? Brian hadn't mentioned a woman in his life; in fact, he'd left her with exactly the opposite impression. She couldn't believe he would... Elizabeth stopped the thought. She should be glad Brian had someone in his life. He deserved to be happy.

She leaned toward the door, wanting to be sure she caught Brian's response.

"It didn't work out," Brian said.

"Aw, Brian, I'm sorry to hear that. I know you liked her. What happened?"

"What usually happens," Brian said. "I told her I had a record, and, you know. That was pretty much it."

"I swear, I don't know what's wrong with these women who can't look past that."

"Dad," Brian said quietly, "it's fine. She was very nice about it. She's got a 13-year-old daughter, and she didn't think..."

"What's that got to do with anything? You're not a child molester!"

Elizabeth found herself nodding in agreement with Mitch. Brian had so much to offer, and any woman who couldn't see that was an idiot.

"She didn't say it like that," Brian said. "It's more that her daughter's at an age where she's got to talk to her about being careful who your friends are, and then, you know, she's dating someone who was in prison..."

Brian trailed off, not bothering to complete the thought.

"I know you feel like it's real important to tell the truth early on, so nobody feels misled," Mitch said. "But sometimes I think it would be better to let things go on a little longer, let these gals get to appreciate all your good qualities, then..."

"Dad..."

"I'm just saying there's such a thing as being too honest, Brian. That's your problem. You're too honest."

The sounds that came next were hard to identify—a crash and what sounded like a muffled cry.

"Brian? What's wrong?"

Elizabeth's heart began to beat faster.

"Sit down, son, simmer down and let's talk about it. Let me get some paper towels and we'll get the coffee cleaned up..."

Elizabeth heard rustling sounds, then the lid of the trash can opening and closing.

"I know I meddle sometimes where I shouldn't," Mitch said. "I don't mean anything by it, you know that."

"It's fine, Dad. Sorry." Brian's voice was low and resigned. "I'm not mad. I just..."

He's going to tell him right now, Elizabeth thought.

"There's something I've never been honest with you about," Brian said.

Trapped in the attic stairwell, Elizabeth leaned her head against the wall and waited.

"We've never talked about why I was hauling drugs," Brian said.

"Honestly, son, that's so long ago that I'm not sure it matters anymore. You did what you did and paid the price. You should be focused on your future and..."

"Kevin asked me to do it."

It all came out in a rush then: Kevin's gambling troubles, Brian's initial refusal, the threats, then, finally, his arrest.

Brian stopped talking. Elizabeth held her breath.

"You... you say Kevin got you into that mess," Mitch sputtered, "and then he didn't lift a finger to help you?"

"He was worried about Lynn and Ashley."

"Bullshit," Mitch said. "He was worried about Kevin." His voice rose. "He's never worried about anyone but Kevin. I know your mother and I did just about everything wrong with you boys, but I still can't for the life of me understand how he ended up with no conscience at all."

"It's not your fault, Dad."

"How could he do that to his own brother? Why didn't you say something?"

"When I realized he wasn't going to step up, I figured what was the point of us both going to prison? It was better for everybody if it was just me," Brian said.

"Oh, Brian…"

Mitch began to cry, and Brian tried to calm him.

It only lasted a few minutes, but it felt like an eternity to Elizabeth. She clamped her hand over her mouth, and hot tears splashed onto her fingers.

"Let me get you some water, Dad," Brian said.

Elizabeth heard the scrape of a chair, then water running.

"I got on you boys for crying when you were little, told you it was for sissies." Mitch choked out the words. "Look at me now."

As soon as Mitch caught his breath, he said, "It's because you thought we loved you less, isn't it? Because you didn't do as well at school as Kevin, because you weren't a star at football. You thought *I* loved you less, didn't you?"

Elizabeth's heart broke for Brian. How could he answer that question?

"Yeah," Brian said softly. "I thought that then. I know better now."

"I'm sorry, son. I'm so, so sorry."

"There's something else," Brian said.

This is going to crush both of them, Elizabeth thought. *I should have let it go.*

Then she thought about Missy, dead on her condo floor because she was hungry for attention, dead because she couldn't keep a secret.

She thought about Kevin. She'd pleaded with him that day she'd called from Kansas City, desperate for once last chance to see Brian. He'd lied to her, because that was what he did. He let others face the consequences of what he'd set in motion.

"It's bad," Brian said. "I don't know what to do but say it: I think Kevin killed Missy."

"What?" Mitch's voice was shrill.

"Missy knew," Brian said. "I think Kevin killed her so she wouldn't tell."

"I don't understand," Mitch said. "The police said the person who killed her was the fella she was seeing on the sly, that crooked cop."

"I think it was Kevin she was seeing," Brian said. "They... they had a history. Kevin slept with her in high school."

"Are you just guessing here?"

"I'm pretty sure," Brian said.

Disbelief edged into Mitch's voice. "You thought your brother murdered that girl, and you kept quiet about it all this time?"

"No," Brian said. "I didn't think it, not then."

"I don't understand," Mitch said. "Did you think back then that Kevin was sneaking around with her?"

"No." Brian's voice was growing softer.

Leave him alone! Elizabeth wanted to shout. She jammed her fist into her mouth and bit her knuckle so hard that she drew blood. The metallic taste filled her mouth.

"Why, Brian? Why now?"

"I'm not doing a very good job explaining," Brian said. "I just... I know it, OK? I don't want it to be true. But it is. I can't explain. I need you to believe me, because..."

Elizabeth sat on the stairs, helpless, as Brian's words trailed off. She thought of her last visit to Brian at the jail, how she'd sat on her side of the glass, watching him cry, powerless to help him.

That was the worst feeling in the world, watching someone she loved suffer and not being able to help.

She hadn't known what to do back then, but she knew what to do now.

Elizabeth rose to her feet, pushed open the attic door and walked into the kitchen.

ABOUT THE AUTHOR

Shawna Seed is a writer and editor whose work has taken her to both coasts and several spots in between, working for organizations ranging from *The Dallas Morning News* to ESPN.com.

Originally from Kansas, she has lived in seven states and every continental U.S. time zone. She and her husband—and their two cats, Gus and Lulu—now make their home in Dallas.

Identity is her debut novel. Her next project, *Not In Time*, is a suspense novel about looted art.

You can learn more about the author at:
www.shawnaseed.com

Like Shawna Seed on Facebook:
www.facebook.com/shawnaseedauthor

Follow Shawna Seed on Twitter (@shawnaseed)

Discuss the book (#identitythenovel)

Find Shawna Seed on Goodreads (www.goodreads.com)

Representation: Dystel & Goderich Literary Management

Cover design: Heather Kern at popshopstudio.com

ACKNOWLEDGMENTS

My sister, Gaye Coburn, read every variation of this manuscript and offered endless encouragement, which is her special gift.

Lauren Abramo at Dystel & Goderich Literary Management picked me out of the slush pile, provided crucial feedback and deserves much credit for helping me bring Brian into clearer focus.

Belinda Allen, Trish Rodriguez Terrell and Cynthia Wahl are great early readers and even better friends. Barbara Morris designed my website and taught me to tile a backsplash, which has nothing to do with writing a novel but deserves a shout-out all the same. The husband-wife team of Mark Davidson and Sarah Duckers advised me on the Texas criminal justice system and directed me to Brian's neighborhood. Everything I got wrong is my fault, not theirs.

I am grateful to my parents, Joe and Karen Seed, who never chastised me for having my nose in a book.

Finally, I couldn't have done this without my husband, Rick Holter, who read the first page I wrote and said, "Go write more."

DISCUSSION GUIDE

1. If you could give Sharlah one piece of advice, what would it be?

2. Are Brian's actions noble or foolish? Both? Neither?

3. After the hurricane, what did you think happened to Sharlah? What clues led you to that conclusion?

4. Several characters are motivated by guilt and shame. Can those ever be positive influences?

5. How do you think Sharlah's childhood influenced her decisions? How did Brian's background affect his?

6. Which character do you think changed the most over the course of the book?

7. Which character did you identify with most?

8. Describe your favorite part of the book.

9. If you could ask the author a question, what would it be?

10. Cast the movie: Who would play Brian? Sharlah? Mitch?

11. If you had the chance to create an entirely new identity, what would you do?

12. Which character do you wish you knew better?

COMING IN FALL 2013

Read Shawna Seed's new suspense novel, *Not In Time*

It seems like a dream come true. Art historian Genevieve McKenna, who just lost her museum job, lands an assignment: Track down a drawing the Nazis stole in wartime Paris. Plus, there's Julien Brooks, whose family owned the drawing. She's eager to get to know him better. A lot better.

But a series of bizarre flashbacks has Genevieve doubting her sanity. Mental illness haunted her mother's life. Is that Genevieve's fate?

On a research trip to Paris, Genevieve and Julien confront their growing attraction and the truth about her recent episodes. What they learn will reveal the true story of Genevieve's mother, the heroism of Julien's family and the heartbreak of a doomed romance.

It may also cost them their lives.